notes of a desolate man

Modern Chinese Literature from Taiwan

Modern Chinese Literature from Taiwan

Wang Chen-ho
Rose, Rose, I Love You

Cheng Ch'ing-wen
Three-Legged Horse

notes of a desolate man

BY CHU T'IEN-WEN

Translated by Howard Goldblatt
and Sylvia Li-chun Lin

COLUMBIA UNIVERSITY PRESS • NEW YORK

Columbia University Press wishes to express its appreciation for assistance given by the Chiang Ching-kuo Foundation for International Scholarly Exchange and Council for Cultural Affairs in the preparation of the translation and in the publication of this series.

COLUMBIA UNIVERSITY PRESS
Publishers Since 1893
New York   Chichester, West Sussex
Translation copyright © 1999 Columbia University Press

Library of Congress Cataloging-in-Publication Data
Ch'u, T'ien-wen.
[Huang jen shou chi. English]
Notes of a desolate man / by Chu T'ien-wen ; translated by
Howard Goldblatt and Sylvia Li-chun Lin.
p.   cm. – (Modern Chinese literature from Taiwan)
ISBN 0–231–11608–X
I. Goldblatt, Howard.   II. Lin, Sylvia Li-chun.   III. Title.   IV. Series.
PL2852.T48H9313   1999
895.1'352–dc21   98–32400

Printed in the United States of America
c 10 9 8 7 6 5 4 3

contents

translators' preface

The translation of *Notes of a Desolate Man* has been a treasure hunt that has taken us back to books and writers and thinkers we haven't encountered for years, has sent us to musty corners of video rental shops, and has enriched our collection of resource materials. Full of challenges and rich in opportunities for the translators, this novel has opened new vistas in fiction that we have tried to convey felicitously in a second language.

As in all translations, particularly those in widely divergent languages, the greatest losses to the non-native reader are experienced in the language itself. While we have striven to adhere as closely as possible to the often idiosyncratic semantics and grammatical structure of the original, for the sake of readability, we have rendered standard Chinese into standard English, wherever that took us. Where either the cultural or historical nuances in the narration or the intentional opacity of the text require explication, we have supplied notes at the end of the novel. Western-language words appeared in boldface in the Chinese edition of the novel; here they are in small caps. The pinyin system of transliteration has been used throughout (the name Ah Yao being the sole modest exception); Taiwanese place names, on the other hand, are given in the local postal spellings.

We have been aided in our work by several colleagues and friends. Our thanks to Joyce Wong Kroll, Carlos Rojas, Kyoko Saegusa, Stephen Snyder, Kumiko Takahara, William Tay, and John Weinstein. Thanks, too, to the Chiang Ching-kuo Foundation for International Scholarly Exchange for supporting the translation, and to our excellent editor, Leslie Kriesel. Finally, we are in debt to the author for her gracious, meticulous, and timely responses to our requests for clarification.

notes of a desolate man

chapter one

This is an age of decadence. This is an age of prophecy. I am securely bonded with it, sinking to the bottom, the very bottom.

I use my naked body to mark the nadir of all the most morally corrupting behaviors the human race can tolerate. Above me, moving from darkness to light, is rampant human desire and sexuality. Below me, there is nothing but an abyss. But since I have never believed in heaven, there can be no hell. Yes, below me, there is no demonic world. There is only, there is only the eternal, the everlasting abyss.

It stops here, it stops with me. The Bible says, Thou shalt not tempt the Lord thy God. This is where it stops.

I have reached my fortieth year, the prime of a man's life. So why have I already experienced the entire cycle of birth, aging, illness, and death, all that humans are fated to pass through, and become like a dead tree?

Who is it who said one should cultivate one's heart until it is like a dead tree and cold ashes, then have it sprout new leaves? But I am not like that. Nor am I like the monk, Master Hongyi, who could turn the splendor and charm of the first half of his life into dew to nourish the branches of tranquil asceticism of the second half.

I think, though I was once afraid of the raging desires that besieged me like moths drawn to a fire, and after the desire subsided, felt a deathly loneliness, and was terrified of facing that kind of loneliness, that now, at least, I can live with the loneliness. Living and dying serenely with that loneliness, looking death straight in the eye, I am no longer afraid.

chapter two

I boarded the first plane to Tokyo, then took the Ome Line train to Fussa. At the Fussa Clinic I saw Ah Yao, sunk into the hollow of his bedding, and spent his last five days with him. I can still say that AIDS is horrifying, but the price of loneliness is higher.

In the videotape he had sent me Ah Yao was shouting with a crowd of demonstrators, ACT UP, FIGHT BACK, FIGHT AIDS. But that had neither moved nor convinced me. He believed in organizations and movements, while I was such a pessimist I never participated in any gathering of more than three people. Garbo said, "Leave me alone." I said dejectedly, Let the world forget me. Ah Yao fought AIDS valiantly, but his life was slipping away like sand in an hourglass, and on the TV screen I thought I'd seen an ocean boiling red with madly copulating octopi as numerous as the sands of the Ganges. Just like Ah Yao's lifetime of insatiable, indiscriminate mating.

I needed to go out for a walk. Ah Yao's mother was dozing in a chair next to his bed, as typhoon rains fell silently beyond the tightly shut window. Ah Yao was a congenial man who treated other people with warmth and passion, dumping all his violent anger on his mother. That undisguised abusive attitude toward her always disgusted me. He brought his lovers home with no regard for her feelings. Ah Yao, I said, the house isn't yours. We often fought over such things, as I criticized him for disregarding other people's feelings. Pouring his frustrations onto his mother was no better than stabbing a defenseless snail with a sharp object. I said, Ah Yao, your mother will never understand the wild, desolate world we inhabit, not as long as she lives. It's not that she doesn't want to, she can't, she simply can't. Most people can't, because their ordered universe is just as fragile.

Endless arguments that never resolved anything, fallen petals and dead people unable to understand each other. Fate had decreed that Ah Yao, engaged in a tug-of-war with time, would fervently lose himself him in carnal pleasures, preaching comradely love, comradely counterattacks, comradely space, comradely rights. He was the photograph of a street demonstration. And me? I was nothing more than the negative, representing hypocrisy, as I hid in a dark closet like a coward, reversing night and day, living ignobly amid the norms of the human world.

Ah Yao's mother treated me like her own son. Way, way back in time I called her Auntie, then later I called her Mama, just the way Ah Yao did. Every time I said the word *Mama,* I adopted a narrative tone, as if I respected her so much I felt unworthy of conversing with her without benefit of an intermediary. I left Mama and the sickbed, and the clinic, which was quiet as snow, and exposed myself to the gusty winds and pouring rain. By the time I opened the umbrella, I was drenched, but I really needed to go out for a walk.

I fought off the wind and rain with my umbrella. The rain was like cosmic dust blown from a bellows, one gust after another, stopping for a moment, then cascading like a waterfall. The wind suddenly changed direction, whipping my umbrella inside out, as if scraping off my scalp. But I needed to go out for a walk.

Yesterday morning, Ah Yao awoke from his deathlike enervation. When I say awoke, for him it was nothing more than a moist glimmer of light welling up in his sunken eye sockets to form a shallow pool barely big enough to reflect my face. Then he saw me too. Having waited for this moment for a long, long time, I held my breath, afraid that the slightest exhalation would blow that light away. The past, the past was like dew, like electricity. If not for Ah Yao, my teen years would have been a vacuum. Ah Yao's eyes moved past my face; probably he wanted to see the light behind me. But it was too late. The blindingly bright, cloudless, pristine, white pre-typhoon rays of sunlight were enough to extinguish him. The light in his eyes dimmed, then disappeared, and he slipped into a coma from which he would never emerge. His wakefulness lasted only an instant and was gone; we were lucky not to have missed it. That fleeting moment was our final farewell, and I was beyond tears.

In 1990, Ah Yao lost a great deal of weight with a cold and went in for a checkup. As feared, he had the disease. He'd had it since 1988, when he was living in New York and San Francisco. He couldn't remember who his partner was at the time. For seven months he took AZT; his hair fell out, he lost his appetite, and he was always nauseous. After he stopped taking the medication, his condition stabilized somewhat and he regained a bit of his appetite. Last spring, I visited him in Tokyo. He was weak already, but he let me talk to him for two whole nights. I went on and on about our youth and our teen years, every movie, every theme song, like fallen nobility airing embroidered silks and satins under a winter sun. I sang the theme song from *The Man of La Mancha* with Peter O'Toole and Sophia Loren: "To dream the impossible dream, to fight the unbeatable foe . . . to right the unrightable wrong . . . to reach the unreachable star." We were always singing their song, while thinking our own thoughts. When 60 percent of the cherry trees were blooming and the newspapers reported their progress daily, we finally solved the puzzle of something that had happened years before.

The summer we passed our college entrance exam, we went to Shih-fen Falls on his family's 100 cc Suzuki, taking turns up front. The Falls recreation area was a popular spot for barbecues. Stone walls, blackened by smoke, twisted and turned; we climbed past a cave and peeked inside at the litter of garbage, as if it had been home to prehistoric dwellers. Imposing ferns with umbrella leaves blotted out the sky. Streaks of sunlight, here one second, gone the next, frolicked like imps in a forest, sometimes stopping on Ah Yao's hair, sometimes flying over his cheeks, and sometimes blinding me. Faster and faster we walked, as a thick layer of rotting leaves foamed and squished under our shoes. Pretty soon we were stepping all over the place, no longer sure if he was chasing me or I was chasing him. The close-in pressure of a Brian de Palma lens shot forced us up to the water's edge. With my path of retreat cut off, I leaped onto a rock in the water, paused for a moment, then jumped over to another one, and then another. I turned to look for him. Unaware that he was nearly stepping on my shadow, I was forced to give up that rock and jump off. We both fell onto a mossy rock ahead of us and had to clutch each other to keep from slipping off. The water sprayed over our heads; sunlight splashed around like an imp, creating thousands of rainbows; and cold water splashed our faces. I thought that if we fell into the water, we'd sizzle with opaque steam. But I moved off the rock and landed at the water's edge. Clambering to my feet, I went over to stand under some broad-leafed bushes, the drumbeat from my pounding heart making me giddy. A darkly sweet aroma permeated the air; white orchid blossoms erupted from snakelike vines. Ah Yao hadn't followed me. He was under the falls, head thrown back, gulping mouthfuls of water. A long time passed, so long that he was doused and I was crestfallen. Not knowing exactly what I was waiting for, I experienced a hefty sense of emptiness that sank painfully to the bottom of my gut.

In silence, we walked out of the damp forest. I grew quieter than ever; he was even more dejected. Tourists were still having a great time, but we scurried back to Taipei.

For many years afterward, I recalled that scene. In that brief, flickering instant, Ah Yao's breath had fallen on my face, but he hadn't kissed me. I wonder why.

At that instant, I had been terrified by intense feelings for someone of my own sex, a startling fear that seemed like God's secrets revealed. I'd seen something I wasn't supposed to see and tried to block it out, but by then it was too late.

I spent that long, hot, stuffy summer holding my own darkness carefully in my hands as if it were a box of radioactive material. Its energy bounced around in my heart, ready to produce the blinding light of a nuclear blast as soon as I dredged up what had occurred beneath the waterfall. It had the power to destroy the narrative order of cause and effect. I had no means of recalling anything, my recollections were empty. So I resigned myself to exhaustion that summer, as the girl across the way kept playing the same song over and over, practicing dance steps to TIE A YELLOW RIBBON.

Face to face with Ah Yao, I retreated into denial. No, I hadn't seen anything. I was innocent, I didn't know a thing. I pretended that nothing had happened, so adamant in my denial that my memory gradually underwent a revision. I erased facts I was reluctant to accept and began rewriting the text, until I was able to truly and completely forget what had happened at Shih-fen Falls. The lost horizon changed into a lost timeline; that day disappeared and nothing at all had happened between Ah Yao and me.

Until last year, at our final, night-long talk, when he said offhandedly, Remember Shih-fen Falls?

Yes, there was such a day; he was still healthy, I was still young.

At the time, I almost kissed you, Ah Yao said.

Oh! Really? I was surprised.

Ah Yao said, But you didn't have an erection, and just like that the impulse was gone.

Erection, yes, erection. The word, like a magic curse, summoned that lost day back from the realm of nothingness. Beneath the waterfall, during that brief moment while we were pressed against each other, I could feel Ah Yao's full erection against my belly, like a clenched fist. But we separated after that momentary touch, and every time I indulged myself in the process of hopeless recollection, I wished I had something with which to freeze the sensation, to look at it, observe it, understand it. The unwitting awakening of my unconscious was abruptly scared off and hounded into hiding in a deep cavern, until I met Jay six years later, that is, and it broke free to consume me. How could I have known that Ah Yao, who wasn't even twenty at the time, had already experienced everything?

Ah Yao told me that on the rough mountain road, when I was sitting behind him on the motorbike, he had fantasized about having anal sex with me. He got so turned on his arms and legs went numb and he had to stop. He asked if I remembered that we stopped by a cliff to look at the rock rising from the sea like a turtle shell. The cliff was San Tiao Chiao, or Three Marten Corners, which the Spanish had named San Diego. After we rested for a few minutes, I took over on the motorbike. He was sweating as he held me around the waist, then the wind dried his sweat and he was tamed. He said it had felt like he'd just done it.

Now, finally, I understood what I'd seen in his profile as he gazed out to sea. From my own rich experience over the years that followed, I knew that was the face of a man who had just enjoyed terrific sex. The blood had receded and the sweat had dried, but the face, not yet replenished with oxygen, was white as congealed fat, in contrast to his jet-black eyebrows and moist red lips, which looked painted on. Then, too, his eyes, framed by thick lashes, were misty, as if peering at ecstasy cooling off like the dimming glow of sunset. At the time, that expression unsettled me and made me turn away and concentrate on the sea.

So that's what it was. Finally awakening to the realization after twenty years, I chewed on this excavated historical data, and its taste was bitter as green olives. I said, Ah Yao, so that's what it was.

But Ah Yao could no longer sustain a long conversation. After a while, he could only utter single words; but I always knew what he wanted to say and finished his sentences for him. When he said, upstairs, I continued his thought: the old are sent upstairs. Ah, *8½*! Our days of film screenings. The oyster noodles in the alley where Taiwan Film Studios were located. Such authentic oysters, not the intestines they use as a substitute nowadays. So, Ah Yao, Fellini belongs to the past. The master aged, and we will be sent upstairs, too. Then I began reciting fragments from *8½*. What I mean by reciting is describing a series of scenes. Ah Yao closed his eyes and listened like an opera fan immersed in familiar arias and dialogue. Review and renew. Ah Yao and me, a couple of gray-haired palace maids, gabbing till dawn.

Ah Yao's place in Japan, a two-story Western-style house, belonged to his mother. Behind it three or four families lived in the shade of an old cherry tree. Each time I went to Tokyo I stayed with Mama, except for this spring, when I made the trip to visit Ah Yao and the two of us were actually together again. In the past, whenever I'd come to Tokyo, he'd been in Taiwan, and when I returned to Taipei, he'd have already taken a tour group to Amsterdam. After he got sick, he rarely came downstairs. Mama placed an overseas call to Taipei, asking me to phone him. Mixing Taiwanese with Japanese, she said to call collect, that she'd pay for the call. She wanted me to tell Ah Yao to get some exercise, and not be so lazy. He needed to walk around, even if he was tired. Following my advice, Ah Yao walked around on the tatami, stretching his neck, rolling his head, and shaking his arms. He did it for me, to show his gratitude for my visit.

He called himself a dying spirit. When he wanted to go outside, he rested his hand on the doorknob for a long time, lacking the strength to turn it. I'd known he was weak, but had no idea he was *that* weak.

I served as his crutches as we walked across the yard and down quiet streets to the riverbank in the park. Stopping every three steps, he lacked the strength even to raise his eyelids. His eyes gazed down at his nose, his nose gazed down at his heart, as he struggled to keep going. Suddenly, cherry blossoms showered down on him. He held his breath, concentrating on holding his emaciated body together, trying to keep it from falling apart under the weight of the flowers. The strain seemed to reduce him to a single line formed by his tightly closed mouth. Not daring to touch him, I just stood there beside him. Amid cherry blossoms fluttering down like a rain shower, waiting for the wind to die down, I felt like the wife of Rhodes, who, thousands of years ago, could not resist the temptation to look back at the burning city and was turned into a pillar of salt.

Every time Mama came upstairs with tea and food or to make the bed or with some extra bedding, she would instruct me in the wisdom of the Lord Jesus. But Ah Yao, who wouldn't listen, was her true intended audience. She was anguished over the fact that he had yet to confess and repent, and the sole purpose of the second half of her life was to get Ah Yao to come to God. Deprived of all alms-givers, she turned to me as a last resort to get her ideas across to Ah Yao.

It was always: Mama would open the sliding paper door and walk in, deliberately and carefully. Although her movements had slowed with age, she still moved with the grace of an actor in a Noh drama, like a dance but more ritualistic.

Mama bent over to place tea in front of me, following the custom of turning the porcelain cup halfway around before handing it to me. Each cup had a front and a back. I don't know how she could tell which was which, but it was important to her to have the front of the cup face her guest.

I treasured every cup of tea Mama presented to me, finishing it like a monk drinking down porridge given as alms. The seaweed flavor of Japanese tea took me back to Ah Yao's house on Taipei's Chang-an East Road, where the refreshing odor of disinfectant used in Western medicine filled the walled two-story house, with its brick facing, terrazzo floors, and baroque façade. It was at his house that I first tasted golden rice puffs sprinkled with bits of seaweed, placed in a jade-colored dish with artistic nicks in the rim. A serene, almost imperceptible fragrance emanated from Mama, who treated me like a grownup.

Japanese mother, Taiwanese daughter-in-law. Referring to the Epistle of Jude, she would say that any man who uses his positive traits in negative ways will suffer the torment of eternal fire and damnation.

Ah Yao called her Infinite Mother.

In Tokyo, I often took the last electric tram back to Fussa. Mama always left a light on in the living room, with a pot of hot water for tea. When I awoke in the morning, she was usually gone. My dirty clothes from the night before would be washed and hung out to dry. On the table, a basket of fruit. Mama knew I didn't eat anything in the morning, just a cup of tea. But rather than disappoint her, I'd force down an apple, or some strawberries, or a summer tangerine. She'd even lay out honey, and a knife and spoon, which I'd need for the tangerine.

I've always been fond of duck and chicken gizzards, and in my letters to Ah Yao, I praised her boiled leeks and stir-fried silver bean sprouts, as a means of expressing my gratitude to her. And she never forgot. She'd spend a whole morning or afternoon in the kitchen, pinching off the ends of bean sprouts one at a time, as if doing fine embroidery, keeping only the juicy, tender middle sections. She also brought home duck and chicken gizzards, which the Japanese don't eat, and laboriously scraped the rough, yellow insides, as if creating a work of art. I was speechless with gratitude. But Ah Yao said it was an honor for Infinite Mother, something she liked to do.

Occasionally, when I was in the same room with Mama, I'd suddenly feel as if we were on a Noh stage, grunting and chanting, submerged in a prolonged silence that felt like a painting whose colors bleed into each other. Our conversations were often reduced to intonations or sighs, but then we really didn't need to say anything. *Tatami* [grass mats], *fusama* [sliding partitions], *shoji* [sliding paper screens], the veranda and eaves, a

slanting pine, like the familiar frame composition of the director
Ozu Yasujiro, where nothing seems to move at all. In his old age,
the camera seemed to be stationary, jump cuts the only punctua-
tion. Within such a silent perspective, with the rhythms of Noh
drama, I enjoyed becoming part of Ozu's scenes.

In reply to a relative who had made a wisecrack about Ah Yao's
not marrying, Mama had said, My son's not marrying is only a
problem of bachelorhood, but your son's marriage has produced
a great many problems. She gleefully repeated this to me in a
mixture of Taiwanese and Japanese that I could barely understand, but that's the gist of it.

Even though she hated the men who phoned Ah Yao and
invariably turned them away, she was always polite. I'm so sorry,
he's not home. When Ah Yao brought one of his lovers home,
she'd politely excuse herself to go shopping. Carrying a handbag
with a paramecium-and-seaweed design, she'd either go to help
out at church or take the fifteen-minute tram ride to Tachikawa,
which was a little farther away, for some snacks and green tea at
Takashimaya, then buy some half-priced but still fresh salmon
sashimi at Yiseitan Supermarket before it closed at seven. She'd
return with a bagful of groceries and stock the fridge with Bud-
weiser beer. But she'd stay downstairs, taking sanctuary behind a
screen, the last spot she could call her own. Sometimes she'd hear
footsteps on the stairs, which meant that Ah Yao and his partner
were coming down to look for something to eat or drink. She'd
turn the TV volume up to let them know there was someone
behind the screen. But, powerless to stop them from fooling
around, she would prostrate herself on the tatami in the grip of
unimaginable torment, and pray. Sometimes it lasted only a
night, at other times two or three days. But only after the
stranger left would she emerge from her sanctuary and go
upstairs to clean with the ferocity of someone ridding the room
of a pestilence.

Mama walked slowly upstairs. The shadow of her hunched figure showed through the screen before she arrived. A giant ghostly shadow. The outline of Infinite Mother.

Ah Yao said, I think we are in rats' alley.

Where the dead men lost their bones. I silently recited the line from Eliot's "The Waste Land," the favorite poem of our youth.

Mama knelt down when she reached the screen door, and I watched the giant shadow shrink until it merged with the actual person. I couldn't help but recall a certain scene. I still remember his name—Xiaoyu. We were on our knees on the hardwood floor, arms around each other as we kissed passionately. Suddenly he bent backward and fell into a corner, alongside an artificial landscape. The floor lamp shone upon the small rocks and slender bamboo. He reached out and turned the light around so that our shadows, cast on the wall and ceiling, looked like giant deities. He was so, so incredibly turned on by the sight of our dark, gigantic, tangled shadows, he nearly went crazy and took me with him as far as we could go.

I looked at the porcelain cup, shaped like a Fuji apple. With no glaze, it felt rough and grainy, as if its days of glory were past. Somehow, I thought, I can tell which is the front of the cup and which the back. One side is a deeper color owing to a greater absorption of heat, unevenly distributed by the burning pine in the kiln. As for the face of the cup, it was the creation of destruction, a Buddhist fire, a Taoist flame.

It was April, the season when cherry trees bloom like raging fires. The philosophy of cherry blossoms dying at the height of their beauty is too mannered. I scrutinized the patches of brownish green and bluish purple around Ah Yao's mouth and wrists; they looked like bruises. Soon the Karposi's tumor would spread to his internal organs and swell his lymph nodes. I sighed. Ah Yao, you still won't repent, will you?

Ah Yao said, Repentance is a far greater evasion.

Approaching forty, we gradually gave up trying to bring each other around to our own way of looking at things. He figured he'd lived a dissolute life, and when it was over he'd go to hell. To say more was a waste of time.

So our conversation during the second half of the night stopped abruptly at a heated moment, when we were both agitated but not yet angry. His body, it simply couldn't take any more.

The light bulb suddenly brightened. I adjusted the shade so the lamp would shine its light out the window onto the cherry blossoms, turning them almost white. As Mama slowly read passages from the New Testament, Ah Yao pushed open the window and grabbed some of the flowers to eat. Cold air rushed in, a spring chill. When I went to close the window, I noticed Ah Yao's deathly ashen face, his mouth stained with pale yellow pollen, his lips trembling as he chewed the flowers. In the depth of night, the windowpane reflected a scenery of quiet flowers and a pale face. Once Ah Yao fell into silent oblivion, his tightly drawn face was like a knife cutting into my heart.

I was watching the sun set, while others were waiting for it to rise.

I walked into the stormy rains down Fussa streets, and was soaked to the skin.

It was an odd street. Tall stalks of bamboo stacked at an angle in front of the doors of houses were tied with colorful ribbons. From one end of the street to the other, the bamboo seemed to blot out the sky. Maybe they had been put up for the Festival of the Dead. I vaguely recalled, several days before, hearing the beating of drums and the shrill sounds of flutes piercing the clouds, followed by groups of ghost-dancers rushing in like the tide carrying schools of tumbling fish to the river, sweeping the shopkeepers and pedestrians on both sides of the street along with them. But now there was no one in sight. The wind and rain set the bamboo leaves rustling noisily and made the ribbons snap in the air. I scurried along beneath them, feeling the awesome power of nature. Suddenly the rain and wind stopped, and the ribbons hung slack, snowy white, vermilion red. The exquisite colors seemed not to belong to this world. I walked among them, wanting, longing to turn back.

Never before had I yearned to see another person as much as at this moment. Anyone, even footsteps from behind, would have been enough. People, people who need people, as Barbra Streisand sang. Someone like me, solitary as a monk, couldn't help but feel this way. My tears were falling; as the wind and rain died out, then returned, I wailed in agony.

Ah Yao, he was already gone!

h Yao was gone. Cold, hard reality confronted me. Gone, what does it mean to be gone? Michael Jackson said, I was born to be immortal.

This resilient moonwalker from the West, who had become a member of the Jackson Five at the age of five, mysterious and childishly innocent, had paid millions of dollars to achieve the chiseled, waxlike face of a statue. Whenever he made one of his rare appearances before the media, I stared anxiously at the TV screen, afraid that the exploding flash bulbs and the heat in the crowded room might melt and distort his face. The locks of hair hanging over his forehead, alongside his nose, and down the sides of his face, like seaweed, made me suspect that he might be trying to cover up a defect. One of my nightmares was that one day he would actually begin to melt under the stares of the whole world, like the supernatural Ayesha in Rider Haggard's *She*.

Guards were stationed in every hallway and at every turn of his secret, secluded residence. A fear of ghosts forced him to stay in his bedroom, and every inch of the house was monitored by surveillance cameras. Laser stereo equipment, set up all over the place, could be turned on to scare away the ghosts and demons. He received no guests except young boys. He played with the children: water-pistol battles, electronic games, pillow fights with feathers flying. He was bosom buddies with the little menace Macaulay Culkin, who became one of the highest-paid actors in the wake of the box-office hit, *Home Alone*. Bodyguards dressed up like gods ringed Jackson's bedroom to prevent demons from stealing his soul while he slept. The cover of his latest album featured a collage of giant faces of baroque and exotic figures from *The Arabian Nights*, and of various nationalities, a replica of the palace bedroom of a secret cult. I could hardly believe that in this day and age, I'd actually see anyone so afraid of aging and dying, so afraid of being gone, that he would imitate the pharaohs in building his own pyramid. The severity of his desperation must be regarded as one of the most intriguing spectacles of the century.

To be gone, for Ingmar Bergman, was simply no longer to be here. No excuse for it and no way to avoid it. No more.

Nevermore.

When Luis Buñuel was growing old, day by day, he faced death without fear. The only question left unanswered was what the world would be like without him. He had no means, no means at all, of knowing. How he wished to be able to rise up from his coffin every ten years to read that day's newspaper!

Those two at least had the chance to age; some people die young.

A while ago, I saw a Mel Gibson remake of an old movie. Hamlet, dying in the arms of his dear friend, says, I am dead. Thou livest. Report me in my cause aright to the uninformed. Things standing thus unknown, shall live behind me. If thou didst ever hold me in thy heart, absent thee from felicity awhile, and in this harsh world draw thy breath in pain, to tell my story.

Such an insignificant, yet magnificent wish! He could not have known that a single phrase would be misinterpreted as "The cat has fainted on the piano." How much more misunderstood, then, a person's entire life. Hamlet was a disturbing figure, but I was always deeply moved by his wonderful dying words, which showed how he brooded over his own deeds and his reputation, and that ultimately helped me understand what people mean when they say, When a tiger dies it leaves behind only its skin; when a man dies, he leaves behind only his name.

A name, a name, an eternal signifier. A person spends a lifetime casting it, polishing it, in hopes that it will shine like a diamond through the corridors of a million light-years. It is a religion without followers, a heavenly kingdom for pagans. Yet I hold out no hope even for that, because we, Ah Yao and me, are doomed to be people without names, without miracles.

It's tough to stay alive, but dying isn't any easier, as with the nameless fish in my fishbowl.

Originally there was a whole school of them, each one the size of a nail. At first glance, you'd have thought they were those tiny big-bellied fish we commonly saw in ditches when we were kids. When my students had barbecues on the mountain behind the school, they caught vast numbers of them in the creek with butterfly nets. On their way home once, they stopped at my place and let themselves in after knocking first. They had stopped by specifically for some coffee brewed in my Krups coffeemaker, making themselves right at home. Afterward, these decent, sensible kids did the dishes before they left. But without asking permission, they left behind a plastic bag filled with fish, along with the suggestion that they could be a treat for my cat Gigi. One of them was actually about to feed the cat, but I quickly put a stop to this violence, and so the fish were left for me. Their lives were now in my hands; I was responsible for them, and that was sheer torture. I never joined the students in their outings, since while everyone was waiting to eat, no more than two or three of the more responsible among them stayed back to tend the fires, the rest of them just hanging around, the smell of slowly roasting meat making them so restless they were constantly arguing and making each other unhappy. Being young and energetic, once they spotted some fish or crabs, they'd jump into the water and dig in the mud like wild animals, not stopping until they'd snapped off the leg of an unfortunate crab. And if that wasn't enough for them, someone would hop on his motorbike and go to the nearest store to buy fishing nets, then they'd go half-crazy scooping fish out of the water, while their barbecue fires seared the rocks on the riverbank, the smoke blackening tendrils hanging from trees. This time, along with their youth, they abandoned both the fish and their nets at my house. Three of those nets, their labels still intact, were left behind with the live fish. This pained me deeply.

First I scooped the fish out of the bag and put them in a basin. Those purple-and-gray-striped plastic bags, which had flooded the market, were the ugliest and the very worst you could find; they wouldn't biodegrade in ten thousand years. That day I went to every store that might carry usable containers, and stumbled upon a messy stationery store that sold glass potbellied fishbowls. All different sizes, with billowing mouths like lotus leaves, they looked like women's derrieres, with bows tied around their middles. The thick layer of dust covering them was a sure sign that they were left over from an earlier fad of raising fighting fish. Several of my fish died even before they were transferred to the fishbowl, and I tossed them into flowerpots on the balcony for fertilizer. Then, using what little knowledge I had in the area of raising fish, I filled a bucket with tap water and, once the chlorine had sunk to the bottom, added a little to the river water already in the bowl, in hopes that the fish would adjust more easily to their new environment, while I pondered what to feed them.

They scattered at once, swimming off in all directions. From above they were a dull gray color, but when I peered through the side of the bowl, I saw they were flat with shiny tropical stripes. A day and a night later, they were still alive, much to my surprise. Only a couple had gone belly-up at the bottom of the bowl. I picked them out with chopsticks. One was almost too small to be called a fish. They too wound up in a flowerpot—dust to dust. I made a special trip to a tropical fish shop in town, at the foot of the mountain, where I bought a can of the most common variety of fish food, little red bricks, which, I was told, were ground-up shrimp. I also brought back a large but very ordinary bowl, shaped like a crystal ball, preparing to raise them on a long-term basis.

I crushed a piece of shrimp brick with my fingernail and spread the powder on the water. To my surprise and delight, the fish scurried up to the surface to fight over the food. Apparently these common fish were going to be a snap to raise. Me, an earth mother type, happily watching her kids and husband clean their plates of food and heaping on more and more, until they couldn't eat another bite. Prodigious consumption produced a prodigious amount of waste that now muddied the water. Concerned about all that nitrogen, I changed the water diligently, always keeping half the original water. Whenever the water was changed, the fish swam along the sides in bunches. Was that because they weren't used to the new water, or because they were so happy to have clean water? I couldn't tell. Only when they finally settled down and started to swim leisurely was my mind at ease. I decided to control the amount of the food in order to reduce the frequency of their restless activity.

After a week, when the fish and I seemed to be forming a pattern of interaction, a bunch of them suddenly died.

The first sign of their demise, a loss of equilibrium, had them struggling to keep from tipping over. If they tilted more than 45 degrees, they'd burst forward, straining to right themselves. Then, having regained their equilibrium, they'd swim off steadily, until they started to tilt again. After several attempts they'd quit, but before giving up completely, they'd flip over and plant their mouths on the bottom of the tank, swimming swimming swimming, until at last, they'd let go and float off, turning slowly, as if performing a slow-motion somersault, then sink to the bottom, belly up, and stop moving. Their life-and-death struggle wore down my willpower like a millstone.

Afraid that what was causing them to die might be contagious, I changed the water more often. They scuttled along the walls of the fishbowl, circling circling circling and stirring up a layer of egg-white mist. Figuring that the deaths might be attributable to population density, I transferred some of the fish into the ugly lotus leaf bowl. It was like moving mountains and emptying the sea, a sort of chemistry experiment that caused me great anxiety, as I assumed I lacked sufficient knowledge of fish to tend to them. I agonized constantly over whether to change the water or feed them. In the end, I stopped sprinkling shrimp powder on the surface, since they no longer showed any interest in it, and as the powder soaked up water, it began to look like poisonous fungi.

One bunch of fish after another died, and I could no longer dump them into the flowerpots for fear of attracting flies and other bugs. With a last look at their persistent luster, I calmly washed them down the drain. Only two survived the disaster.

Amazingly, I found the larger of the two in a groove in the window frame. I had no idea how long it had been there. Scooping it up with an index card, I put it back into the bowl for the time being, not daring to hope that it would live. It remained motionless, as if in a daze; then, surprisingly, it flapped its fins and tail and started to move. Its resilience baffled me. Dared I believe that it possessed the magic power of the carp that leaped over a threshold and turned into a dragon, escaping the bowl to avoid the calamity that befell the others, then somehow surviving out of water? To the smaller fish as well I paid my highest respects; perhaps it was blessed with a streak of resistance in its genes.

In any case, I admired their ability to survive and willingly continued to care for them.

I enhanced their environment with some golden creepers, creating comfortable living conditions as the fibrous roots spread throughout the water to form a sort of arboretum; the peach-shaped leaves extended over the edge of the tank. After a while, a green film began to coat the sides of the bowl, the roots turned fuzzy green, and fish waste accumulated at the bottom, as the bowl developed its own ecosystem.

Oftentimes, I'd gaze at the fish with such concentration that I'd forget to eat and sleep. As they threaded their way through the leaves, their bodies sometimes glistened and sometimes darkened, like shards of shattered gems. Sometimes they turned into sanitation workers, spending an entire afternoon busily tidying up their living quarters. They pushed the accumulated waste off to one side with their mouths, meticulously nibbled the vine roots clean, and vacuumed the sides of the bowl from top to bottom, until they shone. Occasionally they faced off at opposite ends, like Kendo masters mustering inner strength. Then they'd explode forward and shoot right past each other. I didn't know what this was all about, but they quickly returned to their original positions to start over, until I couldn't help but burst out laughing. If I didn't shake the bowl and stir up waves to stop them, they'd keep at it as if possessed. Or they'd float, resting their fins in the water, as if meditating, wanting not to be bothered. But as soon as I sprinkled shrimp powder on the surface they'd show their true colors, mean and voracious.

Look there, the larger one gobbles up most of the food, then turns to attack the smaller one, stopping only when the latter seeks refuge at the bottom. Then the big fish rushes back to the surface to finish off the powder in one final sweep. What a tyrant. More than once, I intervened by dividing the food with my hand. But then I heard of a similar occurrence when a Japanese emperor was feeding his carp, or was it swans? It was always the strongest one that grabbed most of the food and ate more than its fair share. When the palace attendants complained about the inequity, the emperor stubbornly clung to his impartiality, spreading the food all around, just as the sun shines on both the good and the bad. Since infancy he had been taught to dislike nothing and fear nothing. Recognizing neither terror nor danger in the mundane world, he would probably have treated a cobra courteously if he had met one. An ordinary person like me could never reach that level.

I raised a pot of mosquito larvae out on the balcony. Each day I'd scoop out a few and drop them into the fishbowl. The larvae, the color of red moles, squirmed in the water. Quick as a flash, the two fish, like baseball outfielders, rushed up to devour them. They must have been delicious. I knew I was spoiling my fish, but I couldn't help it. Early summer was the season for mosquito larvae, and I got a full scoopful whenever I reached into the pot. The fish kept growing, their lustrous scales proving that they were in good health. I yearned to know if one was a female and the other a male, for that would have really made me happy.

And so it went for a while, until one day I discovered the larger fish tilting to one side as it swam. That threw me into a panic.

The small one pecked at him as he fought to swim on, like a drunk struggling to appear sober. I'm not drunk, he says with a laugh, I am not drunk. Was the small fish harassing him or cheering him on? It moved closer, then backed off, then one quick peck and off it went. Helplessly, I watched the distressed fish turn upside down, showing his white underbelly, as he gradually changed into a different creature. The smaller one was harassing, but lost interest when it realized the other fish no longer posed a threat.

He must have died from overeating. That's the only possible explanation. I gave them too many larvae, and he monopolized the largesse. He ate so much he couldn't get rid of it in time; he literally stuffed himself to death. But this was human error, and my remorse went beyond words.

The last remaining fish died the following February; it froze to death when a cold front moved in. Up till then, every time I looked at it, it seemed so incredibly lonely. I let out a sigh like Jehovah when he said, "It is not good for this man to be alone, so I shall create a mate to assist him." I seriously considered going to the creek in the foothills to find the fish a companion.

The fishbowl held a patch of sunlight and reflected the clouds from beyond the window. The single fish in that large bowl was like a tiny planet in a vast solar system. It moved through its dominion differently now that its sometime playmate, sometime rival was gone (even though its companion had been a bully). It roamed through the water listlessly, in a state of zero gravity, like a man-made satellite successfully launched into the sky to settle into orbit. This was how it would be from now on, living on unless I happened to break the bowl it swam in. It slipped through the water seemingly devoid of anger and happiness, unaffected by enmity or love. Wasn't this nirvana? But then, wouldn't the life of an immortal fish be incredibly boring? Every so often I bent down and blew on the surface to create ripples, and sometimes I was even able to stir up currents toward the bottom. It always made me feel better to see the fish actually swim a bit.

Whenever I paused to think as I was writing, my gaze fell naturally on the fish. It swam in and out of the outer curve of the fishbowl, changing shape at each reflected angle. Slowly moving out of the frame, trailing its magnificent tail of colors like a comet, it would reappear in an aura like the sunrise in one of Monet's impressionistic oils. Then it would disappear completely, leaving a prolonged emptiness in the frame. I'd wait for it to reappear, but the wait was often longer than I could stand; suddenly feeling apprehensive, I'd leap up from my chair and run over to peer into the bowl, afraid my fish might have jumped out and landed somewhere nearby. By then I'd have broken out in a cold sweat, and was relieved only when I saw it floating near the top in fine fettle, blending almost invisibly into the fluorescent-gray surface tension. It continued to tidy up its environment, pushing the waste into a pile with its mouth. I pitied it for the way it reminded me of Chang'e, the lady in the moon, who sweeps her Vast Cold Palace all alone.

I assumed, of course, that it would live and die with me, since it had become such an integral part of my daily life. As time went on, we more or less forgot about each other. Which is why, when I found it lying belly-up that day, I couldn't believe it! I had just read in the newspaper that great numbers of milkfish had frozen to death in the south, but hadn't connected that in any way with the fish in my warm room. Separated by death, just like that. Lulled into thinking that nothing could go wrong, I was caught by surprise when Death paid a visit, and the flesh was too weak to resist.

I buried it in the flowerpot, digging a hole with my fingers and covering it with leaves to commemorate the intimate year of life we had shared.

I kept the fishbowl for the sake of the golden creepers, whose photosynthetic characteristics were impressive. Every few days I rotated the bowl so the emerald green leaves always faced me. How strong the force of life.

On TV I watched a BBC production about the death of an elephant. The feeble animal crumpled to the ground like a collapsed tower as its companions formed a circle around it, straining to help it back to its feet with their powerful trunks. Several times they nearly succeeded, but the elephant always slumped back to the ground. After exhausting themselves, the elephants abruptly dispersed and trumpeted loudly. Then they paired off in twos to rub against each other. One would place its thick forelegs onto the other one's back, imitating the behavior of mating. Were they trying to stir up a will to live in their companion by displaying the pleasure of the sex act? The dying animal lay on the ground, staring blankly ahead, while the underbrush around it split and cracked under the trampling feet of its despairing companions.

I've also witnessed the last glance of this world by a person dying of starvation. Completely exhausted, she lay flat somewhere in the wilderness, her glazed black eyes opened wide. The grass around her swayed in the wind, like spring waters flowing toward the horizon. Dragonflies flitted over the grass as tender, cool evening breezes extinguished the last flicker of life in her. Thunder rumbled in the distance; it was a death scene filmed by Satyajit Ray in a green village in northern India, where food supplies were cut off by Japanese occupying forces in Burma. There was water and there was grass, but the people died silently and miserably, like withered flowers, disappearing from the face of the earth. The Indian way of death.

A woman said, One must be happy while alive, for death lasts a very long time.

Faustus said, Nothing has been proved, nor can anything be proved. New errors are found in every set of ideas I taught. The only certainty is that the purpose of our existence is existence itself; what matters is the process we go through.

While I was out walking madly in the typhoon, Ah Yao was suddenly gone.

I saw a sign pointing toward Seigangyin [Clear Rock Court] and decided to head that way, assuming it was a Buddhist temple or a Shinto shrine. I was totally unprepared for the sudden appearance of a fence surrounding a field of tombstones, so surprising me that I was abruptly freed from the grip of my water-soaked, denuded emotions. At that moment I was able to see my surroundings and me within them. I was soaked to the skin, even my bones were wet, yet I ceremoniously held up my umbrella like a complete fool.

But this time, clear-headed, I chose to continue my foolishness. I began surveying one tombstone after another, carefully scrutinizing the epitaphs. Precisely because I was clear-headed, I felt a chill run up my spine. So I looked up to stare into the distance: over there a bridge and broad avenues; over here apartments. Yes, I could not deny that I was living in a modern society, one I'd so often cursed. But at this moment, it seemed so friendly, so captivating. Composed again, I went back to reading the epitaphs, all alone in a vast cemetery that was shuddering in the wind and rain. I needed to overcome my initial angst by means of this almost masochistic tomb-surveying ceremony.

Ah Yao was dead, which meant that a large chunk of the things we'd shared would go with him. What was the significance of memory if we couldn't share it, or if no one knew about it? It might as well be buried in oblivion. I had to let myself succumb to the rain and the cold wind and fall seriously ill if I was to survive this period of unbearable grief.

The people beneath the tombstones had probably died of old age, good deaths. Ah Yao was too young, so this might not be the place for him. In the foreseeable future, death will fall upon more men and women still younger than Ah Yao, even children. In the memorial of December 1 the year before, the camera gave a bird's-eye view of antlike demonstrators holding up a gigantic banner. It was a quilt patched together from clothes or blankets donated by the families of deceased AIDS patients. The rapid expansion of the quilt shocked the world. Ah Yao will find his place there on that splendid memorial quilt. A warrior, that was Ah Yao.

I left Seigangyin and returned to town. In front of the train station I spotted the golden arches of a McDonalds, hovering above the city like a demonic beast. I'd always avoided eating at McDonalds, but now I ran up to embrace it as if meeting a long-lost relative. This was the first time in my life I'd eaten at McDonalds, and it dawned on me that on this stormy day, when no people seemed to be out, they were actually congregating in a fast-food restaurant lit up like a greenhouse.

As I sipped the lousy coffee to warm up, I took off my socks to dry them, and was shocked by the sight of my ghostly blue feet. I'd bought the socks at Seiyu Department Store the day before, when I left the hospital to get something to eat. I never expected them to fade so completely when wet, even though they came without an inspection tag. I should write a letter of complaint. From my window seat, I watched the typhoon ravage the city, which bowed before its might. As for me, safely indoors and part of a smelly crowd, I didn't have to worry about being beaten or cursed. I was alive! Like a primitive man who, after escaping to his cave from a lightning storm, checks his hands and legs and finds them still intact, I felt very lucky, lucky that I, unbelievably, amazingly, was not HIV-positive. In New York City alone, some three to four hundred thousand people were. Ah Yao was dead, I was still alive.

Not long ago, there was a widespread rumor that KYON was infected with the AIDS virus. KYON, Koizumi Kyoko, one of Japan's first-generation supermodels. Her sweet, friendly smile, which was everywhere on TV, had all of Japan in thrall. She never caused trouble, nor did her name appear in gossip columns; even the most notorious tabloid reporters could find nothing to report on her. This uncrowned queen, who had captured the heart of a nation, could not be dethroned, except by AIDS. Alarming rumor, weapon of destruction, the Pale Horseman of the Apocalypse.

I once saw a Kirin beer ad she made for the Barcelona Olympics. The text went, "Those who will supply me with memories of Barcelona are now sweating away somewhere in Japan." Across the top of the ad: "I want my mellow Kirin LAGER."

I also happened upon the phenomenon of Golden Grandma and Silver Grandma, a pair of centenarian twins who lived in Nagoya. When their ages were combined, Narita Kin and Kaiie Gin were 200 years old. Golden had lost all her teeth, which made her slur her words, while Silver still had her front teeth, enabling her to speak intelligibly. Discovered during Respect the Aged Day, they became overnight media sensations. They made a commercial that was simplicity itself:

Golden said, I never get sick.
Silver said, I'm always in good health, too.
I like red sashimi.
I like white.
I usually do my own laundry.
Me, too. I still do all the housework.
Then a male voice-over: These hundred-year-old grandmas are still housewives. Their names combine to form a symbol of good luck—gold and silver. Lion King, a company established in the twenty-fourth year of the Meiji Period, when men still wore their hair in the samurai style, is also a hundred years old. It has been exactly one hundred years since cleaning products by Lion King entered Japanese households. These products continue to be a great help in your daily life.
Golden said, I still have lots of fun things to do.
Silver said, Me, too. I feel my life has just begun.

Golden's response to a reporter regarding her hundredth birthday was used in another commercial, for DUSKIN, and it immediately became the phrase of the year. She said, It's a feeling of happiness but also one of sorrow.

A mixture of sorrow and happiness, the last writing of Master Hongyi.

I am still alive. I feel as if I should do something for people like me, for those who have died. But I really can't do anything for anyone. I must do it for myself, I must write.

Write in order not to forget.

Time will eventually wear out, erode, annihilate everything. I cannot bear the thought that my memory of Ah Yao will slowly disappear as time goes by, to the point of total oblivion. If I could, I'd crystallize my grief, turn it into an indestructible amulet to wear around my neck. My only option is to write; in the continual process of writing, I will gouge my wound over and over, lash the scars of my sins, and lock up the memories with pain, so they will never slip away.

I write, therefore I am. When I can no longer write, I will throw down my pen, and to hell with it, for I'll no longer be able to lay claim to emotions, consciousness, or form.
And that's all.

chapter four

The greatest archetypes for people like me are Jesus and his twelve disciples.

Jesus was forced to bear the cross in his sacrifice for others; those who betrayed him branded his body with a kiss. His look of perpetual thoughtfulness and his tightly knit brows created the perfect image. His naked body, bloodied by thorns, became an aesthetic standard. When we were at our best, we were just imitating him.

But I never took part in Ah Yao's comradely movement. Ah Yao came close to saying, The revolution hasn't succeeded yet; the comrades must continue the struggle.

The so-called comrades: QUEER. A new breed of homosexuality, a proud break with earlier times. There is no link between pre-AIDS and post-AIDS. The essential difference is the creation of a new age, a rectification of names. Therefore, it is important to make a clear distinction: It's not GAY, it's QUEER. Ah Yao taunted, QUEER, so what? I am that word. You people and we are fundamentally different, so why split hairs?

Ah Yao insisted that GAY is white, male. The term *homosexual* is politically incorrect. QUEER is not like that at all. Male, female, yellow, white, black, bisexual, transsexual, there's room for everyone, that's QUEER.

Yes, I agree. The use of language itself is part of the message, as stated by my cherished Lévi-Strauss.

The most obvious exemplifying event, for instance, was the recent celebration of Columbus's discovery of the New World, no no no, not discovery, *encounter*. The former reveals a Eurocentric worldview that relegates American Indians to the periphery. The new, multifocal view, and the politically correct expression, is that the American continent encountered Columbus. As a member of the Yellow Race, I castigated myself for having been brainwashed by White Europeans. After emerging from my formative years, which were replete with terms like *Far East* and *Near East* in all the histories and geographies, I became the embodiment of the language that I used. It was hard for me to be as active as Ah Yao. My situation was much like that of an old man whose teeth and bones have calcified, fleeing in embarrassment from a smiling dentist approaching with corrective braces.

Early on, when Ah Yao was already a happy GAY man, I was lost and tormented in a labyrinth of identity: Was I or wasn't I? Later on I faced up to cold reality, but not until recently, when the ferocious beast named desire, which possessed me, began to withdraw after realizing that my body was a deteriorating old edifice, did I have the courage to proclaim that I could accept the lonely second half of my life without a partner—the fate of a GAY man. I said, I'm fine, I'm happy.

Ah Yao looked at me with a lecherous sneer. Oh, so you're happy and you're fine, are you? His smirks always succeeded in enraging me. He had abandoned the term GAY, treating it like garbage, while my foolish attempt at gentility and cultivation, wearing an outdated top hat, was utterly ridiculous.

He said, FUCK THE GENTLE. Toward the end of his life, he became more and more aggressive, mistreating his mother to the point of taunting, even assaulting her. I couldn't stand seeing him expose himself on the front line, and I vowed never to claim his body if he perished under siege.

Prior to his death, a memorial for AIDS victims was held in Washington, D.C. in 1987; in 1988, protesters in Manchester demonstrated against Clause 28 of the Local Government Bill; in 1989, Denmark passed a law allowing same-sex marriages, but did not approve adoption. Nineteen-ninety was the year of KISS-ING IN, when public kissing was tolerated. The year 1991 witnessed the OUTING CAMPAIGN. Silence is death, ignorance is fear; medical care is an inalienable right. Protests against Glaxo-Wellcome forced the manufacturer of AZT to lower the cost by 20 percent. This year, according to British law, Hong Kong lifted the ban against anal sex. Ah Yao witnessed all these changes, and he regarded them as great victories.

I later realized that his activities toward the end of his life resulted from an unconscious premonition that his days were numbered, and that in turn caused his confusion. If I'd known that earlier, I wouldn't have argued with him or acted so disagreeably. God, how we argued during our New York–Taipei phone calls! I've forgotten what we fought about, but it was mostly insignificant stuff that often ended in anger and resentment. Once he asked if I'd read the material he'd sent me. I said no. He asked why, and I said I didn't feel like it. It was afternoon over there, two o'clock in the morning here. We fell silent, separated by the thousands of miles between day and night and listening to the sound of coins falling as they noted the passing minutes. I couldn't handle the silence like he could, so I said, OK, enough already. This is long distance. To spite me, he hung up without another word. The unresolved conflict cost me a night's sleep.

I later realized too that he would call for no other reason than to hear my voice, which connected him with his past, like a safety rope thrown just in time to prevent him from falling into an abyss. Our conversations preserved for him the feeling that he was a human being, not an animal. Cowering in a phone booth on some street in a foreign land, cradling the receiver to his ear, he was like the tragic protagonist in *The Fly*, who, after finally finding his girlfriend, begs her to help change him back into a human being.

That image often surfaced in my mind. I recall a phone call I received one Sunday afternoon. Out of habit, I asked, What time is it over there?

He said, I don't know.

I looked out at a majestic caterpillar kite soaring in the yellow autumn sky. My cuckoo clock informed me that it was a little after four. I quickly calculated the time of day for him: Saturday night—no, roughly three in the morning.

He said, It's not important, it doesn't matter. What are you doing?

I said, Nothing, just reading. What about you? What are you doing?

He said, What *would* I be doing? What *else* do you think I'd be doing?

I said, Hey there, you'd better take care of yourself. You're not getting any younger.

He said, What are you reading?

Tristes Tropiques.

Never read it.

I knew he hadn't, since he probably stopped reading when he turned thirty. I mumbled the author's name, feeling somewhat guilty about finding a new heartthrob, thus excluding him. Even in the case of movies, he'd seen only the works of Wim Wenders, the last of Germany's three great directors. Old friends and new acquaintances, after we were grown and began to live separate lives, I treated with caution those parts of our lives that didn't overlap, so as not to offend him.

Not surprisingly, he said, Never heard of him.

He does structural anthropology, I explained apologetically, as if Lévi-Strauss were my lover.

He said, Never mind who he is. Read a little to me.

Oh? I was suddenly tongue-tied. Where do I start?

He said, Start with what you're reading now. Read it aloud to me.

As if summoned from on high, I picked up the book and, after telling him a bit about Lévi-Strauss, gave him a brief overview of the chapter I was reading. It was about the Caduveo tribe in the Brazilian jungle, whose deteriorating circumstances had forced them to preserve some distinguishing qualities from the past—a tendency exhibited most clearly in their art of body painting. They believed that to be a man it was necessary to be painted; to remain in the natural state was to be no different from the beasts. Forgetful of hunting, fishing, and their families, these Indian men wasted whole days in having themselves painted. Facial paintings confer human dignity on the individual; they ensure the transition from nature to culture, from "stupid" beast to civilized man. And since they vary in style and pattern according to caste, they express differences in status within a complex society. This means that they have a sociological function. Caduveo art is characterized by a male/female dualism—the men are sculptors, the women painters. Suppressing my fervor, I revealed my new heartthrob to Ah Yao, then stopped.

Ah Yao said, Very good, I agree. Go on.

Tristes Tropiques, I softly uttered the name of the book in

French before going on to caress the next passage like a lover. I read, page 255:

> In the last resort, the graphic art of the Caduveo women is to be interpreted, and its mysterious appeal and seemingly gratuitous complexity to be explained, as the phantasm of a society ardently and insatiably seeking a means of expressing symbolically the institutions it might have, if its interests and superstitions did not stand in the way. The female beauties trace the outlines of the collective dream with their make-up; their patterns are hieroglyphics describing an inaccessible golden age, which they extol in their ornamentation, since they have no code in which to express it, and whose mysteries they disclose as they reveal their nudity.

Before I'd finished reading, the line was disconnected. I waited for him to call back, but he didn't.

Even thousands of miles could not keep me from detecting the hoarseness and edema in his voice. It had to be the result of weekend bar-hopping followed by musical chairs with a dozen or more men in a steam bath. Before his member had turned completely flaccid, desire flared up again, but his worn-out dick forced him to give up. I knew only too well the frenzied rites of sucking and touching after spitting on your palms and getting down on your knees. It was unstoppable, like the girl who, after putting on the red shoes, couldn't stop dancing until exhaustion set in, and finally died.

All those merging fluids sucked out of other bodies to smear on their own bodies, and on his, congealing to form a veil that smelled like foul mud in a ditch, impossible to get rid of, entangling him like a spiderweb. On that early morning–late night, with trash gusting all around and opaque steam rising from street-level subway vents, the image of Ah Yao, flitting around the streets like a human fly, burned into my mind.

The remake of *The Fly* in 1986, with its technologically advanced visual effects, graphically displayed the transformation process, with shattered body parts, mutating limbs, and pustulating skin; yet it lacked the dramatic tension, the terror, and the tragic beauty of the 1958 version. For the tragedy was that even if Ah Yao turned into a human fly, the experience was something

we, me included, knew only too well, and we both belonged to
the 1958 version. In other words, we were too classic. When new
phrases in commercial ads took youngsters by storm, their innocent and ignorant faces declared defiantly, "Anything goes, so
long as I like it." It was like spitting in my face, but I just turned,
as poised as I could manage, took out a handkerchief, and wiped
the spit off.

When I happened to turn on the TV, the face of a "new person" burst onto the screen, changing and shifting through a con-
vex lens. Making a face, he yelled, "I really—like—I like—my
face," so shocking me that I hit the button and obliterated it. A
commercial for some soft drink or instant noodles, that face violently invaded my bedroom and enraged me. When Ah Yao
stepped out and taunted, QUEER, that's what I am! I wanted to
jump up, wrap him in a blanket, and drag him off the stage. The
kids, they had their youth, but Ah Yao, you and I, with our mangy
hides, why display our ugliness for all to see?

When our mutual friend, Parrot Gao, set up a studio at home
and sat in front of his computer eight hours a day, the preserva-
tion of life was all that kept him going. He never shied away from
announcing to one and all that he would see no one before
noon. He would strip naked, smear skin-tightening lotion all
over his body, and wrap his belly with plastic after applying fat-
reducing oil. Then he'd sit in front of his computer terminal for
two hours before taking off his "battle dress."

One day I decided to get off the bus at his stop to return a
book on southern Fukienese architecture. He sounded very
unhappy over the intercom that I had come unannounced. The
iron gate, mirroring his reluctance, opened slowly, just a crack.
When I reached his third-floor apartment, he hid behind the
door to let me in. He was, I discovered, giving himself a facial;
reduced to two large circles around the eyes, another circling his
mouth, and a pair of dark nostrils, he looked like some kind of
mountain beast. I was going to leave after dropping off the book,
but since I'd already seen him in this getup, he asked me to stick
around and try some of his homemade kumquat tea. He lifted a
corner of his terrycloth bathrobe to show me his belly, all bundled up in plastic wrap like German pigs' feet. I thought you did
this in the mornings, I said. It's almost evening.

My comment unleashed a flood of complaints. He said he'd turned in some stage design sketches two days earlier, and after going over them late into the night, he and his friends had gone to a beer hall for a late-night snack; he hadn't gotten home till nearly dawn. He'd slept most of the day, and when he awoke late that afternoon, he looked at himself in the mirror and saw how his face sagged after an all-night get-together. Feeling depressed, he'd gone for a swim, then come home to play with the computer for a while before heading back to bed, then getting up late again. He was upset that going out just that once had so completely disrupted an orderly schedule he'd taken such pains to establish. Which was why he was forced to give himself a facial so late in the day—he was worried he'd sleep in late again tomorrow, since he wouldn't be able to fall asleep before midnight. He counseled me that a good night's sleep is better than any skincare product, since you age the most between 11 P.M. and 1 A.M., when the *yin* and *yang* cycle changes. Sound, dreamless sleep during this period is the most efficient method of preserving your youth. Do you give yourself facials? he asked me.

I can't, I said. I'm allergic.

He leaned over and whispered, Ever hear of ocean-mud masks?

I touched the gray sandy cream on his face with my index finger. Is that what this is? All I know about is volcanic ash.

He nodded and said, You're right, there's volcanic ash in this, also some potter's clay and spring water, but the main ingredient is mud from a certain place in the Atlantic. No added fragrance, completely natural and hypo-allergenic. You should give it a try.

He showed me an array of bottles and jars in a vanity area next to his bathroom, patiently explaining the benefits of sea salt and seaweed therapy. He informed me that the live placenta extract that had been on the market years earlier—the name itself was enough to scare you away—was tested only on animals and not environment friendly. The best skin-care products are extracted from the ocean, since they contain eighty-four minerals, a bunch of trace elements, and amino acids. For instance, potassium balances electrolytes and aids the normal functioning of neuro-wave circulation to produce energy from carbohydrates, proteins, and fat. Magnesium, with its restorative qualities, moistens and softens the skin. Calcium and zinc have a calming effect; the latter, in particular, can induce chemical reactions from the hundreds of enzymes in our body, to speed up metabolism. Mineral salt is very effective in exfoliating dead skin cells. There's also a massage cream extracted from Dead Sea crystallites that is highly rejuvenating. A full-body skin treatment with mud from the Dead Sea should follow applications of the massage cream. He took out an ordinary two-liter bottle half filled with Dead Sea water, a souvenir from a former lover who had personally taken it from the sea on a pilgrimage to Israel. Caught up in fond memories of the past, he said to the bottle and to me, The Dead Sea, did you know it was the skin-care swimming pool for Cleopatra and the Queen of Sheba?

After his exhaustive edification, I couldn't be stingy and hold back my own secret formula—diet therapy, which emphasizes revising dietary habits in order to alter the body's system. A friend of mine, who had a nasopharyngeal tumor, turned vegetarian after vainly seeking help from famous doctors everywhere. He survived by fighting the cancer cells with diet therapy. Owing to my fragile constitution, I needed to start with internal restoration, supplemented by baby oil, which my kid sister had recommended.

The "Cocoon Dwellers" promoted the popularity of sit-down baths. In fact, Parrot Gao's bathroom and his bed took up two thirds of his apartment; the remaining space was occupied by a food-preparation island and a bar, which, like the steel dining table and four swivel chairs, as well as his filing cabinet, came with wheels so he could move them around. In the bathroom, he had a potted Chinese palm (not your common palm tree); a brick wall with glass inlays to let in natural sunlight, which was partially blocked by a folding screen; plus lounge chairs and rattan stools, all of which gave the illusion of colonial style in the South Sea tropics.

As we intimately exchanged hygiene secrets, Parrot Gao and I were like cast-offs from a shipwreck, sharing experiences of our escape from death. We'd both lived a life of wild abandon. Survivors, both of us, we no longer dressed or made ourselves up to chase or be chased by prospective partners. As survivors, we did it only for ourselves. Fearing death more than other people did, we protected our health almost morbidly, while Ah Yao, who refused to surrender to either age or condition, was still fighting the good fight. I shuddered at the thought of how much violence and humiliation he had been forced to endure from the "new people," the "new new people," and the members of Generation x he encountered.

We talked about Ah Yao, who was so far away, but were reluctant to say too much, as if he were a terminally ill patient whose image could only cause us more pain.

Parrot Gao went to make his kumquat tea behind the bar while I picked up a CD that was lying around. It was New Age music, a synthesizer perfectly reproducing the sound of rain falling in the hollows of a mountain, with breezes blowing and a stream gurgling by. The clinking sounds of spoons and glasses emerged from behind the bar, where Parrot Gao was working. He was wearing a purple-iris terrycloth bathrobe and a sunflower-yellow shower cap wrapped around his head like a bandage; his thinning hair was pulled back to reveal a mask of gray mud, the face of a shaman. He handed me a small porcelain crock of golden liquid, the elixir of immortality.

The synthesizer suddenly released sounds of whale calls and tiger roars over rivers and mountains. Parrot Gao said, You ought to learn how to use Chinese word processing, it's a real time saver.

Glancing down at his desktop computer, I said, No, there's little enough joy in my life as it is. I want to hold on to the pleasure of writing. Each stroke brings me great joy.

He walked over and pointed to the computer. There are at least a million words stored in there, he said.

Take some out to show me, I said.

With considerable enthusiasm, he showed me how it was done, pressing several keys that brought up a line of words on the screen: *Master Zhiding's Treatise on the Sutra of the Ksitigarbha Bodhisattva's Original Vow.* The line was erased and replaced by a densely packed text that appeared to be an explication of Buddhist terminology.

I moved up to get a closer look at the strange combination of words, which were comprehensible only when I read them out loud. So I read: *puti sachui, mohe puti zhidi sachui,* shortened to *pusa* [bodhisattva]. *Puti* is *jue,* which means "awakened," and *sachui* is *youqing,* which means "beings." Oh, so *bodhisattva* means "awakened beings." *Puti* is also *dao,* which means "enlightened," and *sachui* is *zhongsheng,* which means "sentient beings," so *mohe puti zhidi sachui* can also be "enlightened sentient beings." *Mohe* is *da*, which is "big," and *zhidi* is *xin*, which means "mind," so *mohe puti zhidi sachui* even means "supreme enlightened mind of all sentient beings." I started to laugh because reading this was like training my jaw muscles, mobilizing those not used in daily speech. I said, Parrot, what's the point in keeping this stuff?

He was doing some stage design for the Prajna Dance Troupe at the time, and had collected all kinds of materials, whether they were relevant or not. So I put him to the test: What does *prajna* mean?

He hit a key and another string of words popped up. I read: *Prajna* is knowledge. There are three kinds of differentiating knowledge: There is no differentiation in concrete objects, there is no differentiation in abstract ideas, and there is no differentiation in all realms. I mulled over those phrases like chewing on a stalk of rush weed. Very interesting.

As if under my hypnotic spell, he started to read too: *Tipo* is heaven, the realms of desire include the six heavens of desire, while the material realm consists of the four meditative heavens, which include the eighteen heavens of form, the deva Mahesvara, and the four heavens without form. The so-called four heavens, we read together, are: The land of infinite space, the land of omniscience, the land of nothingness, and the land where there is neither consciousness nor unconsciousness. I sniffed his sparse hair, through which his scalp showed, and asked, Are you still using 101?

He turned and gave me an annoyed look. That stuff's bogus. You're better off using raw ginger.

Back when we were shocked and dismayed to find our hair coming out in handfuls, like autumn leaves, we passed around all kinds of folk remedies. Whenever someone we knew was going to mainland China to visit relatives or take a tour, we'd ask him to pick up half a dozen bottles of 101 Hair Restorer. Even though there were rumors of fake products, we hoped we'd be the lucky ones: we knew it wouldn't kill us, and it might actually grow some hair. We were on an emotional roller coaster each time we tried a new product: from the anticipation when we began, to the obsessive examination for signs of new hair, to the numbness in our scalp from all that rubbing, and to the ultimate disappointment that came with failure. To get quick results, we resorted to covering up the bald spots with fuzzy perms, regardless of the damage it could do to hair. Our hearts sank as we watched our hair get sparser day by day, split ends cropping up everywhere, and turning dry and discol- ored. Eventually we had to admit to ourselves that there was no true hair restorer anywhere, just as there was no elixir of immortality. We admitted that our youth was gone and that we were paying the price for exhausting our energy and vitality as young men. We aged earlier, developed addictions, were afflicted with hidden illnesses, and died young.

More and more people in our circle began meditating and studying Buddhism, or placed their faith in New Age beliefs, or advocated the holistic approach to health maintenance, hoping to unify body and spirit via metaphysical concepts. I was excluded from their secret rituals, while my friends Fairy Slave and Tang the Gourd were happily caught up in previous-life regressive therapy, hypnosis, rebirthing, kundalini, winds rising, shakti, prana, and svabhavika. It was as if they held passports to the next life and pitied me for being without one. I was angry and jealous, not over the passport, because I had no interest in going wherever it was, but over all the unfamiliar terms they were using. They had lost sight of how to treat a friend. Annoyed, I said, Why can't you just admit that the only therapeutic value of this New Age stuff is psychological, that they are all spiritual placebos?

I left when I read in Fairy Slave and Tang the Gourd's faces that they considered me thickheaded, unworthy of being instructed in the Tao. But I wished I'd stuck around to finish what I wanted to say. Given another chance I'd say, New Age? Back when we were young, good looking, and healthy, who gave a damn about the New Age? The reality is, there's no previous life, and no afterlife; only aging and death.

Ah Yao said, Redemption is the worst example of placing blame on others.

The New Age nature music captured the migrating whales' resonant calls in the deep waters of the Atlantic and Pacific. The electromagnetic vibrations in the vacuum of outer space were converted into magnetic pulses, then transformed into galactic music.

The survivors, Parrot Gao and I, awash in therapeutic New Age music, were drinking rich, aromatic kumquat tea, while Ah Yao, in his far-off foreign land, was carrying out the ideals of a gay man, squandering his life in casual sex like the poor mantis, unaware of its own folly.

Ah Yao was having sex with a string of casual lovers, while our friends and I were fleeing to tall mountains and vast oceans to escape the arrival of the Pale Horseman, whose name was Death, and I heard Ah Yao calling out to me from behind, a place of fire and brimstone, whether it was called Sodom or Gomorrah. It could be an international phone call or some Jamaican Blue Mountain coffee he'd asked someone to bring me; I couldn't help but turn around to take a look, and the instant I saw smoke rising above the place like a blazing kiln, I too turned into a pillar of salt.

But I did it willingly. Standing between hermetic reclusion and burning degeneration, whipped by the wind and eroded by the rain, only then would I feel I hadn't betrayed Ah Yao.

I maintained my composure and remained as motionless as Mother Earth, immersed in quiet thought and pondering the treasury of profound wisdom, whose name is Ksitigarbha. Parrot Gao's computer data bank decoded the meaning of the Dhyani Bodhisattva for me.

This is how it was: Guanyin's twelve vows, Samantabhadra's ten great vows, Sakyamuni's five hundred vows, Ksitigarbha's original vow. This is where friends can be found. "When all sentient beings have been saved, the Bodhi's existence will be proved; not until hell is empty will he become a Buddha." It was the *Sutra of the Ksitigarbha Bodhisattva's Original Vow* where this appeared, and I was so delighted I gave Parrot Gao's hair a little peck.

It was too late to tell Ah Yao that, several weeks after I returned to Taipei from Tokyo, some bumper stickers he'd sent me had fallen out of a stack of papers I was going through. There were all sorts of symbols and slogans: Silence Is Death; Ignorance Is Fear; ACT UP, FIGHT BACK, FIGHT AIDS. They were scattered all over the floor—insignificant people with their inconsequential mutter-ings, insistent upon issuing warning and threats. I picked them up one by one and put them in a safe place. I wanted desperately to tell Ah Yao it wasn't that I didn't want to participate in their comrades' movements, but that in the final analysis, I was afraid, afraid of shouting slogans. I was always embarrassed by having to shout and wave my fists in a crowd, for it felt like I was standing naked in the street, disgracing myself. It was too late to say, Ah Yao, forgive me for being a helpless loner handicapped by his own body language.

chapter five

Ah Yao would forgive me.

Many years ago, we stood in the square in front of the Presidential Office amid a vast, enthralled crowd beneath a sea of flags and a tide of paper flowers. We craned our necks to look at the Great Man, who finally appeared on a platform decorated with resplendent Double-Ten bunting. A very small Great Man, he was waving a white-gloved hand to salute the roaring citizenry below, who responded with shouted slogans. At the time, I didn't realize that the Great Man, subject to the same cycle of birth, old age, sickness, and death as everyone else, was already in his eighties. His thickly accented voice, with which I'd grown familiar through radio broadcasts, was shriller and more feeble in person, and was immediately drowned out by the surge of slogans rising and falling below. Hearing the Great Man's voice in the flesh, I realized that a Great Man was just a human being. All around me, tens of thousands of people raised their fists to shout "Long life," which quickly grew into a torrential chant. A loud boom behind me sounded like the sky opening up to release a meteorite shower; it was a cloud of doves flying over our heads. Balloons soared so close I could almost jump up and touch them as they rose gracefully into the western sky like a flock of colorful birds, then languidly floated away. A single balloon went straight up, and I followed it with my eyes as it drifted higher and higher into the sky, taking with it my heart, which was so full it nearly dripped water. Finally it soared over the highest point of the Presidential Office and became a tiny spot that disappeared into the clear blue firmament.

Wearing blue canvas baseball caps, we were assigned to the area representing the blue sky on the national flag. The sophomores lined up as the twelve rays of light, while students from other schools formed the red background. Students from girls' high schools, in strawboard wreaths decorated with carmine paper flowers, spelled out the words. Ah Yao's cousin's school was assigned as the top of the character for *China,* set into a background of yellow paper flowers. There were also Double Tens and plum blossoms. From a bird's-eye view, the square was covered by a fabulous tapestry that rippled every time slogans rose into the air. What a stirring scene for everyone present. Those were happier times, when we believed in everything and doubted nothing.

There was no identity issue, for God was in his heaven, all was right with the world.

It was orderly, mathematical, the world of Bach, with the golden structure that Lévi-Strauss had pursued all his life. A world I longed for, one I thought might exist only in the collective dream of the human race.

I didn't have a chance to explain to Ah Yao that I wasn't unwilling to support his movement, I was simply confused and concerned: while we praised the beauty and solemnity of the endless order, did we have a space of our own in the orderly realm of Bach's music, where everything has its place and its master, where men are men and women are women and the planets move silently in their natural orbits? Or were we simply exceptions, something to be excluded?

I wished that Lévi-Strauss could give me the answer—I often doubted that he belonged to this world, that he was someone whose discourse I could actually listen to merely by buying a plane ticket to Paris and going to his anthropology lab at the Collège de France.

$E = mc^2$, the final formula of the universe, the fruit of lifelong research from the great masters. Even Sakyamuni had only one phrase: "All phenomena are ephemeral, that is the way of karma; karma is the annihilation of the self, calmness and extinction is joy."

I wanted to ask Lévi-Strauss about his matrix algebra model, and the binary opposition of his culinary triangle. The three-element kinship system, comprised of blood relation, adoption, and marriage, is transformed into a complex web of relationships by multiplication and inheritance. And this web is what separates humans from nature; it is unique to them. Animals, on the other hand, have no way of distinguishing themselves from nature, for they have yet to break from it. This system, an independent unit that is on a par with nature, is opposed to nature yet united with it. As the ultimate master of anthropology, Lévi-Strauss wanted to unearth the deep structure buried beneath the entanglement of time and space, which was a profound reality-transcending experience, with a durability and externality that cannot be eroded by the passage of time.

I was anxious to know about people like us, maybe 10 percent of the human race. Where would he locate us in his matrix? How would his structure explain our existence? Were we the odd components screened out by his system?

Are we the single man in central Brazil's Bororo village, where ancestors are as important as living people? Those with no offspring are considered unfit as human beings, and can never ascend to the ranks of ancestors, since there are no progeny to worship them. The same is true for orphans, who, along with single men, are placed in the categories of the handicapped or male shamans.

The *bari* [shaman] is an asocial character. The personal link uniting him with one or more spirits gives him certain privileges: the knowledge of diseases as well as prophetic gifts. But the *bari* is also governed by his guardian spirit or spirits. They use him as a means of assuming bodily form, and when he is thus acting as a medium, he falls into trances and convulsions. The shaman and the spirit are so jealously interlinked that it is impossible in the last resort to know which of the two partners is the master and which the servant. Even the revelation by which he is summoned to accomplish his mission is painful: he first becomes aware of the fact that he has been chosen by the stench that pursues him, and from which he cannot escape.

No choice, and no way to change.

Like most of those summoned, we wailed, Why me?

What, exactly, is the existence of the self that has no choice? What happens if it is changed? Is changing oneself a negating act? What is the meaning of existence if the self is negated?

One year this unanswerable question threw me into a

depression that lasted all fall and into the winter. More often than not, the pungent smell of ammonia overlay the dusty, moldly odor of moth-eaten books. Leaving all the books unread, I sat alone in my office in the library, ideas coming and going one after the other and transporting me all the way to the barren trash heap of wild fantasy. Eventually I could think of nothing, and could only stare blankly at a square of dusty sky through the air vent above me, like an empty heart submerged in desolation. When it got dark, the vent chattered in the gusty wind. Few people came to the office, and whenever the door was opened a nauseating stench poured in from toilets at the end of the hallway.

Of course there can be no answer. Whether we exist or not, the answer can never emerge from cogitation. Lévi-Strauss pointed out early on that existentialism is overindulgent in the contemplation of the self, elevating personal anxiety to the level of a serious philosophical issue, which can result in a kind of salesgirl metaphysics.

The answer can only be encountered purely by chance as one stumbles along. Each existence and its type has its own unique answer.

Little Bird, my dear comrade, attempted suicide twice. He had always thought that the demonic black hole appeared as a result of pressure from society, relatives, and parents, and he sought his answer in suicide. He told me, The demon is part of you, so welcome it and talk with it when it comes. You'll get used to it eventually.

An English translation of the biography of Michel Foucault, who died of AIDS at the age of fifty-eight, appeared in London. In the photo published in the newspaper, he is caressing his bald head with both hands, perhaps a close-up of him dressing in front of a mirror. A pair of oval glasses perched on his white face makes him look like a panda. In his early years, he suffered all kinds of torment. He would often go out in the middle of the night to hang out in bars or on street corners in search of chance encounters. But when he returned home, he was overcome by guilt to the point of paralysis. Only by having the school doctor come over was he able to suppress his suicidal urges. Over a decade later, he exiled himself to places as far away as North Africa, and didn't return until the early 1970s to teach at the Collège de France. He died before he was able to finish his *Histoire de la sexualité.*

In my opinion, his abstruse and tedious history of sexuality was nothing less than a personal confession. The relationship between sex and power that he proposed has been extensively quoted, expanded upon, and given new spins by scholars, for it is so easy to use. But these scholars are simply playing with language; no connection occurs between the signifier and its object, because there was never an object. They are simply performing mental gymnastics; their narrowly defined specializations replace facts to enable them to remain in academia.

But not Foucault. He had an object—himself, that and the world he lived in. He badly wanted to find an answer somewhere between the two.

For others, finding an answer was mere sophistry, but for him, it was a matter of life or death.

He was also sex, indelible sex that gave him rapturous pleasure and excruciating pain, to which he devoted his life. By the time he began to perceive, understand, and explain it, he had reached the end of his life. It was buried with him, like a priceless treasure that appears briefly, only to drop out of sight once again. Treasure hunters of later generations will have to start all over, for everything.

The answer can be obtained only by trading one's life for it, and since every answer is destined for a specific individual, it cannot be transmitted to anyone else.

It is depressing to think that we are old and near death by the time we finally grasp our answers, after such a long, arduous trek. The fruit we harvest after so many hardships—a lifetime of experience, vision, and the ability to appreciate it—will simply turn to dust, completely useless to anyone. We are eager to teach the next generation, but are considered outmoded. The young, in particular, have no idea why old crocodiles like us care so much. There was a period of time when I was so sad that I'd stand in front of a classful of students and be unable to utter a word. After a long silence, I could only put on a good face and tell them, Go out and enjoy the sunshine.

To be sure, the history of sexuality differs radically from Lévi-Strauss.

The answer for Lévi-Strauss was already there, had become a

living attitude, a profound, crystallized, and gracious existence. Lévi-Strauss, who published yet another masterpiece—*Jealous Women Potters*—seven years ago, said that while the thesis remained the same, what differed was the sensitivity of the contents. The master was alive and well, and since I was living in his time, I had the good fortune of seeing him constantly present new and, as always, insightful ideas. I was so happy I had to turn away and dry my tears of joy.

But Foucault was different, for he could not hide his discontent. Facing the stately institution of sexuality built upon the intertwining relationship of sex and power, first he mocked it, then he lashed out at it, thrust his hands into the sticky mix and couldn't pull them out. He discovered that he was part of that institution, from which he in fact sprang. He never imagined he would actually turn his attack on himself.

He dragged himself out and confessed that the first to be encircled by the institution of sexuality and then sexualized was the idler. Let us not forget that he came from a well-to-do bourgeois family.

He readily admitted that the working class had never been controlled by sexuality, for they live in their own marital system—legal marriage, fertility, and incestuous taboos.

He believed that sexuality evolved from Christian confession during the Middle Ages. To state it more clearly: the codification of the sacrament of penance in the early thirteenth century ordered all Christians to confess periodically without reservation. The core of confession was, of course, sex. In the sixteenth century, confession became asceticism, spiritualism, and mysticism. The hundreds and thousands of methods employed to analyze and describe sex have developed into a set of rich, detailed skills. For centuries, the truth of sex was transmitted through this kind of discourse.

It once belonged strictly in the domain of religion, remaining secret and traceless. At the end of the eighteenth century, it began to separate from the Church. The truth of sexuality could no longer be presented through the earlier discourse of sin and redemption, death and immortality. Instead, it was replaced by another discourse: that of medical science, psychology, and psychoanalysis. Sex turned secular and entered the realm of law and order. Language itself and the semiotics of sex endured violent assaults.

It became a health issue, not the philosophical issue of final judgment. Sexual desire descended from heaven to the human world and attached itself to the human body. Now there was a whole new set of skills and techniques relying not on power but on technique, not on prohibitions but on normalization, not on punishment but on management. The body became the source of knowledge, and knowledge produced power, a complex and multifaceted construct that gained popularity in the far corners of the earth.

Hence, in the guise of scientific discourse, sexuality disseminated sex in the open, while at the same time avoiding it. Sexuality became a public matter, not only free from repression, but spreading more and more beyond matter and the body to stimulate and explain sex, to give it a chance to speak out, to order it to tell the truth. Sexuality became the will to gain knowledge for a whole generation, chattering nonstop and raising false alarms. Foucault said, "We 'Other Victorians.'"

Foucault, in a word, refused to be labeled.

Even now, when the sexual power structure has become so open-minded and benevolent, it has eliminated iron and blood and replaced them with the more refined instruction and conditioning. Particularly when treating so-called "unnatural" behaviors, it painstakingly maintains medical diction in its descriptions, which are neutral and devoid of moral judgment. As if making botanical classifications, that structure places a label on a whole range of sexual behaviors: sodomy, bestiality, fetishism, pedophilia, voyeurism, exhibitionism, transvestism, auto-eroticism, old-age sexaholism. It covers everything, while constantly inventing new terms. The "unnatural" has now become an area of specialty that enjoys its own autonomy. This is the first time in any society that everyone's sexual fantasy has been solicited in such an egalitarian fashion.

But Foucault didn't appreciate it at all.

He adamantly refused to be managed because of his inner disturbance and his homosexuality. He disliked psychiatrists and specialists, ridiculing them by saying they rented their ears out to snatch away sexual secrets, and were the first to become sexually aroused by them. He became extremely restless and agitated every time he thought about how the power structure tried to take benevolent charge of his sexuality, to gently touch and caress him, and he wracked his brains for ways to fight back.

He habitually inserted warning signals in his writing about the insidious, the very very insidious institution of sexuality, which encourages us to jubilantly follow its totalitarian control, while having us believe that we have been liberated by sexual openness and transparency, that we have obtained freedom through sexual pleasure.

He spoke with vehemence and wrote with passion. He picked up a lance and brandished it as he rushed forward to lift the veil and reveal the true identity.

But he was in for a shock.

By then, the institution of sexuality he thought he knew had turned into a colossus by self-transformation and inflation. At some point, the institution of sexuality that had been entrusted to the marriage system was no longer bound by the need to procreate. It freed itself from the control of reproduction while concentrating on heightening physical sensitivity and the quality of sensation, in pursuit of elusive traces of feelings, building a pleasure dome that permits total sexual abandonment.

He seemed to foresee that the institution of sexuality would bring with it a Faustian temptation in which a society would willingly pay any price for sex and sexual dominance. Sex would be worth dying for.

He did not have time to say more; like a murdered witness, he was only able to provide a lead. He breathed his last and said, with prophetic bluster, Sex, everything is sex.

The unfinished *Histoire de la sexualité* stopped here.

He appeared to have been liberated, but was not. He seemed to have found the answer, but had not.

I followed him up to the lofty mountain crags, but the road ended at the edge of the sky, and there he disappeared. I shouted his name, but there was no response.

The earth goes on forever until it reaches the sky. No no no, that wasn't the stone sculpture at the summit of Mount Tai; nor was it the blank stele. It was Palisades Park of 1943.

Ah Yao visited Palisades Park once. During World War II, when he was working for MGM, Tennessee Williams lived in Santa

Monica, by the Park. Palm trees everywhere; a stone fence marked the cliffs' edge. During that golden summer, blackouts were ordered for an area seven miles inland on the California coast to prevent Japanese air raids. Every evening after dinner, Williams would bicycle out to the Park, which was swarming with young soldiers. The Pacific Ocean reflected the dimming sunset as he rode by, looking for phosphorescent eyes in the dark. He would double back when he saw someone who struck his fancy, then stop by the roadside and pretend to watch the sea. He would strike a match to light his cigarette, using the instant the match flared up to study his prey. If things worked out, he'd invite the man back to his place. If not, he'd try a second one, then a third. It continued like that night after night in his Ocean Avenue apartment in a place called Palisades Manor.

Ah Yao told me, If Williams hadn't recorded this in his diary, no one would ever believe that he had had sex with a marine seven times in one night.

From atop the palisade, a brief glance down was enough to make me dizzy. As I stood there, I felt something that maybe Foucault had experienced: erotic utopia.

There, sex would not have to shoulder the mission of procreation, so there would be no contractual demand on either partner, and gender difference would no longer matter. Women with women, men with men, in a sexual realm where all barriers would have been dismantled, exploring sex together and the borders of the borders of sex, as far as they wanted to go. Sex would now be removed from the primitive function of childbearing, sublimated until sex became its own objective, an erotic nation built upon sensuality, artistry, aesthetics. But was this the ultimate realm for us? Was this the dreamland so earnestly sought by those of us who comprise 10 percent of the human race?

Foucault was silent.

Standing there, I seemed to understand that many erotic nations must have appeared in the course of human history. They were like exotic flowers that disappeared after blooming but once. Later generations could only dimly detect their existence amid vanishing, decaying texts, for they could neither expand nor grow. They became extinct in the frozen sorrows of indetermination and slow degeneration.

Yes, this was probably our sad yet beautiful destiny.

The past, or the fleeting present, or the future all sail toward Byzantium.

Sail toward an erotic utopia. In ancient times, tiny nameless countries that dotted the area around the Mediterranean like stars, those that didn't pass down any myths, were terminators. We are the terminators of the kinship system.

chapter six

Sail toward the Mediterranean.

We were ocean glow-worms that laid our eggs between sunset and sunrise, a whole patch of shiny eggs that Columbus mistook for land.

Our wedding, after all, something Ah Yao didn't know, was held in the biggest church in the world, St. Peter's Basilica, where the Pope resides.

I was writing postcards on a balcony whose trellis was filled with the leaves of honeysuckle and roses. It was the end of August, but I was filled with such happiness I could almost smell the flowers' rich fragrance; every once in a while I had to stop and take a deep breath, like a swimmer coming up for air, before resuming my writing.

One of the postcards, a close-up portrait of Pope John Paul II, holding an elaborately carved crozier and wearing his white embroidered miter, was for my younger sister. I was sure she'd read it over and over. The other, a picture of the Sistine Chapel, was for Ah Yao.

I wrote, Dear Ah Yao, I want your blessings. I'm in Rome. His last name is Yan, and we love each other very much. . . . Even now, just as when I wrote that line, I find it so hard to continue, I have to get up and take a walk.

The smell of that morning's cappuccino with cinnamon assaults my nose like a hurricane, so I flee to a corner, waiting for the smell to drift across the room and disappear through the walls. Then I turn around, covering my nose with my sleeve, and gaze at the devastation in the hurricane's aftermath. I see the low, menacing clouds of this morning's Taipei outside the window, while on that morning Yongjie was sound asleep on the big bed with its blue sheets.

Yongjie and I, at the time of Ah Yao's death, had been together for at least seven years. Seven years! I hadn't even told Ah Yao Yongjie's name.

As I leaned against the door, I looked at Yongjie as if in a trance. My God! As he slept, he was as handsome and flawless as Michelangelo's Adam. The day before, we had lingered in the Sistine Chapel, admiring the actual frescoes. In this vast universe, God created man. God, on this side of the ceiling, and man, on the other side, reach out to each other, their index fingers nearly touching in midair. Several hundred years later, this image inspired Steven Spielberg to create his classic scene of the first contact between E.T. and the little boy. But I perceived, sadly, that the expressions and gestures of God and man told not of contact but of parting. In order to establish and continue the world, "A man shall leave his father and his mother," an ironclad law for all places and all times. But for us, the terminators of the kinship system, A man shall leave his man, one man or one man after another.

It was invariably during my happiest moments that I felt the inconstancy of life.

Silently enduring the sentimental attachment filling my chest to the bursting point, I stopped myself from disturbing Yongjie. Let him sleep. I closed the door enough to block the sun's rays streaming in from the east. His thick, naturally curly hair, black and glossy, reflected traces of neon light. Near his scalp, the hair was damp from perspiration. Stir not up, nor awake my love, till he please.

I sat back down in front of the white wrought-iron table. My chair's back and legs curled out like the tips of vines. I continued to write: Do you still remember the line from that poem, Separated by long rivers and high mountains, I am deeply saddened? That's how I feel at this moment. We went to the Vatican. Japan's NHK sponsored the restoration of the Sistine frescoes, while turning the project into a documentary. The front part was completed and the renovation of the vault was underway. I heard that from 1988 to 1992 they would clean the section featuring the Last Judgment. Of course, we also visited the Spanish Piazza, where we took pictures of each other at the same spot, and imagined what Audrey Hepburn looked like in 1953. We planned to visit Rimini, Fellini's hometown. We'd also go to Venice, Florence, then return to Taiwan before school started.

The postcard was sent to New York, which, except for Mama's place in Tokyo, was the only address I had for him. But Ah Yao could have been out making revolution or wandering the streets almost anywhere. I wasn't sure he'd get it, although his partner, who couldn't read Chinese, probably kept his things together. In the end, I never received his blessing, not over the phone, not in the notes tucked in among the packages he sent, not even during the time I kept a vigil by his deathbed.

The only exception was the time Yongjie answered the phone and handed it to me. It was Ah Yao. Obviously drunk, he wanted me to guess where he was. I said, You're drunk.

He said, I'll give you a hint, listen carefully, I'm on Bour—bon Street.

Oh, I said, you're in New Orleans.

He was overcome with joy, and kept kissing the phone. Then he began reciting something. It was all a jumble, and the only thing I understood was something about when cotton is king and sugar is queen. . . . In the gibberish that followed, I heard him say: Who was that? The guy named Yan?

I thought I heard him wrong, so I asked, What?

He shouted something, then recited Blanche's classic line in a somber voice, I've always relied upon the kindness of strangers.

I held my breath, waiting for him to continue.

But he vanished in silence, just like Blanche exiting the stage, leaving a dial tone hanging in the air. Anxiously I called his name, but there was no response, nothing but static. I wouldn't have been at all surprised if an old crocodile like him got robbed, or killed, or simply dropped dead in the French Quarter, where the bars made those powerful hurricane cocktails.

I jogged my memory. Did he actually say it? The guy named Yan? If so, did that mean he got my card? Or had I simply heard wrong?

On several occasions, it was like a fish bone in my throat. I could have simply asked if he'd received the postcard I'd sent from Rome. But I never could bring myself to say the words, all because of my cowardice and indescribable pride. I'd already blurted out that I was in love, and if he didn't bring up the subject, I'd never mention it again. I'd have told him, but only if he asked, and even then it would depend upon how he asked.

His cavalier attitude over the phone made me wonder if it meant anything at all to him. Could he tell somehow that our union was fleeting, based upon illicit sex, and that we'd each go our own way before long? I could almost see him trying to anger me again with one of his smirks. In many of my imagined exchanges, we went round and round until we were blue in the face. Yongjie always tried his best to listen with patience and good humor, but invariably dozed off during one of my tedious, almost hysterical monologues. Tossing and turning all night, I finally fell out of bed, waking Yongjie, who sat up, gave me a good-natured smile, and said, I've never seen anyone quite like you.

I moaned and sighed, until Yongjie forgot about sleeping and got up to make something to drink.

My darling Yongjie pranced over to the kitchen counter, confidently revealing his tight, chiseled body to me, as always. That never failed to draw sighs of admiration from me. I said sadly, If only Ah Yao could get to know you.

Yongjie turned his face slightly toward me, a profile that made him look like a Greek statue. Aren't you afraid he'd steal me away?

Suddenly I understood everything. Now, two months after his death, in the process of writing, the words themselves told me that Ah Yao had been jealous.

That was because Ah Yao and me, our feelings for each other, were like the memory of a ninety-year-old man. Old folks have odd memories: they can't remember recent events and can't forget distant ones. The past was like pearl-colored still frames, while recent days blurred like high-speed motion pictures. That's how we were. We grew more and more estranged as the number of new people and new events entering our lives outstripped all the sweet memories we had shared; we became even more stubborn in holding on to what we had in common instead of looking at our differences. Later on, during our infrequent reunions, after reminiscing, we reminisced some more, and then some more. Those reminiscences, which cleansed us in the cruel world in which we lived, were so wonderful, yet so fragile. Once we strayed into the present, we'd begin to argue because we cared so much for each other, yet were unable to agree on anything. It was agony. And I didn't realize until now that I had forsaken a dear friend in the pursuit of sexual fulfillment. The way I'd giddily confided in Ah Yao about my new love had dealt a serious blow to our friendship.

In many ways, Ah Yao was my mentor, my elder in matters of love. At the time, I had this pipe dream that I'd like to take Yongjie to meet Ah Yao, because I yearned for Ah Yao's praise. That would have meant more to me than all the blessings in the world. If I'd eagerly brought my love to him and he had admired Yongjie, I'd have been unimaginably happy. But if he had desired him, would I have given Yongjie up? I don't know, but I was so proud yet so indifferent in front of Ah Yao that I believe I might have. I muttered dreamily, Yongjie, the two of you would get along beautifully. He likes Fassbinder and so do you. You two could have wonderful discussions about *Alexanderplatz*.

Yongjie protested by stuffing my mouth with a gin and Coke. Can you stop talking about your old lover for one minute? He couldn't believe I'd never slept with Ah Yao.

My mouth was dry and my tongue was parched, so I gulped down the gin and Coke, enjoying the sensation of icy-cold bubbles spreading from the tip of my nose to my eyes. I sneezed. It felt wonderful. I looked at Yongjie, who sometimes teased me about Ah Yao. Ah Yao, who was on the other side of the world, unexpectedly became our love potion. No wonder that small amount of gin in the Coke was enough to turn my face red and make my eyes burn with desire.

Yongjie, a good drinker, rinsed his mouth and poured some tequila. He sprinkled salt on the back of his hand between his thumb and forefinger, while holding a slice of lemon in his other hand. Then he licked the salt, tossed down a shot of tequila, and bit into the lemon. If he'd eroticized the process just a little, it would have been such a turn-on I'd have embraced him passionately. That was the only way to purge my mind of Ah Yao's pesky image.

In the early autumn of that year we stayed with Momo in Rome. During the day we went to all the city's historic sites, then frolicked in bed till dawn. The days were too short; so were the nights. When dark circles appeared under our eyes, we agreed to take a day off, not going anywhere, just staying home to listen to music, sleep, read, and cook.

Momo often rode over on his bike, bringing some of his girl-friend's homemade rosemary sauce and peach preserves for us to eat with crackers while drinking Yunnan Pu'er or Iron Guanyin tea. Momo's girlfriend, a Polish Jew, was very cordial to Momo's two Chinese friends, so we arranged a time to meet for dinner at a nineteenth-century restaurant. That night we ordered fried fish and iced vodka and sat down to wait for her. As an employee of the Ministry of the Interior, she was kept busy interpreting for Polish refugees who were applying for political asylum. She couldn't make it that night.

Another time, when we were standing on the street outside her apartment, she opened her window and tossed a tourist guide down to Momo. She waved to us, then disappeared behind the window like a princess in a castle.

I suspected that Momo's place had once been a butler's quarters, for the ground floor was a small room next to the gate in a large courtyard. It was lower than the street, so the lights had to be left on all day long. Momo had partitioned the room with shelves and cabinets into an area for the kitchen, one for his stereo and rocking chair, and another for his desk, typewriter, phone, and fax machine. A metal spiral staircase in the center of the room was barely wide enough for one person, but Yongjie and I climbed it together, our limbs entwined like tangled vines. The stairs gave out onto a spacious second floor, with a large mattress and a bathroom. French doors opened out to blinding golden sunlight and a rooftop trellis with a sea of green leaves. I'd sit out there and look up at the ivied castle tower, which was now home to two families who shared the entrance with Momo. Or I'd read from Momo's selected works of Mao Zedong and sip moldy tea—the cheap tin it came in had a very poetic name: Cloud and Mist of Mount Lu. It was green tea.

I read a poem from the collection: Mountains/Whip my speedy horse, don't dismount/Look back, surprised/The sky three feet three away. The note said, This poem, in the style of a sixteen-word song, was written as we passed through Skull Mountain on the Long March. So one good poet and one lousy one had settled on opposite shores.

Momo recommended some music to us—stirring marches praising the red sun and the socialist homeland. The times had changed and the rousing chorus of men and women seemed comical, but it still excited Momo, who sang along: Chairman Mao is the helmsman of our proletarian homeland! He told us to listen carefully. These are Tibetans singing, now the Kazakhs, these are Uzbeks. . . . The way he was gesticulating—Italian style—the whole thing seemed totally absurd. Like a man afflicted with St. Vitus's Dance. What could not be suppressed was the shadow of his passing youth calling to him.

We had to muster all our patience to appear interested, so as not to offend him. Momo also proudly played the theme songs from Chinese movies like *Street Angel, Singing at Midnight,* and *Song of the Fishermen,* which led to another round of praise from those who knew the songs, while we played the role of appreciative friends. When Momo sang the aria "Su San Departs Hongtong County" in falsetto along with a tape recording from the Peking opera, Yongjie's eyes caressed me from head to toe through the misty smoke from his Russian long-filter cigarette. I looked away and tried to hide my smile, but Yongjie, seeing my puffed-out cheeks, started to laugh. Momo, thinking we were making fun of him, turned red. He opened another bottle of liquor, a long-stemmed porcelain bottle, and, saying it was imported from Holland, insisted that everyone drink a glass, no matter how many different kinds of liquor might be sloshing around in our bellies already. Yongjie and I waited until Momo dejectedly rose to leave and walked his bike out, stopping every few steps to shout, Chairman Mao is the helmsman of the proletarian homeland, then finally disappeared around a dark corner before we went back inside, already burning with desire.

It was a day of rest, but Momo didn't show. We would have kept him company, and anything would have done, from comic dialogue to Shaoxing drama, not because we were staying at his place, but because his naive infatuation with China hadn't subsided, even at his age. In 1974 he'd gone to China to attend Liaoning University. There was picture of him in his Mao jacket, crouching in a vegetable field, but it wasn't clear if he was actually planting anything. The photo was black and white, but you could almost see the Mediterranean blue in his eyes transported to the Great Northern Wasteland, where the sky's edge hung so very low.

His house was filled with odds and ends, like a Dharma statuette, embroidery from Guizhou, Zheng Banqiao's bamboo painting and calligraphy, woodblock prints from Suzhou. Also lion and dragon dolls made of bright red cotton by old women in northern Shaanxi, little donkeys, shoes with tips shaped like tigers' heads, white Buddhist vestments. Paper puppets for shadow plays hung from a lamp; there was a movie poster for *Woman Basketball Player No. 5*; and above his bed hung two framed calligraphic scrolls in the flowing cursive style, both ghastly. He even had a bedspread made of blue tie-dyed fabric from Yunnan that covered the big mattress; when we slept on it, we felt as if we were floating atop dense seaweed and coral. When I looked at all this, I couldn't help feeling that I was witnessing the carcass of my own youth scattered all over the place.

One day early on, the word went out for a group of friends to get together to listen in secret to mainland music someone had recorded from somewhere—folk songs, ditties, "The Butterfly Lovers" performed by a string orchestra, and "Mu Guiying Becoming a General." As if on a pilgrimage, we turned off the lights and lit a single candle. Sitting in front of the tape recorder, Jay was not only in charge of the music but also controlled everyone's breathing, like a spiritual medium. For a while, all we heard was the *sha-sha-sha* of the tape brushing across the recorder heads, then suddenly, a shouted "Hey" that could have belonged to either a man or a woman. Goose bumps erupted up and down our spines. Then came a man's voice, loud and clear: The skeleton's cries rise a thousand feet into the air/The silent, windless sky makes the sound brittle. Jay's burning eyes were fixed on me, and I believe it was at this precise moment when we felt the electrifying attraction that led to the future, our future. Later, whenever I thought about this, my tragic first love, it was like opening up an old wound.

There was a time, whenever I heard the Shaanxi melody "Xintianyou," particularly those crackling notes from the Chinese panpipe, that my heart would tremble and hot tears would stream down my face. I even developed a fetish over the blue dyed robes from northern China. I reencountered all these at Momo's place in Rome, but somehow they had become the sediment of an emotional cleansing! It was like the Monk Tripitika of the Tang, who was shocked to see a corpse floating by as he crossed the River after reaching Spirit Mountain. It was his own mortal body, which he had shed.

Recently I've become less and less attached to worldly desires, a clear sign of aging.

I remained aloof from the world. I was close to paradise, but in no danger of descending to my destruction. Yongjie said no one understood how *cool* I was better than he did. He said it was like the music from Miles Davis's trumpet, like walking on eggshells.

Don't play what you know, play what you hear, Davis said.

Yongjie found, to his surprise, that Momo had a CD by Davis, and he played it incessantly. He told me the album called WALKING was made when Davis was recording with PRESTIGE RECORDS. It was 1954 in New York, when the twenty-eight-year-old Davis had kicked his drug habit, and he changed his cool jazz style to play a harder-edged bebop.

Yongjie taught me how to listen to the music of Davis, who rarely used vibrato, the sound more like a human voice, sometimes distant and sad, sometimes clear and bright. It had a spatial feeling, clean and neat. Davis had said he was always listening to his own music to see if he could eliminate something.

Yongjie showed me how Davis played his trumpet with a mute, how he seemed to breathe into the microphone. There were no obvious starting notes, for his music just rose up and, in the same way, stopped without ending. Yongjie turned his back to me and said that Davis often played with his back to the audience, then left the stage after his solo. As if entering a place where only he existed, Yongjie stood in front of the rose trellis and swayed to the erotic rhythms from downstairs, oblivious to everything else.

With his terrific sense of rhythm, he seemed to be making love to the music, the caresses taking him to the point of orgasm, before he pulled back to prolong the pleasure. The music patiently circled him and submitted as he began anew. A phantom kiss brushed against him; he seemed to welcome it, yet refused it, letting it cover his body, which went limp, like cotton wadding, soft and fluffy. But still he withheld his consent, and the kiss began to get anxious, there but not quite there. When it reached its limits of patience and submissiveness, he turned around and became docile. But then the melody slowed and led him in a leisurely pace, groping and hesitating. Like this? Is this right? He was searching. Then he sensed that the moment of truth was near, and his excitement mounted. Yes, yes, it's so close, it's right there. He started to run, and the quickening melody rising above the beats chased after him. Yes, almost there, almost there. They were kissing amid the brilliance of truth.

I was overcome with envy and jealousy, but I wiped the tears from my eyes so he wouldn't see them.

Yesterday we went to a mass at St. Peter's Basilica. It was the five o'clock evening service, so there weren't many people around. The pipe organ started up first, like angels' wings descending from the towering ceiling. I took Yongjie's hand and held it tight. A line of clergymen in white robes and red vestments walked past us up the aisle on their way to the altar. Yongjie responded by squeezing my hand even tighter; we were like a bride and groom joined together before God. Since we had no place in the marriage system of this world, why not join our lives together here in this domed church, designed and begun by Michelangelo, even though it took a hundred years to finish?

We'd been together three and a half years, during which we were faithful to each other and treated each other with respect and consideration. But I didn't dare think about the future. Was it love that created this kind of monogamous relationship? Who knows? Love is more short-lived than summer flowers, and each touch further reduces its magic.

It seemed as if we met at a time when we had both just recovered from mental instability; more than anything else we sought stability, a worry-free life with substance. We were fortunate to be in sync in so many ways, so we could maintain a sort of balance. Bound to each other, we were like those beautiful maidens of classical novels who turn down their suitors by saying, "I am promised to another."

Only those who have lived a life with no constraints know the pride-filled joy of being constrained.

Having willingly agreed to those constraints, we empowered

each other, and that was what our contract meant. As long as the contract remained valid, he belonged to me, body and soul, and I was obliged to reward him with total satisfaction, inside and out.

"Privilege is to march foremost in war." Remember? This definition so surprised Montaigne that he devoted an entire chapter to it in his essays. When he met three Brazilian Indians who had been brought to Europe as prisoners, he asked about the privilege their king derived from the superiority he enjoyed among his own people.

No, not king—captain, one of the Indians, a captain, answered proudly. My privilege is to march foremost in war.

My privilege was to satisfy him sexually. I was able to show my generosity, the manifestation of happiness.

During those unrestrained days of the past, I'd had sexual contact with hundreds, maybe thousands of bodies. But young, beautiful harem girls are all the same in the arms of the sultan. Wanting to satisfy my desires, I had turned into a sex maniac caught up in the vicious cycle of insatiable desires. Such a long, long time, until I forgot how it felt to make love with a soul. Yongjie, whom I had never expected to meet, and I were willing to give ourselves in exchange, out of a sense of mutual admiration. Our bodies were the ritual altars upon which we proved that, while everyone was alike physically, subtle differences in the soul, hidden inside the body, made each person unique.

So we made a contract, promising to nurture each other. And when the summer flowers of love began to wither, we still possessed a sufficient amount of curiosity to expand the territory of our relationship, enough to retain our interest for the time being.

But me, I still dared not think about the future.

Were we pagans? Or were we apostates, sexual perverts? How could we take such solemn vows? We were living our lives like the phrase that became popular during the first oil crisis: Enjoy today, for tomorrow it will cost even more.

See, not even the gods are immune to destruction, so what chance do contracts have?

Even in St. Peter's Basilica, the Chair of St. Peter, who holds the key to eternal paradise, cannot hide the fatigue on his face as he looks down on the devout during mass from his place on the apse. When rituals become a system and a habit, God is about to die. Now let us, the apostates, project our sweetness and good cheer onto the soporific mass, changing it by bestowing upon it beautiful colors, as at the beginning of all rituals.

See, there behind the main altar, in the center of the nave, a bronze chair radiates doves from the Holy Ghost, thousands of rays of brilliant light. Above the main altar, four giant pillars support the bronze canopy, like the four poles Nüwa erected by cutting off the legs of a turtle. Thirty or forty years ago, the body of St. Peter was discovered in a tomb beneath the main altar, which houses a confessional chapel where ninety-five oil lamps burn day and night, like the two candle dragons guarding the poles of heaven and earth. Remember the poem? Ladling fine wine with the Big Dipper/Toast the two celestial dragons/Wealth and fame are not what I seek/I want only eternal youth. We wanted to live to a ripe old age and make love until the very end, never tiring of it.

We didn't let go of each other's hand or leave the nave until we had taken communion. After passing through the atrium, we stopped to look at *St. Peter Crossing the Sea*, a thirteenth-century mosaic. It was already dark; the lights in the Pope's residence high above us had come on, and the orange lamps of the piazza were lit. It had been drizzling when we came, and now a rainbow appeared on the edge of the piazza. It had two shades: the brighter of the two, called *hong*, the primary rainbow, is male, while the darker one, the *ni*, or secondary rainbow, is female. We were like the ni and hong to each other. In current society, where our relationship could not be legally recognized, we hoped to live like the occasional rainfall, transforming the brilliance of sunlight into rainbows for everyone to see.

We counted the Bernini colonnades in the oval of the piazza. They say there are 284 columns in two facing semicircles. After counting over half of them, we stopped to share a sentimental kiss in the shadow of a row of columns when no one was around. We nearly lost self-control; listening to sounds like sudden rain, as doves flew home to the west, we forgot where we'd left off in our counting.

After a long time, our raging passion slowly cooled and blended in with the rare silence around us. The columns, their shadows, and the Egyptian obelisk moved here in the first century A.D. crisscrossed like the Grand Canyon, breathing in incalculable

quantities of time, to the point of overflowing. We were startled by the tomb of time made of silent floating sand that submerged us.

Without a word, and still holding hands, we ran as fast as we
could, not daring to slow down lest the enormous, silent shadow
catch up with us.

After fleeing down streets bustling with shops and the pilgrimage road, all paved with marble, we walked slowly along the
Tiber to the bus stop. Yongjie said, That's why I never like to visit
historic sites; they only remind me of the presence of death.
Feeling the sorrows of separation and death, he was choking on
his tears.

Yes, I know, I said, also feeling an ache in my nose. That's why
we must keep our bodies in good shape, so we can still make love
when we are very very old.

We agreed to choose an auspicious day to take blood tests after
we returned to Taiwan. We also agreed to stay together, even if
one of us tested positive.

"Love and respect in everything," was the inscription on the
inside of a silver ring, the meaning of which we sort of guessed. In
stores that sold all sorts of lovely religious objects, we picked out
the cheapest keepsakes for each other. I took Yongjie's finger and
started to nibble it, with no sexual implication, letting the silver
ring on his finger bite into my gums with a numbing sensation.

I remember seeing him sway and lose himself in the music of
Miles Davis's trumpet. While I looked on, I felt that my heart was
left defenseless in my body, softly dripping water and drying
under the sun.

I t was invariably during my happiest moments that I felt the inconstancy of life.

I often feared that Yongjie, who was created by heaven, with a remarkable sense of rhythm and a beautifully proportioned body, was fated to die young. I frequently found myself wishing that he were a little duller, and would willingly have covered him with mud and dirt to hide his beauty. When he danced to the music in front of the rose trellis, I could almost see Zeus descending from heaven, transforming himself into a magnificent swan, then raping him. There were times when I intentionally loved him a little less, trying to appear indifferent for fear that the Creator would lie in wait and snatch him away from me out of jealousy.

We were shopping in a supermarket, walking past the shelves with a shopping cart. He was in front of me; suddenly he disappeared at the end of an aisle. I rushed over with the cart but couldn't see him anywhere. In a panic, I turned west and walked all the way to the end, but couldn't find him. So I turned and walked back, but still couldn't find him. I was so anxious I nearly knocked over a towering display of potato chips. Then I spotted him, standing there picking out cheese crackers as if nothing were wrong; meanwhile, I felt as if my hair had turned gray in the blink of an eye.

Not long ago, I saw a Hong Kong movie called *Dream Lovers*, which was roundly panned. The reviewers were right when they called it vapid, anemic, aesthetically indulgent. But I saw it over and over again; I was hopelessly hooked. To my utter disbelief, it included one highly emotional scene that had nothing to do with the main plot. In a supermarket, Chow Yun-fat did exactly the same thing with Brigit Lin that I had with Yongjie. Chow's anxiety and desperation so surprised me that I thought I might have directed the scene in a dream or that the camera had infiltrated my consciousness and snatched the scene from me. As for the film's overall mood, involving previous and present lives, the madness and depression were the results of unfulfilled desire burning its way into the next life, the inevitable outcome of fruitless, childless sex. I believed that only someone like us could make a movie like that.

Indulgent aestheticism. I was reminded of a young man who looked like Nijinsky, with high cheekbones and upturned emerald-green almond-shaped eyes. The morning after their first night together, as they were walking amid seaside dunes, he said to his lover, Last night you showed me the true meaning of exquisite pain.

Yes, exquisite pain. That is the true face of indulgent aestheticism. Masochism and indulgent aestheticism are twin sisters, after all.

The existential body that is offered up as a sacrifice to be gazed upon and moved is hidden yet replete with storms and rain. It is like the pain of bereavement experienced by a teenaged girl as she buries her childhood and bids farewell to her single-minded solipsism, in order to pave the way into adulthood. If the pain is so strong it overflows the dam, she can become masochistic, doing things like eating mud, chewing on chalk and charcoal, drinking salt water, or pricking her hand with needles. That's how we are. Maybe because we have been mired so long in the karmic cycle of betraying and being betrayed, we are inclined toward masochism and indulgent aestheticism.

On the darkened, closed stage, under a spotlight, stands the twelfth-century dancer Shizuka Gozen, abandoned in the Taira-Minamoto War. She is wearing an elaborate dress with as many as twelve layers, like a wedding dress, which, along with her long silky black hair, is draped across the stairs. Covering her face, she turns back to look: men are being killed, the women taken prisoner; her city, her kingdom is going up in smoke.

On the face of Monet's dying wife, Camille, was the last light of life. An oil painting is like a sketch, with rapid strokes, but Camille's features darkened, underwent a change, turning from yellow to white, then to blue, and finally to a gray darkness; Monet wasn't quick enough to capture the vanishing color and light. His wife, the love of his life, turned into an object no different from any other object, illuminated and ultimately abandoned by light.

Five years before Rodin died, the skill he displayed in his sculpture of the dancer Nijinsky was simply breathtaking. Yet how absurd to think that a piece of clay formed into lines and a skin surface could capture the instantaneously changing poses whose intensity and closeness kept rushing toward him. Attempting to approach eternity with the human figure, Rodin was never able to break free of the goat's horns and hooves of his pastoral themes, even though he lived to seventy-seven. Such futility.

All those like us, denied permission, consent, and blessings, can have no good ending, as if evil monsters had been cast down to make our journey impossible. With the faithful love that Yongjie and I stole, we were careful, so as not to allow the Furies to catch us and take away our mutual trust. Insecurity, like a preservative, forced us to work hard toward a disciplined life, but it also surrounded us like a light fog so that we could only sit across from each other and worry.

Like a miser, I hoarded the good fortune and the person I had for now, slowly squandering what time we had together. Without prior agreement, whenever Yongjie left on one of his trips, we showed no reluctance and never kissed good-bye. We would treat it as something as ordinary as if he were going to the corner convenience store to buy something to eat—he'd be right back—or as if I were going to the office to meet with a student while he was developing film in the darkroom he'd set up in the bathroom. We even avoided each other's eyes, lest we see our own weaknesses reflected. We never made love the night before a trip, because—because it was too traumatic. We'd make love a day or two before and with intentional haste, so as not to be destroyed by the terrifying desire aroused by sadness over our impending separation. Then we'd spend the night before the departure with married friends. Experience taught us not to stay with our own kind, for the puerile banter and flirtation or the alcohol and the music in KTV or in bars could ruin our mood and make things worse.

Often, I'd take Yongjie to my kid sister's place, where I'd watch videotapes while my sister prepared food and drinks. Her two kids would ask me to be a big bad wolf and chase them around, but I'd frighten them and they'd be bawling before long. Her husband would play Chinese chess with Yongjie in silence, neither of them making any noise all evening. After the kids went to bed, my sister would shower, then sit down and watch the videos with me. She'd smell wonderful. She'd be busy the whole time, either peeling fruit for us or stringing beads. Or she'd be sewing or embroidering, which gave me a sense of comfort and security. The world would not crumble just because Yongjie and I were separated, and we'd be together again soon. Then we'd go home in a happy, healthy mood, where we'd busy ourselves before bedtime, like an ordinary husband and wife living their routine life. That way the routine would, of course, get us through the time until we were together again. There was no room for accidents. Yes, we'd be together again and as wrapped up in love as ever.

We were cautious to the point of superstition, afraid that something might happen when we were unprepared. Once, before he left, Yongjie said, I'm leaving, which nearly tore my heart apart. That is why they say, Be careful what you wish for. I'm leaving. Precisely what I was afraid of. Always prepared to be notified of an accident, I answered every phone call with a trembling hand. If I'd heard, Please come to the hospital, I wouldn't have been surprised. That day, Yongjie, as if sensing something, called me more often than usual. Phone calls reached me at home, at school, at a café, at home again; I trembled each time I picked up the receiver. The mixture of fear and joy at those moments turned us both speechless. It was terrible. After this incident, we created another taboo—we were careful never to use words like *leaving, going,* and *bye.* We held on to each other and made our way down a treacherous, mine-strewn path, scared to even think about what one would do if the other were gone.

The longest he was away was the time he went to film the southern portion of the Silk Road in Sichuan, Yunnan, and Burma. As usual, I didn't see him off; we just hugged like a couple of run-of-the-mill good friends, free of entanglements. After he ran down the stairs with his suitcase, I closed the door and sighed. But I was able to restrain my impulse to go to the balcony and watch him walk away, afraid that would be the last time I ever saw him, that my action would somehow confirm the power of fate to play with our lives. With my eyes closed, I ruminated over his words. One time he called from Orchid Island to tell me how terrific it was to have someone to think about. The feeling of fidelity was also wonderful, like a white camellia waiting for the true admirer to come before opening its layers of snowy petals. Yongjie was never stingy with words like that, and they always brought tears to my eyes. I'd engrave his words on my heart like a scarlet A, until he returned to remove them himself.

I got a haircut after he left. Each gust of wind chilled my exposed neck, turning my heart barren, like a field overgrown with weeds. Nothing filled my eyes but loneliness, loneliness, vast and endless loneliness.

In earlier days, in my inexperience, I'd been crushed by this sort of loneliness, to the point where I no longer felt human. I've come a long way since then, and am more or less capable of dealing with it.

I often visited my sister to take part in her family life, which helped me maintain a healthy spirit, like a raspberry bush standing tall among hemp plants. I turned down all invitations to evening gatherings. No heart-to-heart talks, no partying or drinking, no sex, and no daytime naps. I didn't even read. I made a point of going to bed early and getting up early, then jogging in the early morning sunshine so I'd have enough energy to get through the days when Yongjie was not around. I restrained myself like the unbetrothed maidens in ancient tales.

Then, when the evening fog drifted over and loneliness loomed large, I opened the door and let it in.

Loneliness is not something you can simply ignore or drive away. I knew that all too well; if you ignore it, it will return before long. And when it does, it will be even more unbearable. The only way to deal with loneliness is to bind yourself to loneliness.

It possesses you, body and soul, makes it so that there are no books to read, no music to appreciate, no videos to watch, and no words to write. I could almost hear it eating away like a termite at my heart, my bone marrow, and my brain in its quest to annex my body. I sat on the floor like an idiot, guarding a houseful of Yongjie's traces, while the bed had never looked so empty. I played with my penis; but why was it so tiring, so boring? D. H. Lawrence once said, Sex is all in your head. That's the truth. Loneliness had eaten away at my brain, clearing my head of all sexual desire.

So I abandoned mental activity for physical exercise. In the middle of the night, I turned on all the lights and started cleaning the house. Later, I learned that the reclusive Michael Jackson had finally allowed Oprah Winfrey to interview him in Neverland. In the evenings, he walked outside in a cool breeze, and I was puzzled over how neatly tended and how artificial his estate and playground were, like a well-maintained public facility or a model to be buried with the dead. Playgrounds always reminded me of circuses, of clowns and holidays and childhood, sad memories. When the music ended and the people were gone, the merry-go-round sounded unbearably sad, like the spirit of a dead person, unwilling to leave, lingering to pay homage to a glorious past. Looking into the camera, Michael pointed out his merry-go-round and his Ferris wheel, its blazing lights shining through the black velvet of night like a pair of diamond-studded platters. He said that sometimes at night he'd ride the merry-go-round by himself. My God, he must be the loneliest person I've ever seen.

Sometimes loneliness is more than psychological; it takes a physical toll as well. For me the most common manifestation is a sudden, unexplained heart palpitation. A powerful current surges through my chest, as if portending something terrible, and disappears only after I lean against a wall, gasping for air, and somehow manage to take a few deep breaths. But before long it reappears. And there are times when it sags heavily, sort of like a hernia. If I've been standing too long or working too hard, suddenly the back of my neck and my shoulders feel as if they're being squeezed by pincers, and the excruciating pain forces me to lie on my back in bed. With wide-staring eyes and an exhausted body, I can only wait until the loneliness is worn out so I can embrace it and take it with me into the river of sleep, two corpses bound together.

Day after day, I shambled through life like a zombie, with only instinct to guide me along. The primitive and uncivilized nature of my life made me feel like a giant reptile during the Cretaceous or Jurassic periods.

In my days as a reptile, the only thing I was able to read was an article on color, some research on the visual imagery of red and green in Chinese poetry.

I carried it with me like a rosary and read it over and over again. In fact, the work was more like a volume of exhaustive research on a color periodic table. It listed names for reds and greens from several color systems. A Japanese book on Chinese colors alone has 140 different reds, which, based on the MUNSELL Color Chart, are listed in order of shades, and within them by tints. Just look at the reds in row 5 on chart 7: moist red, light primrose red, fingernail red, vale red, light peach red, light poppy red, apple red, cheek red, melon pulp red, molten iron red, strawberry red, distiller's red, escargot red, cassia red, pomegranate red, mercury red, cooked-shrimp red, blush red, and crab-pincer red.

The greens on 10 GY in the Green Chart: mugwort-back green, Jialing River green, tender lily green, grasshopper green, water green, hydrangea green, mantis green, pea green, chalcedony green, leafy green, Parisian green, plum green, fluorite green, rice sprout green, cabbage green, bean green, glaze green, algae green, tussah silkworm green, wheat-wave green, snake gallbladder green, green bean green, light gray green, dark glaze green, duckweed green, grass green, and yew green.

When we escape the logic of words, abandoning even their semiotic functions, they become shards of colored glass in a kaleidoscope that form magnificent visual scenes. I lost myself in this color garden of pure sensation, as if flying in a world seen through the multiple-lens eyes of a fly, and forgot to return to the real world.

Whose phrase was it? What I enjoy about a story is neither its content nor its structure, but the scratches I add to its clear, smooth surface. "I moved along quickly, I omitted, I searched, and I sank into it one more time." Ah, the pleasure of the text! Yes, *veni, vedi, vici,* the comment of Julius Caesar as he entered Rome, a sigh that has been handed down through the ages.

How to deal with sorrow? Only writings in Chinese characters will do.

But Goethe said, The key to the study of color lies in strictly separating the subjective from the objective. This is the mantra, the haiku from Goethe, who studied color so extensively.

Do the colors of the natural world exist by themselves or through our seeing eyes? Or is it in between, like with Monet, who developed cataracts in his later years and had to rely on labels to choose colors for his paintings? After painting lilies for over twenty years, were what he painted the colors in his memory after his eyesight had dimmed, or were they the colors he saw in the absence of vision, light, and color?

Am I, or am I not? There was a time when I was completely

lost in the pursuit of this unanswerable question. Now I was still lost, but there was no longer any need to ask the question. I was like the Buddhist faithful who read the *Diamond Sutra* several times a day; they don't have to understand it, for as long as they recite the sonorous passages until the day they die, they will reach the other shore, like blood running through the body in rhythmic pace, as if pursued by dancers throughout the life of the host. I would recite my own sutra, the red and green color table.

Whale fin red, the red color of whale fins shining over the city.

Lips just turning red, the young red beak of a house parrot.

Red under the water, the round morning sun turns the water red. Barbarian brocade red, a narrow blouse with short sleeves in barbarian brocade red. Spoiled peach red, putting on make-up in spoiled peach red. Flapping fish red, startling drumbeats make the fish jump and flap its red fins. Cut flower red, light fragrance from red cut flowers caressing the sleeve. Beast fire red, pine-flame red, lodge-burning red, big valley red, red on the cheek, red after the frost, azalea red, mermaid silk red, Buddhist relic red, lonely red of the palace flowers.

Peeking undergarment red, five-foot red, a window of red, a speck of red, a smiling red, the burning red of the candle at song time, red on gold hairpins at the temples, the twelve kinds of red that fly in from nowhere.

A whole window of clamorous red.

Redlike, floating green and redlike, but nothing happens.

Chaotic red, someone submerged in chaotic red and terrifying green. Terrifying green, startling green, pallid green, decadent green, fatigue green, drifting green in a windless sky, someone returning in colliding green, blowing green deepening daily.

Rush leaves green as the sword of Wu, looking at the Han River from afar and seeing green duck heads. Bronze rust green, green between gold, greenish cinnabar, green left from a frost, clothes-staining green, green of an opened letter, don't praise the green in the blue robe.

Narrow narrow red, narrow narrow red boots walking in the snow. Geranium-bud red, lofty red, daily red, midnight red, last year's red. Flowers in bloom not as red as ancient ones. Tomorrow's red can't compare with today's. Skeleton red.

Red crimson vermilion scarlet maroon cinnabar.

Green jade emerald.

Golden well jade, hairpin beam jade, wine grease jade, sandalwood jade, pearl stone jade, heavenly wine jade, peach blushing
jade, Mandarin duck jade, winding river jade, Xiao and Xiang
Rivers jade, weedy jade, Qinhuai River jade. Blooded jade, green
from vermilion.

Vermilion from jade, complexion vermilion, two-ribbon vermilion, cannot vermilion, twice-proscribed vermilion, powder
vermilion, lip grit vermilion, cold water vermilion, raise the roof-
beam vermilion, poplar vermilion, my vermilion, dimples vermil-
ion, two-horse vermilion, twisting vermilion, lead vermilion, silver
vermilion, gold vermilion, purple vermilion, yellow vermilion,
cinnabar vermilion, blue vermilion, black vermilion, vermilion
vermilion. Vermilion is too crimson, blood is not crimson, thou-
sand-drop crimson, three-month crimson, rush-to-rainbow crim-
son, sun crimson, sword spirit crimson, beard resentment crimson,
jealous gentleman crimson, empty desire crimson . . .

chapter eight

A bud of red, January grows a bud of red.

Turning-to-dust red, old folks are partial to turning-to-dust red.

I recited my own sutra to get through the days and brave the
storm of loneliness, in the fashion of Ah Yao, the human Fly, who
telephoned for my help from the other side of the world. Goethe
once said that if he hadn't had a background in the plastic arts
and natural sciences, it would have been extremely difficult for
him to keep going and not give up in the face of the terrible age
in which he lived and its effects on everyday life.

What a great person Goethe was. In a time of disintegration,
he used poetry, the study of colors, and biology as his formula for
calming the storms, allowing him to live to the highest standard.
Insignificant people like us, who indulge in writing and reading,

have learned a bit of magic or an incantation to escape the flames, and now we can vanish into the magic state of words without having to worry about the demons' fires raging outside.

Outside, from outside came a young man with slanting eyes, appearing in front of my table and asking crisply, How about buying me a cup of coffee?

I'd been sitting at the window seat for a long time, wanting to avoid the rush hour. I could see all the bustle, all the foot traffic and the street vendors in the corridor beneath the second-story overhangs, and I could stare at the layered reflections in the window of moon-shaped light bulbs suspended above shadowy objects. That's where the young man emerged from, and walked up to me. I'd been observing him for the longest time.

He'd apparently misunderstood my behavior, for he sat down across from me and waved to the waitress to bring him a glass of Mexican iced coffee, which he recommended highly, saying it was available only at this particular coffee shop. He said it had Kahlua in it and was very potent. Nondrinkers had to be careful not to get drunk on their coffee. What an embarrassment that would be. He asked if I wanted a cup. I said no.

He could tell I wasn't interested in conversation, but that didn't bother him. Opening his backpack, he took out a length of wire, which turned out to be attached to a pair of earphones, and a darling little royal-blue Sony Walkman. After fitting the earphones into his ears, he pushed a button and slumped down in his chair to listen to a tape, his hands tucked under his legs, feet dangling in the air. From time to time he bent down, showing me the swirl of black hair on the crown of his head, and at other times he turned to look around the coffee shop, rolling his eyes to show both his indifference and his immaturity. Judging from his clothes and accessories, his Swatch wristwatch, a gold necklace, and a jade pendant hanging around his neck by a red cotton cord, the bold little demon was probably a kept man. He wore a white FIDO DIDO T-shirt and had a black plastic backpack from the same company. Several crooked lines in white announced to the world: "Fido is just Fido. Fido never bothers anyone. Fido understands everything. Fido does not judge. Fido means youth, Fido won't age. Fido is innocent. Fido has power. Fido comes from the past, Fido is the future."

Fido was all, so how could we make our voices heard?

The accent of the Fido generation sounded much like the National Language spoken by those born in the 1970s. No, no, a more accurate name for their language would be Pekingese or Putonghua. Nowadays, in the Republic of Taiwan, the so-called National Language is no longer the one we used to know. But Fido couldn't care less about these differences. Several decades from now, we will mourn the disappearance of the mother tongue of the Republic of Taiwan. At that time, the National Language in circulation will be the one used and continuously transformed by the Fido kid sitting across from me. It will be the language heard on every variety show on every channel when you turn on the TV. At that time, the language used by my generation, a relic from the previous century, will die off amid either derision or nostalgia. Our accent will disappear from the face of the earth forever.

I couldn't look the Fido kid in the eye. His youthful body, like the reflection of metal under a bright sun, forced me to don my sunglasses before I dared look at him. Earlier I'd seen him sitting at a table, joking with a group of boys and girls, a group of Fido kids younger than all my students, unfathomable and unapproachable, like the rabbit in the moon. Then they all left, as sprightly as red and blue dragonflies born in the wake of a rainfall. They passed under the overhang and went their own way, accompanied by my heartfelt praise.

When the coffee arrived, Fido looked at me, waiting for orders. I just focused on the cup of iced coffee, overflowing with whipped cream and topped with a cherry; I was half meditating, half nodding, like a man appreciating a work of art. He took that as a sign that he could start drinking.

And so with total composure, he raised the cup to his lips, no longer feeling any need to pay attention to me. I was the lucky one, for I was free to drink in his beauty and youth with my eyes. I was getting a lot for my money. With his earphones, his Fido T-shirt, and the Fido declaration on his backpack, he announced that he didn't want to be disturbed. Content in his own world, why would he need me for socializing?

The Fido kid was pretty, and he knew it. I could tell by his narcissism that he required stage lights when he made love. The

LIMELIGHT, or the spotlights in those little bars where I used to spend my nights. Hydrogen and oxygen burned limestone and created a strong white beam that lit up a stage on which a beautiful sufferer's three-quarter profile, like Garbo's sculpted face, was displayed to be watched, treasured, worshipped. Then it withered, but by then he had already reached an indescribable climax. Rare beauties are born to be looked at; it's the only way they can be complete.

It was as if we all had androgynous souls.

Watched, pleased, but hard to please, the mysterious feminine body. Have you seen the array of earthen male organs excavated in Central Asia and Asia Minor? They filled the palace to please the Earth Goddess during an ancient matriarchal period. Yes, take a look at primitive pornography, which portrays only the pleasure and gratification of the female body, for that is the way to excite and satisfy men. It is the racial memory and collective dream of the male species to strip away thousands of layers of civilization and overthrow the barrier of consciousness in order to expose the odorific female body, to induce the woman to breast-feed, and to use their erect male organs to make the obscure female body cry out, "Yes, give me more!"

I often prolong my climax, obsessed with the face of my lover under the lamplight, a fairy, a demon. As if he weren't connected to my physical body, but exposing himself to play with the force of infatuation that is staring at him. I am only a medium for that force, while he is overwhelmed, dazed by the ether or marsh gas released from the abandonment to passion into which he has plunged. The more deeply he sinks, the more violent I become. Violence and tenderness; with overflowing tenderness I kiss him.

The femininity that is gazed upon and the masculinity that gazes coexist in us.

I am often amazed by the fact that femininity is his own handiwork. He creates himself; he merely displays, but displaying is itself existence; displaying is pleasure. He is like the star-filled body of mythology, which, after swallowing the sun, was transformed into the horizon. As the sun moved past his body, he created the evening, then gave birth to the sun to create another new day.

He never explains himself, so he is a unified entity; his soul is his body, from which it is never separated. At the most exquisite moment, he is that which the dancer treasures and of which he is most proud. Jay's idol once said, "The body is sacred attire, your first and last piece of clothing; it is where you enter life and where you bid farewell to the world. So you must treat it with respect and love, with happiness and awe, with gratitude." A dancer worships his own body, he stares at himself in admiration, in silence. He gazes at his reflection and falls in love with himself. He is like the native Indian song: Now beauty is in front, now beauty is on the right, now beauty is on the left. I walk in beauty. I am beauty.

I am surprised to discover that what we call divinity is in fact femininity.

As for the masculine body, it *is* the rib taken from Adam.

It grew into a masculine form, coexisting with the feminine counterpart of his species, and yet he was so different. Facing this silent and submissive existence, he was both curious and puzzled. He took a long look at it, got close enough to touch it, caressed it, tried to comprehend and explain it. He served as his own self, but at the same time was an observer. As the poem goes: The dead sea had no living organisms/I heard the sound of fish. When the silent ocean finally sent waves crashing his way, he was so ecstatic he was willing to drown himself in it.

Indeed, science is masculine. Virginia Woolf once said, Science is not gendered; it is a man, it is a father, and it is contagious.

Ah, where does myth end? Where does history begin? Lévi-Strauss said, In a society with no writing system or records, myth exists to ensure the insulation of society, so that the future will be the same as the present and the past.

Perhaps all myths describe an upheaval that occurred more than ten thousand years ago.

Myth reveals secrets, nature created woman, and woman created man. But man created history. Yes, history. Man wrote the story of mankind based upon his conceptions. He wrote that woman was created out of a rib from his body. He even wrote that original sin resulted from the punishment of woman for eating the forbidden fruit of knowledge.

But from my point of view, it was man who ate the forbidden fruit of knowledge. Yes, it was he who originated binary opposition. Yes, it was he who originated abstract reasoning. He observed, he analyzed, and he explicated.

He created a system that was equal to nature yet different from nature, one whose constitution bore little resemblance to nature! The male deity usurped the position of the female deity, whose rage then became mankind's original sin.

Remember, said the last female deity, there was a time when you roamed alone, laughed out loud, bathed nude. . . . The female deity turned and walked to the end of myth, yielding to the emerging social order. The sorrowful and disappointed female deity became our Garden of Eden, which would never return.

I dissected myself, the bud of a feminine soul trapped in a masculine body. My mental activities were full of feminine characteristics, but my body, this body that carried the DNA of reproduction, could never escape its biologically determined state. A fate of blood and iron.

DNA blindly moves around to create more DNA. The male and female have different strategies of reproduction. The male is a competitor, while the female is a selector. Millions of sperm cells vie for a single egg's selection. The female, who is in charge of reproduction, needs a cooperative male partner in order to spread her DNA. She slyly, calculatingly selects a donor. The success of the male, on the other hand, relies upon his far-reaching dissemination, so that more females can produce more offspring that carry his DNA. Look at us. Men are heartless toward women, of course, but are even more heartless toward other men, aren't they?

Our feminine qualities include favoring concrete feelings, appreciating the physique, and a fondness for outward appearance. The material is existence, the only kind of existence. There is no meditation and no metaphysics, for what the subjective eye sees is the only thing that exists. Double vermilion red, rosy red, shell red, persimmon red, agate red, gray lily red, ivory red, pink oyster red, silver star cherry-apple red. I recite my own sutra: Steaming red, Bright sun steamed the small peaches red.

Yes, feminine qualities. But we lack the nature to reproduce or the virtue to improve human life. And so the idea that what we see is what exists is pushed to the limit. It is like a Victorian woman howling: I am amazed by the beauty of my body. I want to create this statue! But how shall I proceed? Marriage is the only answer. The statue must be finished before I grow ugly, before I get old. I must marry soon so I can forge this statue.

Beauty frozen in time is a rejection of time, for time creates loss. We become Mallarmé's exquisite swan, which admired itself so long in the icy water that its feet froze and it could never break free.

The reproductive drive in our DNA cannot carry out its function; with no means to spend itself, it is either cast away in sexual consumption or is invested in the building and chiseling of a sensual palace, which we never tire of sculpting. We have the energy and the leisure time to savor every minute detail of this erotic utopia in which we lose ourselves and from whose carnal pleasures we refuse to return.

The Fido boy being observed was a son of that utopia. I shied away from looking at him, turning instead to gaze out the window with a tiny sigh.

I prayed that this pretty young man, who had apparently never loved or had his heart broken, would never ever fall in love with anyone. Falling in love is the beginning of degradation. How could I bear to see the five senses of this heavenly beauty deteriorate? I couldn't keep myself from silently reciting, Let him disappoint everyone in the world, but let no one disappoint him.

Rare beauty is often unkind, for those who are infatuated with this beauty are cast away after being used. At my age, I was living the ignoble existence of an ant or a cricket.

It pained me to think about Yongjie, from whom I'd had no news since he left for southwestern China. After thinking through all the possibilities, I imagined that he was probably dead, buried by the first mountain snow. Tears blurred my vision; I had nearly forgotten what he looked like, what he sounded like, how he smelled. . . . In this corner of the city, gilded by a sea of lights, I sat across from the Fido boy for a long time, neither of us saying a word.

Our eyes finally met when I got up to leave. There were no streaks of red in his clear eyes, which were tinted with the china blue of a baby's eyes. They gazed straight into mine, devoid of emotion, which made me ashamed of my own appearance. I mumbled something as my face started to burn red, in direct opposition to the coldness in my heart. Maybe I said, Aren't you coming?

Fido had already taken off his earphones; now he raised his eyebrows, looking very cool, and said, Sure. He dumped his things into his backpack, then nimbly twisted out of his chair. In his jeans and Travel Fox sneakers, he walked out ahead of me, wantonly displaying his slender, lithe back.

Seeing everything at a glance instead of letting my eyes linger, I took care of the check. But even from that distance, I sensed his x-raylike gaze scanning my body from top to bottom. I smiled and derided myself, Yes, I am a scaly old crocodile.

At the door, I said, Well, then, that's it . . .

Fido said, Ever played snatch the doll?

No, I said, feeling ashamed. He slapped my hand, and waved me next door.

His hand was cool and soft. I followed him, sighing softly. I'd made my intention clear when I said, Well, then, that's it, which meant: I don't feel like it tonight even though I'm lonely. But I appreciate your sitting with me for a while, because, after all, I'm old and useless while you're still young and handsome. I'm indebted to you for keeping me company. Then, that's it. So long. People of my generation often live our lives like Takamine Hideko in Naruse Mikio's movie: she turns to cast a departing glance.

In the few outdoor scenes of Naruse's films, the characters walk and talk in pairs. Sometimes the camera follows them on a track, and Naruse is especially fond of having one character walk ahead of the other, then turn back to look while the other hurries to catch up so the two of them can recommence their conversation. Substituting the action of characters for the movement of the camera, he creates a genuinely subtle atmosphere.

Even for indoor scenes, Naruse prefers a place where inside meets outside, producing overlapping fading scenes and the movement of time with varying shades of light and shadow. He also creates a special kind of camera frame—the Naruse frame—by taking advantage of the openness of Japanese houses and their screens to produce diagonal images and multiple spaces while manipulating the depth captured by a stationary camera. The people inside are like floating clouds, constantly stopping and flowing, coming together and moving away from each other.

Ozu Yasujiro once said, There are only two movies I could not have made: one is Mizoguchi Kenji's *Sisters of the Gion,* the other is Naruse's *Floating Clouds.*

The horizontal style of Ozu is closer to the masculine. His frames are mathematical, geometric, weaving emotional threads between vertical and horizontal lines. The empty frame is his container for emotion.

Naruse is more colorful than Ozu, but there are fewer traces and fewer emotional ties—the flower blossoms then dies—and he is more captivating than Ozu, who observes in silence and is reflective. Naruse prefers to participate in the movement of fate, for he has always been drawn to nature.

As for the Fido generation, they are passive and active at the same time, for they are straightforward, totally cool, and sexless. They prefer good, clean masturbation to emotional entanglements that can be so distressing. They are neat freaks who have stronger and deeper narcissistic tendencies than the other group, the so-called "new new" people.

I had to constantly adjust my views in order to read Fido more clearly and not misjudge him. Apparently, it was not his intention to take anything from me. As a matter of fact, one look would be enough to tell him what I could offer, be it sex or money, and that was so little it was probably not worth even one of his smiles. Maybe he was just being charitable. I'd looked at him through the window for a long time, but the disparity in our wealth was so vast I couldn't even open my mouth to decline his charity. Take snatch the doll, for example. It had become immensely popular, and I hadn't even heard of it.

He showed me where to insert the coins and how to control the mechanical claws to pick up colorful rag dolls in the glass case. Then he said, PAPA, go play that machine. Hurry up, no one's playing that one, go take it.

PAPA, was that me? Still, I followed his order and took over the nearby machine.

PAPA? Pop? Baba? Bob? He called me Papa. With my face reddening and my heart thumping, I frantically started the game, and my coins were gone in no time. I looked over at Fido, who, caught up in his own game, didn't even turn to look my way. Flashing a bright smile, he said, PAPA, get some change from that dispenser over there.

I did as he said, getting ten ten-yuan coins, which I handed to him, then watched him play while looking around at the other machines inside, all vying with each other for volume, with a whole array of flashing, blinking lights. The players monopolized their machines in rapt concentration, as if masturbating, unconcerned about the outside world, even if the sky were to fall. I walked over to a table surrounded by a bunch of kids. It was a horse race game. I bet on a dark orange plastic horse with a blue jockey that was rarely bet on. I lost and continued to lose but stayed with it, abjuring change, as if I'd already bonded with the horse, a single entity with a common fate. Then I didn't know where I was. Was it a world in some future millennium? Or the Vienna of sex and death at the turn of the last century? Or Rome before Nero burned it down? *Fellini Satyricon*?

Around 1969 or 1970, *Fellini Satyricon* debuted at Madison Square Garden. After a rock concert attended by ten thousand young people, with the smell of marijuana hanging in the air, a crowd of hippies roared around on their motorcycles and in psychedelic vans. Snowflakes flew in the Manhattan sky, where the skyscrapers were all lit up. The debut was a huge hit: the youngsters applauded every scene, while some went to sleep and many more made love. The movie seemed to go on forever; what showed on the screen was an enactment of what was going on in the audience, the myth of romance, which found its own time and space in a mysterious, unimaginable way. Many years later, in Fellini's recollection, it was as if the secret of the myth had suddenly been decoded, as ancient Rome, future generations, and the present viewing audience were instantaneously connected. The movie no longer belonged to Fellini, for it had become a geological relic, an ammonite, whose asymmetrical spirals showed how two ages millions of years apart could come together in the same space.

So this was true. Fido came from the past, and he was the future. His Fido pack, snug against his back, with his arms looped through the straps, made him look like a hiker or someone pausing briefly in his travels. His spotless, white high-top sneakers made him look like some of the hermit characters in martial-arts novels, who dwelt in tombs for years and slept on tightropes.

Apparently he, someone who didn't know the meaning of loneliness, had no intention of being charitable to me.

Narcissistic neat freaks want organic relationships that are completely comfortable and totally harmless. Give a little, take a little, but never anything deep, for that is erosive, can bring only destruction, and is thus inauspicious. Now I began to see why the young generation, born under the threat of AIDS and a depleted ozone layer, had such weak constitutions. They were groping for an atmosphere hospitable for coexistence and needed to avoid anything deep, lest they die young. Fido approached me, perhaps, because I represented no sexual pressure. That's it, I was a colorless plant with no smell and no taste.

Compared to them, we were far more rough-edged. In chance meetings, it was common for us to be engulfed in the heat of passion, like fiery Mt. Kunlun, which was ultimately destructive. Yes, so long as the other person was warm and pleasant and was willing, something easy was made even easier.

I told Fido I was leaving. He hadn't played anything else the whole evening, and had snatched only a single doll. He said, Wait, PAPA, let me finish this game. The game had turned his cheeks the hot red of an overripe peach; like a loving father, I felt like planting a kiss on his face. But I just laid my hand heavily on his shoulder to show I was glad to have met him, and to say, Good-bye. I have to go.

Out on the street, I stood for a long while, having forgotten where I wanted to go.

Gusts of an early winter night wind shook the Great Wall that I had struggled to erect in order to keep loneliness at bay. The invasion of loneliness was Genghis Khan soaring over the wall amid the wildwoods and entering the Chinese Kingdom on horseback one dark, windy night. His cherished ambitions and his dreams, all realized in that one towering leap, were frozen in time, and he would continue leaping for all eternity. Only the snorts of his horse and the ageless wind broke the silence. Yongjie must be dead, I thought. His plaintive sobs swept past my ear: If you wait for me, I'll be back, but you must wait for me with all your heart. You must wait until yellow rain falls from the sky, until the big snows come, until the victory of summer arrives, until there is no more news, until memory fades, until you have a change of heart, until there is no more waiting. . . .

A cool, soft hand held mine. It wasn't Yongjie, it was Fido. I was surprised he had followed me. Don't you want to play any more?

Mumbling something, Fido nodded and asked where I was

going.

Finally, I sighed and let my emotions spill out in front of him. Yongjie wasn't home, and tonight I wasn't sure I had the courage to return there alone. A bar didn't interest me, that's for sure. After giving a lecture that afternoon and betting on horses all evening, the thought of going to a bar to listen to the blues or a jazz piano was so wearying I felt like throwing up. As for my sister's house, that kind of happy family atmosphere was all wrong for tonight. Given my shattered mental state, I was like a wandering ghost for whom proper homes were off-limits, since even the slightest movement of a human shadow would send me scrambling away in fright. I didn't have the energy to talk with Fido, either. Besides, what could we talk about? We lived in different centuries. I honestly didn't know where I felt like going.

As if surveying the wilderness and the roads ahead, Fido looked up at the neon sign for the Penglai Hotel on the twelfth floor of the highest building in town. Was that an invitation? My God, he was so young, easily younger than any of my students. I didn't think I was up to it. But Fido, without a trace of emotion, asked in a voice as transparent as clear plastic, PAPA, your place or mine?

I was shocked, speechless. Well, then, but, indeed . . . I'd once taken a lovely one-night stand home. The next morning, while I was swimming in the sweet memories of his smells and his breathing, he was already gone, along with a cash bonus I'd received just that day. I never saw him after that, and I became more cautious, more watchful.

Fido said nonchalantly, Why don't we go to my place. I'll show you how to play First Queen. And I can tell your fortune from coffee.

I said, What about your parents?

Fido pouted. It'd be a miracle if they were home.

I said, Don't they take care of you?

Fido said, They? Are you talking about ATMs?

ATMs?

Yeah, ATMs. I'm their ATM card.

Of course, the relationship between an ATM and an ATM card. Delighted that I'd agreed to go with him, Fido immediately cheered up and chattered with joy. I tell you, PAPA, First Queen is soooo cool. It's a role-playing interactive game, and my version's in color. I also installed an ad-lib card that plays great music. Yeah, yeah, Fido began to yell, waving his hands and giving the V-for-victory sign, like a happy crab.

I had no idea what he was talking about, and didn't much want to know. First Queen—later, when I saw him playing it on the computer, I figured out what the words meant. Out of curiosity, I asked what his father did for a living.

Fido said, My father's in international trade. Even when he does come back to Taiwan, he's rarely home. As a matter of fact, I like my father. He's smart, and he's a first-rate breadwinner. He dropped by once when I was playing Tetris. Out of the blue, he said he'd like to give it a try. He scored over thirty thousand points the very first time. Beat me. Fido stumbled a few steps, acting out the gesture of ramming his head into a wall and knocking himself unconscious.

What about your mother? I asked. Is she rarely home too?

Fido said, My mom's a different story. She suspects that my father has a mistress, but has no proof. She can't find a way to his heart or a way to keep him around. This year she started playing the stock market, and she's addicted to mahjong and ballroom dancing. She keeps busy.

So you're basically all alone?

Fido said, It's better for her this way, since I don't have to worry about her. Before my sister got married, my mother was bored to death and said it was all our fault, because she would've gotten a new husband if not for us. She was much happier after my sister got married, since she didn't have to stick around the house anymore. I can take care of myself, anyway, and I'm never short of money, so it really doesn't matter whether she's home or not. I'm free to do what I want. I'm not crazy about the idea of keeping her company or anything, because we don't have much to talk about.

I asked, Where do you go to school? What grade are you in?

Fido looked at me. You're sure full of questions. I go to a school you never heard of. And I don't want to go to college in Taiwan. After my compulsory military service, I'm going abroad to study. I have no pressure, which is why I'm always out fooling around.

You don't stay home and you don't go to school.

No, I stay away from home, but I don't skip classes. Too much trouble. If I skip too many the school will notify my parents, and wouldn't that be a pain?

Isn't staying away from home a pain?

No. Here's what I do: I'm out of here as soon as my mother leaves to play mahjong or goes abroad. Then I come home the day before she's supposed to return. If there's a problem, I just tell her I stayed over at a classmate's house. She rarely asks me any tough questions. Knowing when my father's coming home is harder. But if there's any trouble, my mother covers for me, because she doesn't want my father to get mad at her. So whenever that happens, she just tells him I went camping.

Where do you go when you split from home?

KTV, MTV, shrimp fishing, stuff like that. And if I have no place to go, I stay in a hotel. I hate being home alone. My sister knows I normally don't come home when our parents are away. That's right, she describes my staying away from home as not *coming* home. I'm like a wolf, a lone wolf.

What about friends? At least you have classmates you're close to?

No, I'm an only son and I like to be alone. People say you can buy friendship, but I don't like people to hang out with me just because I've got money. I don't have any real friends.

How about girlfriends?

Girlfriends? Don't you know that girls nowadays are all opportunists? I'd rather get a call girl in a hotel.

Have you ever done it?

No, not yet. I don't want to catch something. I don't want to be GAY either; it's too much of a hassle.

And no one bothers you? What I mean is, there must be lots of guys chasing you.

Well, that depends on whether I want them to chase me. If you don't want to be hassled, you won't be. At least, that's how I look at it. For example, when I go to KTV, I get a room to myself and sing alone. I'm a terrific singer, and it doesn't matter if there's no one to hear me, because the screen will display Give Him a Hand! When I'm tired I take a nap, then start again when I wake up. I always tell them to begin with the first song, and I keep at it till I've finished the whole songbook.

I looked at the young, innocent face of the Fido kid with

amazement, sort of like Aschenbach meeting Tadzio. In German, *Aschenbach*, a river piled high with corpses, a river of death. Aschenbach, unable to cross the river, dies of cholera in the canal city of Venice, where the air is permeated with the smell of disinfectant. Tadzio, a pure, seductive flower raised and nourished by death and sex. But today, whatever day it was, I followed Fido to his house, where he was going to tell my fortune with coffee.

The house, with no trace of daily living, was more like the set for a TV show, resplendently decorated like a Tainan noodle stand on Hua-hsi Street. It was spotless, since an obasan came to clean every day. The imported liquor bottles lining a glass cabinet were there for display, while the lady of the house's vanity table was covered with brand-name cosmetics, so much of the stuff you could plaster the walls with it. On the bar was a half-empty bottle of mineral water that seemed to have been there so long that moss or mosquito larvae were growing inside, which was probably not far from the truth. I sat in a sofa in the corner and was immediately stung on the neck by a mosquito, raising a red bump that itched like mad. The mosquito flitted past, right in front of my eyes, disappeared briefly, then whizzed past my ears. I slapped at it but never succeeded in killing it. A winter day in a high-rise equipped with elevators—how had the mosquito gotten in? Clearly it had come from the area around the leather sofa, which sank like drifting sand as soon as I sat on it; it had been a long time since anyone had been near the spot. There was no coffeemaker, so Fido made a cup of instant Maxwell House. Out of politeness, I slowly stirred the coffee with a spoon, watching the eerie reflection of my face on the shiny black coffee table.

Not a single book, not in this house. Not a newspaper, a magazine, a flyer printed with jibberish, a DM [direct-mail ad], a catalogue, even a phone book, I didn't see a single one anywhere. I suddenly lost my bearings, as if adrift in a wilderness. Fido, who was holding a can of soda pop, was sitting across from me at an angle, with plenty of space between us. We didn't seem to have anything more to say. He took off his jeans, leaving his long T-shirt to cover his buttocks; I wondered if there was anything on underneath, until he sat down and I saw a pair of pastel yellow shorts. He sat with his legs curled inward, like the Nymph of the Rhine on her rock. We had, apparently, suddenly lost the conversational atmosphere we'd enjoyed only a few minutes earlier. I wished he'd call me PAPA and take us back to where we'd been before. I couldn't keep myself from becoming a piece of algae out of water, turning dry and sticky, about to give off a salty stench. I yearned to get up and leave, to flee before the odor made it to the surface.

Fido finished his drink and, shooting a basket, tossed the can into a trash can with a loud bang that made me jump. He picked up a remote control, thank goodness, and sound shot out of a big-screen Proton TV, followed by the images of a comic variety show. He surfed the channels but came back to the variety show with its singing, dancing, and off-color jokes; it easily filled up the room.

We watched the show in silence until the phone rang. Fido picked up the cordless receiver and walked to the far side of a draped window, where he whispered into the mouthpiece. I could tell he'd been waiting for that phone call, and I was only there to help him kill time. When the birds fly off, a hunter puts away his bow and arrows. Time for me to leave. I gulped down the cold coffee, to show I was leaving.

Fido turned off the phone and said, PAPA, wait a while. My friend'll be here soon, and we can have some fun.

In a pandering, almost ass-kissing attitude, I said, Sure. Fortune-telling with coffee?

Fido said, My friend doesn't dare play with his computer these days. He says there are too many computer viruses floating around, so he shut his down. I told him you need three disks to play this game, since the total space required is over 3 MB. His computer only has enough space for the black-and-white version. As soon he heard mine was in color, he said he'd be right over.

That's right, Fido didn't say *coffee*, he said *computer*. I kept my mouth shut and turned back to watch the show while we waited for Godot. When the show was over, Fido switched to NHK-2, and Godot arrived.

Godot glanced at me. Maybe that was how he said hi. And Fido didn't introduce us. Without a word, they went into his room like a pair of Siamese twins. So they didn't even talk to each other! Shortly after that, Fido called out, Come in, PAPA.

I sort of slinked into the room, then stood meekly against the wall to watch, not daring to go all the way in. OK, the monitor's on, Fido said. Password.

Godot held up a red X-ray film to get the password—4508.

Fido typed the number in and a whirring sound came from the disk drive. Suddenly, psychedelic animation exploded onto the screen; the ad-lib card began playing music. Wow, I cried out in astonishment. Very impressive. But they didn't bat an eye; they were totally cool, like brain surgeons prepping for surgery.

For a few moments they just stared at the screen; then they lightly touched each other, like ants exchanging information with their antennae. Once they'd reached some sort of agreement, Godot sat down and pressed the key to attack.

Fido stood beside him with an open map of six mythological continents, holding a diagram of some sort. Godot's hero ran around on the screen. As he left a village, he ran into three beautiful demons. Godot was slow to react, but Fido quickly released a firestorm that sent them fleeing in panic, which earned the players thirty dollars and five experience points.

As I looked on, I tried to figure out if they were lovers or not, but I couldn't tell.

Fido said he didn't want to be GAY because it was too much of a hassle. My good friend Beibei, she said making love is a pain. Once sex enters the picture, her self is out in plain view, and so is that of her male friend. Sex is nothing but a pressure cooker for both parties, and both wind up getting hurt. She said she's a lover of peace; she pursues peace and wants no entanglements.

My student Haohao said that chasing girls is on the same level as playing computer games. If, at the end of a date, he feels like doing something else, he'd rather go home and play computer games or watch a video than take the girl somewhere or try to get her into bed.

Beibei later told me about something called second virgin syndrome, which has become very popular in Japan over the past six months. It means that young women who are no longer virgins can stop having sex. It's like chicken pox or smallpox—the sooner you get it over with, the better; or you can get a vaccination to avoid it altogether. One of the reasons why this syndrome has become so popular is that published research has shown that many girls are not virgins, and that those who don't appreciate the fact that they are different often go out and intentionally lose their virginity. From these publications they have learned that not everyone has to have sex, so they are quite comfortable without it. Just when you lose your virginity depends upon the climate at your workplace or school, and so does sex. You don't lose your virginity over love; it's just the accompanying result and the memory of making love with someone more experienced that matters.

I was surprised. So heterosexual love has been homosexualized, has it?

We often had stormy sexual relationships with strangers, so our memories of them only began after separation. These memories, like those of every animal after copulation, were melancholic and filled with sorrow.

Was it Schopenhauer who said that the ecstasy and pain one experiences when in love is actually the sigh of racial souls? Racial will is carried out through love in order for the sexes to unite and produce offspring. Just think, how classic! In the wondrous news and anecdotes of heterosexual romances, the female is the selector, carefully protecting the precious eggs while cunningly and cleverly selecting her partner. The competing males must exert themselves physically and intellectually, must be patient and energetic, if they are to overcome millions of obstacles. That in turn puzzles later generations, which evaluate them and say, Foolishness, thy name is man.

From now on, if the majority of males in any one era gradually lose the motivation and the foolishness to reproduce, then this era will be more or less homosexualized. When I hear sisters around me complaining and wondering where all the good men have gone, I concentrate on keeping myself from blushing, never blushing, trying to maintain a casual manner and hide my identity.

When men are no longer unfaithful or moved by beauty, will it be because they think it is too much trouble, or because they're tired, or too busy, or unable, or unwilling? At that time all women will be stilled.

When will the sexless age arrive? 2020? In the movie with the Chinese title *Silver-Winged Killer* [*Blade Runner*], the protagonist is sent to kill androids. At the critical moment when the pursuit reaches its end, the roles of the hunted and the hunter are switched, as the android saves the hero from falling off a skyscraper. Then, as the android's life comes to an end, he turns his sad eyes to the hero, and a single dove soars into the sky behind him; he dies and turns to liquid metal. Naturally, the female android falls in love with the hero, and because of love she miraculously survives.

When Fido and Godot came to a castle where rare treasure was said to be stashed, a very dangerous place, Fido wanted to go in, and Godot agreed to take a look. First he armed himself, putting on the war god helmet, purple boxing gloves, shiny blue armor, and dragon boots. Jade sword in hand, he valiantly entered the dungeon. Oh, no, he encountered a goblin every five steps and a monster every six! Finally he found some treasure boxes, but there was nothing inside. In the end, he got only two glutinous rice cones and a bowl of meat soup; but before he could eat them, he was poisoned and had to crawl away.

As I was thinking about statistics that showed that baby boomers will all have died off by the year 2069, I heard some familiar music, very far away, almost indiscernible. At first I didn't pay any attention to it, for I was wrapped up in the game of First Queen. But the music returned, then disappeared, again and again. Each time was more distinct than the time before, until finally I heard it clearly and it was right outside. I traced the sound to the living room, where the TV was showing a black-and-white movie. I couldn't believe my eyes; it was tuned to NHK-2, and it was Fellini's *La Strada*.

The circus strongman Anthony Quinn and the simple-minded Giulietta Masina, two good old friends, traversed time and space to visit me. Hot tears welled up in my eyes while I sat there watching, as if in a dream.

It was long, long ago, before Ah Yao went abroad, that we saw the movie at the Lincoln Center in Taipei's United States Information Center. It was also the last time Ah Yao and I saw a movie together. Every time Nino Rota's music came on, Ah Yao would start sniffling, as if he had a cold. At the end of the movie, when Anthony Quinn kneels on the beach, his remorseful sobs merging with the sound of the receding waves, Ah Yao and I both wept. We tried to compose ourselves before the lights came on, but we were still shrouded in sadness after escaping to the outside, and we walked in silence. Every building along

Chungking South Road was decorated with celebratory arches and national flags; the golden wind of October gilded the whole city. Ah Yao bought some grilled squid. After we drank some iced sour-plum juice in the park, we sat on the steps outside the museum to eat the squid. Then we began talking about the movie, but arrived at conclusions that were absolutely contrary to our true feelings. We thought that *La Strada* was too sentimental, not pointed enough; at the time, we were obsessed with *8½* and we worshipped *Fellini Satyricon*.

Several years later, when I saw *La Strada* on video, I was caught up in nostalgia, and I knew a bit more about the movie's background than when I saw it with Ah Yao. When the movie first came out, leftist critics hated it because it avoided social problems. Or, to borrow realist jargon, it was a movie of denial, decadent and reactionary. One, and only one, critic said, "What a daring movie it is!" Maybe he detected that *La Strada* had the courage to swim against the current. Nonetheless, I clung to Ah Yao and to my view that the strongman and the simple-minded girl, Fellini's ideals, were overly romanticized.

Apparently, at this moment in time, the movie had finally gained its deserved status, for the screen was acting out what was happening in real life.

The circus performer who rides in a covered wagon and the simple-minded girl he has bought, two marginal figures, start out on a journey to make a living together. When the winter sun comes out, the strongman abandons the simple-minded girl, who has just recovered from a near-fatal illness, leaving her a bit of money and some food. He goes to work for a circus, with a beautiful woman who becomes his companion, and makes a decent living. When he isn't performing he wanders the streets. In the spring, pollen floats in the air, children are outside playing ball. Suddenly he stops, thinking he hears a song nearby; it fades out, then it's back. As he follows the sound, it becomes clearer and clearer. On the outskirts of town he sees a woman hanging laundry out to dry; it is she who is humming the tune. When he asks her about it, she tells him that a woman passing through two years earlier had taught her the song. She had died there a year ago.

Covering my face with my hands, I began to wail like the strongman at the end of the movie. Ah Yao and I, Yongjie and I, sexual deviants who have exiled ourselves to the margins of society, generally come to grief because of the wasteland inside us, even before society dispenses its punishments. How had I gotten myself into this house to be trampled upon by everything represented by Fido?

The simple-minded girl and the strongman appeared at just the right time, beckoning to me with a shared language. Just that tiny bit of familiar accent was the thread I needed to lead me out of the maze. Having lost my dignity, I barely escaped being stripped naked. Giulietta's comical face and her big, round, doe-like eyes were tolerant of Fellini, who, the older he got, the harder he was to get along with, and of my unbearably foolish appearance. She was like couch grass, which calms anxiety; the rhododendron, which calms and quiets; pine rosin, which cures depression; gentian violet, which increases stamina; jasmine, which combats melancholia; basilicum, which relieves stress; and honeysuckle, which alleviates homesickness. People can talk about Bach therapy or aromatherapy, if they like, but for me the written word, word therapy, is enough.

Look at this: the marigold cures toothaches, the eucalyptus is an astringent, the daisy is an antitoxin, myrtle works on bronchitis, orange blossoms improve digestion, wild kudzu stops diarrhea, oats ease convulsions, lilac oil prevents necrosis and aches, rosemary aids memory.

When *La Strada* ended, I turned off the TV and left Fido's house, neither saying good-bye nor, of course, leaving a note.

Fido would never find me again, nor would I see him again. I couldn't fight him, not the Fido generation, but at least I could retreat in defeat with my dignity intact. I held on to the wild hope that I hadn't made a fool of myself.

Afterward, I often thought about Fido's house, whose alley intersected with a highway. As I stood there trying to flag down a taxi, I saw a garbage truck coming toward me. Like a yellow lumbering tank, it was equipped with an array of red lights. Five or six in a row roared past me, stinking to high heaven, like the strange beasts in Miyazaki Hayao's animation film, *Naussica*.

In Miyazaki's animation, the beasts' green bodies are covered with gray-blue viewfinders that turn blood red when they are angry. The beasts' wrath represents the wrath of the earth, barren and contaminated in the aftermath of a nuclear war. Only one person, a girl in a flying machine shaped like a dragonfly, has the power to calm the beasts' wrath. As she soars overhead, her shadow is reflected in their viewfinders. In the end they rush over in a red tide but are stopped by the girl, who calms them. The girl, however, passes out, critically injured. The beasts touch her with their tentacles and lift her into the air, while the sea of tentacles, like waves of golden wheat, emits therapeutic energy that awakens her. She walks on the crest of the wave, in the golden rays. The people in the Valley of the Wind look up at her, and an ancient woman sheds tears of joy. In the legend, which only she has heard, this heroine promised to return, and has finally appeared after generations of people have waited in vain.

On that winter night, I stood in the street, feeling as alone as if I were in a homosexualized utopia, like the array of nameless small countries surrounding the Mediterranean that did not even pass down any myths. I could only recite my own sutra, which went: The West Lake dried up, and there were no more waves. The Leifeng Pagoda fell, and the White Snake reemerged.

chapter nine

The activists of the New Age movement said that the Platonian astrological year requires 25,800 years to complete all twelve signs of the zodiac. Each movement from one sign to the next, one astrological month, takes 2,150 years. With each change of the Platonian month, the new replaces the old; disintegration and decomposition follow. The immortal Ma Gu reclaimed land from the sea three times, then transformed it into mulberry orchards. The next astrological month will occur at the end of the century, when the sun moves from Pisces to Aquarius. Hence we will move from the Christian civilization of the Age of Pisces to today's post-Christianity and, in the year 2001, enter the Age of Aquarius, the NEW AGE.

Tang the Gourd instructed me that Aquarius, represented by the Water Bearer, who sprinkled water down on the world, symbolizes tenderness, tolerance, humanism, and peace. There- fore, the Age of Aquarius will be marked by feminine ecology fighting masculine materialism.

Fairy Slave concurred and added that our consciousness needed to be transformed.

They showed me some books, one of which was *The Aquarian Conspiracy*, handbook of the New Age. Tang taught me how to control my consciousness, saying that consciousness is the only energy in the universe that moves faster than the speed of light; and it softens the hardest steel until you can twist it around your finger.

Tang and Fairy Slave were true believers, more like converts who shared a belief than lovers. They came to our bar parties together and never forgot to preach their ideas. Tang had just learned a song by Zhang Qingfang called MEN'S TALK. He sang for us: You have a friend living by the Tamsui River. You tell him about your worries, why can't lovers be friends? Why don't you answer, why can you tell only him what's on your mind?

Tang was a frustrated G [gay] who spent every penny looking for true love. Over a period of years, he lost his house and savings of several hundred thousand in a series of affairs, yet in the end every one of his lovers split on him. Now he was living with Fairy Slave, who was still involved with another lover. Tang sang to him, You and I are like heaven and earth. You're a floating cloud in the sky, and my tears have become a river. . . .

Tipping a lit candle to let the drippings fall into a water-filled plate, Fairy Slave told fortunes by observing how the wax formed. The candlelight concealed all traces of his age and highlighted the three-dimensional shape of his eyes and nose. Concentrating on reading the candle wax seemed to give him a headache, for he rubbed his temples with his index fingers, like an alluring Peking Opera female impersonator brushing rouge into the hair on his temples. After reading the wax, he muttered his interpretation to himself: Be careful with words and behavior, for your love affairs will be rife with misunderstandings and innuendo.

Suddenly I realized that this must be how Fido told fortunes with his coffee—or was it his computer? So I dropped some

melted wax into the plate and asked Fairy Slave to read my fortune. Watching the wax form into the shape of a boat, he said, You

are a true doubter. You need more confidence if you are to
achieve emotional harmony.

Fairy Slave was always sitting in candlelight. Whenever a new-
comer talked with him, he'd tell his story one more time. It went
something like this: Twelve years earlier, he had gone to New
Park [gay hangout], where he hooked himself an American who
loved him more than anyone had ever loved him before. He studied hard to pass the TOEFL exam so he could go to the United
States to be with his lover, who lived on a houseboat, which he
had decorated with hundreds of enlarged pictures of Fairy Slave
as a welcoming gesture. The houseboat, which never gave Fairy
Slave the sense of security he sought, was invariably blamed for
his outbursts. And after only a month he returned to Taiwan,
resigned to a life here. Over a period of twelve years, his lover,
who spent all his vacations with him in Taiwan, by then had taken
on the support of several Taiwanese orphans, to whom he
brought gifts each time he came. But he never gave Fairy Slave a
cent. Then, a year ago, his lover came with a marriage contract for
Fairy Slave; all he had to do was sign to qualify as his legal heir.
But Fairy Slave said no. Not long after that, a letter arrived from
the United States, informing him of his lover's death. Even now,
Fairy Slave dreamed of the bobbing houseboat, in which his lover
used to fall asleep holding his soft, shell-colored body. Eyes still
open, Fairy Slave would gaze through a porthole at the almond-
colored crescent moon, like a paper cutout pasted up in the dark
blue sky. He was incurably homesick.

Someone started to sing again: You don't need to shout. No
matter where a wild goose flies, it is the same floating world.

I still recall his name—it was Shi. We met every weekend for a
month. Then he phoned me on a day he wasn't supposed to call,
to borrow twenty thousand New Taiwan dollars. I couldn't tell
him I only had about fifty thousand, most of it paybacks from my
fellow soldiers when I was discharged from the military, since I
hadn't found a job yet. But I agreed to lend him the money,
every cent of it. We met at the usual place, a restaurant à la Centre
Pompidou, with exposed pipes and steel beams and pitted walls.
The air conditioner was always turned up so high I nearly froze,
and could barely talk. So even on hot summer days, I had to

remind myself to take along a hooded parka. But Shi always wore too little so he could show off his body, which was as chiseled and muscular as Arnold Schwarzenegger's. And always the same outfit, no matter where he went: a white cotton tank top tucked into a pair of short short denims, high-top sneakers over cotton socks with the Polo logo, and a green canvas bookbag.

Shi beat around the bush for a while, and when he wasn't talking, he was looking at me like a wounded puppy. I knew I'd never get the twenty thousand back. He told me what a hard life he'd lived and what a rat he was, as if widening the disparity in terms of respectability and station would somehow enhance his reasons to accept my gift. He was waiting for me to spit out a string of nasty words, to show displeasure, maybe even a little violence, for then he wouldn't have to feel guilty. I couldn't help but wonder why, from the first time we made love, he was always so eager, so very eager to roll over, a gesture that brought me indescribable pleasure and for which I was immensely grateful. Contrary to what I'd been led to believe, it was never a matter of our bestowing mutual pleasure. He always tried to please me more. Maybe I should have faced the reality that our relationship was no different than that of a prostitute and a client. The only difference was, instead of demanding payment each time, he wanted it all at once, now.

I could only mutter over and over: It's OK. It doesn't matter. Don't worry about it. Don't say that. . . . Tormented by such unfair treatment, I could only hope that this disaster would end soon. But the kinder I was, the more he demeaned himself. Our conversation, which began in the evening and dragged on until after dinner, was like a broken record, the same tune over and over; the air conditioning even had Shi, who never let the cold stop him from baring his shoulders and legs, sniffling to keep his nose from running. Finally reaching my threshold for pain, I said with determination, Let's go.

Panic showed on his face, as if I were about to desert him in the wild.

I couldn't stand it anymore, so as a parting gesture I asked, Where are you going now?

I don't know, he said with a self-deprecating cringe. Then he asked dejectedly, Want to do it?

My God, trapped by my own words again! There was always

such a gap between what I said and what I meant. What I meant was, OK, goods delivered and payment made, so long. But the message Shi got was, Let's go to bed. Of course, what I intended to say was, No, I don't want to go to bed. But what came out was, Time to go. From his relieved, hurried smile, I understood that he'd interpreted that as: Sure. Don't we always go to a bar for a drink after dinner, then to a hotel? Why should it be any different this time?

But the situation had developed to the point where I'd lost my chance to explain. And I was afraid he might burst into tears if I rejected him.

So we went to the same little bar under a highway overpass. I was so depressed I downed two more Manhattans than usual. In order to get a measure of revenge, I kept my hand in my pocket to let him pay for once. He tried to lighten the atmosphere by fluttering about like a butterfly, and it was at that moment that I suddenly saw through him. Why, I wondered, did a swimming coach with a steady income need to borrow money from someone who didn't even have a job? To pay off a gambling debt? A drug habit? Was he in some kind of trouble? Or did he have another lover? In any case, I didn't believe he needed the money for his sister's operation, as he had said. I realized I didn't know a thing about him, and yet I'd actually entertained thoughts of staying with him forever.

We headed off to bed after leaving the bar, but I lagged behind so he'd have to pay for the hotel room. After all, the money would come out of my twenty thousand, so he had nothing to complain about. Alluring as ever, if anything, he was even more accommodating, which melted my resentment and brought me back around. I should have taken advantage of the occasion to enjoy the sex; it was just a game of deception between us, anyway. I wanted to, so why did it turn out so badly? My body wouldn't listen to me; it was all wrong. I never got off, and felt *I* owed *him* an apology. Finally, it seemed, we were even. Neither of us had to try to hold on to the other any longer. The ups and downs of the balancing act between power and sex are incredibly hard to explain.

As usual, we hailed a taxi when we left the hotel. I dropped him off at an intersection near his place. Daybreak comes early in the summer, and street sweepers, men and women, were already at work. His power to attract me so strongly yesterday had van- ished completely, leaving behind nothing but a pile of dried yellow sediment like flower petals in a perfumery after being steamed, cooled, and fried in oil. Up till now, I'd always turned to look out the window and watch him cross the street, longing to be with him again soon, but this time I didn't so much as glance back. I was afraid I'd see how ordinary, ugly, and unsightly he was. So I focused my attention on the street sweepers' vests and yellow caps, a stimulating sight. I'd seen them often before, but today, for the first time, I actually sensed their presence. I'd heard they were at high risk of being killed on the job by drunk drivers. I never wanted to see Shi again.

Shi must have also lost interest in me, the dregs of humanity.

I plunged back into a severe depression, with no idea who might come to my rescue, or when.

I often deceived myself into thinking that this time I'd meet the real one, the steady one. I was terrified of seeing anyone's true colors, for that meant that my hopes would be dashed one more time. Then I'd plunge into depression and weakness, my life hanging by a thread. In the morning, I'd wake up wondering why I didn't just die, crushed by the thought that I had to get through another day. As I followed the sun's slow westward movement, my body weakened inch by inch, until the last light of dusk disappeared and I fell apart. My wandering soul wanted only to find something to hold on to, something to help me, since I didn't think I could make it through the night. But then, what difference could it possibly make?

One Saturday afternoon, when glorious sunlight filled the room, I pored over my address book but couldn't find anyone I could talk to, or meet, or maybe go out with, not even some old army buddies who lived down south. If I were to appear in front of friends in my decrepit, faltering state, it would, at the very least, be an unpleasant disruption, a disturbance. I couldn't find any friends unlucky enough to have to listen to my wretched confessions or spiritual probings. Looking at the last few balcony railings visible in the fading sunlight, on the verge of sinking into darkness, I felt my heart pound madly in my chest, as if the King of Hell had sent thirteen golden summonses to snatch my life away. I nearly called up Beibei to propose to her and beg her to sleep beside me, just so I could hold her hand to pass the long lonely night, which seemed like impending death. I actually picked up the phone and dialed her number. But when her cheery voice came on the other end— Hello, hello—all I could do was gasp like a dying man. But she knew it was me. Is that you, Shao?

I swallowed hard and said yes. I asked what she was doing. She said they were having a family reunion and let me listen to the noise on her end. I heard a loud houseful of people of all ages, including crying babies. She asked me why I'd called.

I said, I was going to ask you out to a movie, but some other time.

She said, Are you OK?

I'm OK, I said, I'm fine.

She was waiting for me to hang up and I was waiting for her. After a long silence she said, Hello? and I answered, Hello. She laughed and said, You're fine. I said, Yeah, I'm fine. She said, Talk to you later, then, and hung up.

And I plummeted into an abyss.

The night had fallen and I was out of options. So I dressed, washed up, and sprayed on some cologne, in a hurry to find someplace to spend the night, like Dracula wandering, searching for blood. Mother was disappointed when I told her I wasn't staying for dinner. The smell of fried green onions and soy sauce wafted in from one of the other apartments in our low-income housing project. In the middle courtyard, some big kids were playing basketball, while smaller kids were riding their trikes. My younger sister had just gotten home from her tutoring job. It was like two realms, yin and yang, darkness and light, coexisting yet separated by an invisible strict law of nature. I could see them but they couldn't see me. They couldn't imagine the kind of place I was going to, a place with no light, a place they could never visit in their entire lives.

It happened once: without warning, Jay said, You have to get used to all this, then left with some other guy for rehearsal. Dumbstruck, I stayed behind in his rented top-floor flat, my heart turning to mud. Burying my face in the jacket he often wore, I sniffed it madly, like a dying man sucking in life-saving oxygen from a tank. I had two days' leave, so I took an express train from Pingtung to Taipei on a night when a cold front was moving across Taiwan. I thought about Jay the whole night, and didn't sleep a wink. My body burned until it was nearly transparent, my eyes were shining. Since I had a key to his place, I entered without knocking and saw him sound asleep in the arms of another man, who opened his eyes and saw me standing there. Then Jay woke up. They both sat up and glared at me, an intruder. I didn't even recognize Jay; he'd turned into a werewolf.

Before the two of them left, we all had some instant noodles. The guy wasn't a bad sort, since he sat unobtrusively off to the side. The way I planted myself on the edge of the mattress, which was on the floor, Bohemian style, must have made me look like a dying sunflower that had lost its ability to gaze skyward. The place was an illegal structure built on top of an apartment building, so the ceiling was very low. Holding my head in my hands, I could only see Jay's knees and feet as he walked back and forth. The room was noisy, messy, and suffocating. I didn't move for the longest time, not even when Jay told me the noodles were ready.

Jay came over, pulled me to my feet, and placed me in front of a bowl of noodles with an egg in it. While we were eating, he told me that the music was for their new dance—some percussion sounds and cacophonous flute drifted over from his tape deck. Jay put some egg white into my bowl, and said they were still revising the score. He always ate the yolk and gave me the white. That was the only thing about him I recognized up to that moment. I nearly lost it, but was able to keep myself under control and, though choking on my tears, finish the bowl of noodles. It was time for rehearsal and they had to leave. Jay told me to lie down and catch up on some sleep. He said, You have to get used to all this.

I fell asleep with my face buried in Jay's jacket, dreaming about my first visit back to Taipei since beginning my compulsory military service. The day before my return, I called Jay to tell him; he was preparing for a show and told me to wait for him at his place. I went there straight from the station, nearly flying up the six flights of stairs, fantasizing the possibility of Jay's showing up at the next landing to greet me. At the doorstep, I reached under one of the potted cactus plants by the window and found the key, which meant he wasn't back yet. I opened the door and walked in; everything was just as if I'd never been away. I could spot no changes in Jay's lifestyle that might have been caused by missing me, nor could I see any preparations to welcome me home. I was feeling a little hurt when he suddenly appeared and gave me a big hug. He had been hiding behind the bathroom door, where he could watch me after I entered the place. Surprised and elated, I asked why he was home, since he was so busy, but he just covered my mouth and said he missed me so much he couldn't wait any longer. That was the extent of our conversation, and we didn't rest until we'd made passionate love, after which he got up to dress and invited me to go along with him to meet someone. He handed me an orange Air Force jacket a pilot friend had given him. We ran downstairs together, stopping constantly to kiss and fondle each other. We both had an erection even though we'd just made love; we pointed at each other and laughed. . . .

I woke up with the laughter ringing in my ears, unable to tell where my dream world had gone. I seemed to be looking down at myself on the bed, drenched in cold sweat like a body pulled from the deep freeze to thaw. I felt as if I'd slept for a thousand years, but it had only been a quarter of an hour or so.

The sun shone in from the east. The real world was too cruel, so I buried my face in the jacket again, sniffing Jay's smell, wanting to fall into the sleep of memory and not wake up again, ever.

Jay was wearing a dark green, unbuttoned Chinese jacket over a checkered cotton shirt that wasn't tucked into his green cotton pants, and a pair of handmade black cloth shoes. He'd bought the jacket and shoes in Hong Kong. It was an old Shanghai-style café, the orange light filtering in through the outside awning turning him into a figure right out of a Rembrandt. His arrogant, rash airs surprised the woman interviewing him; the shock registered in her occasional laugh. I sat off in the corner, finishing a plate of spaghetti and a peach tart and drinking black tea, my eyes never straying from Jay. From the bits and pieces of conversation that drifted over, I could more or less tell what they were talking about. I saw my own reflection in a mirror on the wall. Am I sexy? Jay said my boot-camp crewcut was surprisingly sexy. I lowered my head, smelling the odor rising from my collar, a mixture of Jay and me, of us after sex, since we hadn't had time to shower afterward, and it gave me a sweet, warm feeling, a weak numbness, a hot current . . .

I woke up feeling exuberant. From the ground-level angle of a reptile, I sensed the light, the objects, and the moist, familiar odors around me. Cocooning myself in my eggshell and its wet, sticky contents, I went back to sleep, to the rhythmic beat of blood as it flowed through my body.

The dancer began swaying to the rhythms of the music, listening to his body. His memory had been incorporated into that body, relying upon its vocabulary and its movements.

His face was bonier than those of most people, more rugged, angular. The dancer said, When you're hard at work perfecting your dancing techniques, you can tell at a glance that your facial bones protrude much more than when you started out. When Nijinsky performed his world-famous jetés he had actually leaped thousands of times already. The dancer silently recited a secret incantation to cultivate his skills, chanting something that sounded like poetry or a prose-poem—

Slowly exhaling, shrinking into myself as far as I could go, I seemed to see the sky. Inhaling deeply, opening up to the outer limit, I seemed to see the earth. When my body expanded, I gazed over at a precipice; when my body went aloft, I lived within my own self. When I shrank within myself and swayed, it was like Chinese divination: I cast the bamboo strips but got no answer, so I cast again and still there was no answer. Finally my body arched, my arms spread out, yes, yes, a full moon in the sky . . .

I muttered in my dream, as if praying: The prophet never sleeps. You must possess true knowledge and vision throughout your life. You should not be afraid to die now, for when one's body dies, one lives in God. . . .

I dreamed that he wrapped his arms tightly around me, a powerful, overwhelming force that brooked no debate or hesitation, as if an arrow had thudded into its target; I could actually feel it. I lay back and gave myself to him, and he took me with the tenderness of the Black Sea. While I struggled, as if trying to fight him off, he stirred up a cyclone of passion in me like a windblown prairie fire, immolating both me and him. His lean body was invested with a fatalistic fanaticism. He said he'd never chosen his fate, including being a dancer and being gay. He had been summoned, predestined to be who he was. It was out of his hands, he was chosen to be a dancer. His fatalistic heat entered the prison of my consciousness, leaving no possibility of escape. It was like releasing a tiger from its cage—the pitiful awakening of my sexuality, the sorrowful beginning of a tragic love.

On Jay's bed, which was soaked with our sweat and our desire, I kept waking up and falling back to sleep. The time between each falling asleep and awakening seemed as long as eternal death, but was actually as brief as the time it took a hulking lizard to open and close its heavy eyelids. This was my only reason to exist, the undying hope for Jay's return, for him to enter the room and walk over to me, to bend down and kiss me. That would break the evil spell, and all the misfortunes that had visited me would be nothing but a dream!

Jay didn't come home that night. My slumber and my wait fermented into bubbles. At one moment I suspected him; the next moment I defended him. As soon as I began to hate him, I immediately forgave him. I believed he would be coming back, then that conviction vanished. Ideas moved faster than the speed of light; the bubbles popped, then formed again, an astonishing power of fermentation, like that of the jar of pickled kumquats Parrot Gao gave me later on. I forgot all about it, and it remained unopened in my pantry for a year. When I finally went to get it, I was shocked to see how the fermentation of the kumquats had cracked the squat glass jar in several places. I was like that too. On that pale, gray-flooded winter afternoon, I got out of bed and walked out of the building, having eaten or drunk nothing, and not knowing where to go.

Maybe I took a bus to West Gate. Since I didn't have enough money, I was able to escape the pimps who lined the streets. Maybe I went to the Red Chamber theater to watch a movie whose name I never knew. As I slowly got used to the darkness around me, I experienced the flickering sensation of being surrounded by a thicket of shrubs in the damp night. The sounds of heavy breathing came from behind me, shadows swaying in the wilderness and sending wafts of a disagreeable odor my way. Like the last yellow leaf on a dying tree, I was wracked by cold shivers until the movie ended and the movie-goers had left, and I found myself seated precariously in a stilt house hanging over the edge of a steep precipice, my legs like rubber, my mouth numb. I didn't dare look back, but I did any-way, and saw used toilet paper strewn all over the empty seats and the floor, like a hill of white morning glories.

I walked out of the theater and shuffled down streets illumi-nated by cold, yellow lights.

I walked and I walked, crossing Taipei from east to west. When I got back to Jay's place, I looked up and saw a light inside. I near-ly went into shock! Holding my gut, I took refuge at the street corner, sick to my stomach. I stumbled off, circling the nearby alleys over and over, arguing with myself. Once I'd reasoned out a form of solid, unassailable logic, I returned to the street below his place; but when I looked up this time, I crumbled and turned around; startled by my own shadow, I fled. Wondering if every shadow entering the alley might belong to either Jay or that man, I held my breath like a dewdrop that might dry up at any moment and followed each one. After a while, I dragged my body up one floor after another, stopping at each landing to catch my breath so as not to pass out. When I finally arrived at Jay's door, I knocked softly, prepared to utter the lines I had prac-ticed thousands of times by then. I'd say, matter-of-factly, I came for my things.

For a long, long time, so long I nearly turned into the fos-silized Goddess of the Yangtze Gorge, I waited, but no one answered. So I took out the key and let myself in. It was immedi-ately obvious that Jay hadn't returned. I felt the indentations in the bed and sniffed the air around it to assure myself it hadn't been violated by anyone since I was last there. I was desperate but unconvinced, so I kept looking and sniffing. Fine motes of dust, like tiny raindrops, floated in the light under the paper shade of a lamp that had been on all day and was now hot to the touch. I turned it off and sat dejectedly in the dark, certain by now that Jay had not returned.

I sat like that till dawn, when I decided to write Jay a letter.

Page after page, I tried, but could only get as far as the opening sentence: MY LOVER. Love and hate swept over me like a raging tide, and I couldn't write another word. MY LOVER, MY LOVER . . . I left behind a pile of crumpled, blank paper. I had to get back to camp.

The Red Chamber theater in the winter! I returned to the city.

The downtown streets were even drier and colder, so dry that dust and tiny scraps fluttered in the air; I coughed the whole way. Although I was mentally prepared, I didn't know what I expected to accomplish. Still, I wasn't wearing anything under my jeans.

I recall the strong smell of hair gel during the matinee at the theater, which was about as lively as a deserted warehouse. It moved from the other side of the theater toward me until it was right next to me. Icy cold and burning hot at the same time, I felt like a corpse lying exposed in the wild. Truly boundless. I got up from my seat to go to the bathroom. Standing in front of the urinal, I could smell ammonia while the gray, dusty sunlight streaming in through the high window mixed with my heavy breath to form streams of white mist. The hair gel had followed me into the bathroom and now stood behind me. It quickly began fondling me, then pulled down my jeans. I didn't turn to look, just let it do what it wanted. I didn't have an erection; I just smelled the overpowering hair gel, heard the sound from the movie and the rumbling projector, and watched the dusty daylight stream in through the window. Then the smell of hair gel left me. The whole thing had lasted less than five minutes. I felt a sharp pain in my wet, cold buttocks. I was trembling so much I dropped the toilet paper I took out of my pocket. I looked down and saw my frozen legs and my jeans, down around my ankles and looking up at their owner with disarming innocence.

I fled in terror.

Walking among all the well-dressed people out on the streets, I felt like an imposter, hesitating and watchful, cognizant of the unforgiving nature of the laws of this world. I feared I'd have been completely exposed if the sun were brightened just a bit.

After buying a ticket, I paced the area by the rear entrance to the train station, where I frantically dialed Jay's number, unwilling to believe that he wouldn't go home wouldn't answer the phone wouldn't show up, just disappear. Then it dawned on me that, except for his place—our little nest—I didn't know a single other place where I could reach him, or any way to contact him. I didn't know where he rehearsed; I didn't know his colleagues, his friends, or his family. There was no overlapping in our social circles, nothing but our love. Love had clouded my eyes and led me to believe that this was my whole world, the little nest and the bed in it. All of a sudden, on this day, the fog lifted, leaving me alone in the wilderness, where our mansion of pleasure turned out to be a tomb.

Jay said, You have to get used to all this.

Yes, I'd used up the few years of my allotted golden youth getting used to the laws of that world.

For about a year and half, until I was discharged, I traveled obsessively between Taipei and Kaohsiung. Whenever I had some time off, even a weekend, I'd take the train to Taipei in the evening and return in the morning, like a short-lived flower.

On countless evenings, neither drinking nor eating, I stared at my face in the dark window and at streams of light from trains gliding over the island from south to north, as if revisiting scenes from my dreams reflected in the window. Sometimes I saw flames from oil refineries licking at the evening sky. Sometimes I saw lights scattered around the edge of a large bluish-purple plain, like pearls or diamonds, as tiny nameless stations flowed by like floating islands. Sometimes watery fields looked like land covered by silver mines; sometimes a dozen moons appeared in the irrigation ditches. The scenery swept by, like fast-forwarded movie frames washing over my eyes and my mind, turning them rough, pale, and dry, until the day broke and it was time for me to disembark.

Day after day, from south to north and north to south. I suffered train station depression, and have never gotten over it.

Those rock-yellow waiting rooms were packed like meat markets, but when I came out of the restroom they would be empty, except for some discarded newspapers rustling on the floor with every gust of wind. The peculiar female voices announcing train schedules over the P.A. system plucked out my heart as if by magic. If, at this moment, someone had called out to me in imitation of the Zhou tyrant's concubine, I'd surely have fallen down and expired like Bigan of Chinese legend, whose heart was removed to please the concubine. The hurried passengers waiting for trains or rushing off to someplace had become strangers in paradise, reincarnated and sent on their way to the mortal world. The station was empty, but I, I still didn't know where to go.

That's how it went, situations and events repeating themselves, like the patterns on the underside of a knitted blanket—the knitting of my hopeless, endless waiting.

Gradually I got used to this sort of aimless waiting.

I experienced round after round of disbelief, seeking verification, realization, negation of negation, the achievement of aimless waiting.

chapter ten

Because I didn't believe, after returning to base that time, I tried to find a way to get back to Taipei as soon as possible. And that was because, once I was able to reach him by long distance, his voice was incredibly soft and tender as he explained to me that he hadn't come home for two days because they'd gone to a Zen retreat in the mountains.

Unable to control my chattering teeth, I asked Jay if I could see him when I came to Taipei.

Of course, he said. Then he added, Silly.

I replayed our dialogue over and over, and late at night I let my tears trickle down, quiet tears that formed straight lines as they flowed smoothly out of the corners of my eyes, past my temples, and into my ears, where they dried. Nonstop, straight, silent lines.

When I saw Jay again in his room, I looked at him in a daze, as if I'd escaped from certain death on a battlefield. Back then, I'd been truly stupid, really, and very ugly. The truth was, Jay didn't love me anymore. It was as simple as that.

Back then I hadn't been able to see the cruelty of two people falling out of love. The one with a new love always has the advantage. Not only denied compensation, the one betrayed actually winds up in debt. Jay and I, creditor and debtor. A tender word or a comforting comment from the creditor can produce unrealistic illusions, self-pity, and exaggerated feelings in the debtor, who then begins to dream of something that can no longer be his.

I was unshaven and smelled terrible; complaints poured from my mouth. The debtor in this case was in error, for I said, You could at least have called and told me. I waited and waited, until I had no choice but to leave.

Jay said, There was no phone up in the mountains. How could I have called?

I asked, Which mountains?

Ta Pingting.

Did everyone from the dance troupe go?

Jay didn't answer; he just looked at me.

I waited anxiously for him to tell me what was going on: he and that man, he and I, we, what are we going to do? But he didn't say a word. I reproached him assuredly with a pout, tortured him with a silence that was more severe than the third degree. I was blind to the fact that the more pressure I put on him, the faster my value would diminish. I didn't comprehend the humiliating position of a debtor, or how natural it was for a creditor to be heartless. I should have been sensible enough to leave before he changed his attitude. How idiotic, how foolish I was! So when the situation changed and Jay no longer was kind and polite, I would be utterly pathetic.

Jay started talking about a dancer in the troupe who had the most explosive energy, Jin. Jay said Jin transformed himself into a javelin that would always rise to the occasion and never missed its mark. For example, other dancers would exit stage left by dancing diagonally, but Jin would keep spinning at center stage until the very end. This was a difficult maneuver requiring a great sense of control and awareness of the whole stage, not to mention the dance ending; but Jin was up to the challenge. His talent declared, Wherever I am is the center of the stage. That sort of self-assuredness. Jin never fell just to fall, but to give himself the opportunity to rise up again. In every jump, he accomplished what his body was capable of, like a bronze statue of Poseidon from the pinnacle of Greek sculpture, naked and beautiful.

Jay said the ancient Greeks believed that male nobility could be transferred either privately or publicly to a young man, in ways that included performing sodomy in the Temple of Apollo. OUSIA, Greek for *semen*, has another meaning that connotes material and existence. And so pedophilia became a rite of initiation on the Isle of Crete for young men, a bidding of farewell to childhood. See, that's how a Greek warrior transferred his combat skills to young men under his military and civic supervision.

I began to suspect that Jin was Jay's lover, his comrade-in-arms, his companion. So was the man that day Jin? Wasn't he? Why hadn't he left any impression on me? I was so tormented by my suspicion, I was unable to concentrate; I could see and hear nothing.

Jay said that sex was a quest for knowledge, a sort of enlightenment, not just a means of reproduction and pleasure.

Jay said the mystics of shamanism, the warriors of Japanese *bushido*, and the male aristocratic tribal chieftains of Hawaii are all representatives of homosexualized systems. Even the Athenian palace guards defeated by Philip of Macedon at the battle of Chaeronea were comprised of homosexuals.

Jay said Jin was born with the carefree attitude that declared: I belong to no man. Jay was completely won over by this attitude. Yes, Jin was the femme fatale of the homosexual world.

Jay continued to talk, nonstop and in a very superior tone. He was in complete control of the intellectual atmosphere. How could his elevated speech tolerate any mundane interruption? I couldn't open my mouth, and my heart ached as if melting in a crucible.

One evening Jay took me to a bar. After ordering me a drink, he sat me down on a seat like a potted plant while he mingled. I didn't know if he wanted to pass me off to someone else or so anger me that I'd find a new paramour; maybe he was showing me how to leave home, like a mother bird teaching her youngster to leave the nest. In any event, he left me there and ignored me, flirting openly as if I were invisible. The creditor had changed his demeanor and moved on with complete assurance.

My ugly appearance as a fledgling must have been obvious to everyone. A very very old, tall, skinny guy, who was probably no older than I am now, came over and sat by me. He bought me a drink, repeatedly patting me on the shoulder and leg with his bony hand to show that he understood my situation. Taking silence is golden as his strategy, he merely uttered: It's always like this. You'll get used to it.

After a couple of drinks, I laid my head on the table and kept it there. When I looked up, I couldn't see Jay. Jumping to my feet, panicked, I stumbled. The tall, skinny guy helped me back to my chair, telling me that Jay had left with someone else. Agonized by what he said, and very drunk, I left the bar with the tall, skinny guy, who took me back to his place. Barely holding out till I got to the bathroom, I emptied my stomach into the toilet.

While letting the water run in the bathtub, he helped me off with my clothes, then sprayed me with water and lathered me up. I detected the smell of cold lemon, and his large skeletal hand felt warm and comforting. After lathering, he squatted in front of me and carefully washed every part of my body. As he touched me here and there, it felt like fondling, but then again it didn't. I was only half awake, but I could sense my erection. I stood in the middle of the bathroom, showing off a body with a flat stomach and not an ounce of fat, prepared to let him do whatever he wanted. I assumed he wanted to suck on my erect member, but he didn't. Instead, he laid me down in the tub to soak in the hot water and wrung out a towel to clean my face. For a while, he sat by the tub gazing at my naked body while he gently swished an herbal sachet in the water to release the fragrance of orange. His tender, sad gaze lingered on my body for a long time. Then he got to his feet, picked up the dirty clothes on the floor, and tossed them into the washing machine.

I lay in bed. Before long he came over and lay down beside me. I held him; shocked by the emptiness in my arms, I held him tighter, and he nearly disappeared. Such an empty, lifeless body holding my neck and pressing against my chest. As I touched him, I felt an overpowering longing for Jay, like waves rising up a thousand feet. Jay's strong, slender body aroused a fatalistic infatuation in me. My touch made the body next to me moan and groan, as if in pain and also as if in joy. He came quickly, but I fell asleep in my drunkenness, still erect.

After I awoke the next morning, I looked around the place. It was immaculately clean and neat, with no decorative touches. The bare walls gave it the appearance of a government guest house. My clothes, washed and dried, lay folded on an ottoman. It was nearly noon, but the heavy drapes kept the room so dark it was impossible to guess the time. I couldn't wait to leave. Then the dark shadow of the tall, skinny guy appeared in the bedroom doorway; he told me to eat something before I left.

The fried eggs and bacon, looking almost too good to eat, lay on a white china plate with the picture of a green building and some writing that indicated it was a gift from the provincial government. I looked up at the tall, skinny guy, my first sober glimpse of him. In the musty darkness, our eyes met briefly before we both looked away. It would be our first and last real glance at each other.

He handed me two pieces of crisp toast, soft on the inside, and a glass of freshly squeezed orange juice. He looked at me with such desperation in his eyes, hoping that I'd stay longer, that he spilled half the glass of juice. He wiped the table with a rag and went back to squeeze more oranges. It's OK, I said, I'm fine. Those were, I think, the first words I'd spoken to him. I finished breakfast in a hurry and left, not daring to look back.

After that, we ran into each other several times at different bars, but showed no sign of recognition, like ships passing in the night.

It was never necessary for me and my countless one-night stands to converse; we exchanged information like dogs sniffing each other. We needed language only to get each other into bed and to moan our sensations once we were there. That was all the vocabulary we needed.

I remembered the tall, skinny guy because his body had aged and turned ugly prematurely through sexual overindulgence. With a pockmarked face that seemed to have been eaten away by the plague, the only chance he stood was the occasional pick-up of a broken-hearted, drunken boy, whom he brought home and stripped naked to gaze at, and to lament over how such a fresh young body suffered from the agonies of purgatory. It wouldn't take long for that young body to grow thick calluses, an impenetrable shield of protection. Not showing any true feeling, so as never to be hurt again, was one of the rules of the dark, homosexual world. He treasured this last glance before the young body grew rough and calcified, holding on tightly to the soul inside, which roiled with emotion. Yet all this would soon be lost. Tormented by a mournful emotional entanglement, he was still driven by his debilitating addiction, out every night to look for drunken boys like me.

His dark image, like that of a mortician or of the boatman who ferries souls across the river Styx, was etched indelibly on my mind, until one day it merged with Ah Yao's. I couldn't be sure if I was thinking about him or about either the Ah Yao of long ago or the Ah Yao of recent days.

I gradually realized why, such a long time ago, Ah Yao, who walked beside me after school, would suddenly disappear. I'd take the bus home alone, but it was still early, and I was lonely at home all by myself as dusk settled around me. On occasion I'd ride over to Ah Yao's house on a bike borrowed from the Chen kid across the way. Apologizing profusely, Ah Yao's mom would tell me that he had gone out, and would invite me to wait inside. But unless Ah Yao was home, I was always too shy to go in; instead, I'd circle the area slowly on the bike, hoping to run into him on his way home. Sometimes he'd simply vanish, and even I, his best friend, had no way of contacting him. For a long time we both knew he was gay, but I wouldn't admit that I was. So he hid this side of himself from me, and we continued as playmates. Where did he go when I, or Mama, or other members of his family couldn't find him? Not a trace, no way to reach him, not until he showed up again.

When I admitted I was gay, the places he went became Alice's looking glass, into which I stumbled, a new world just on the other side, where boisterous gays declared that the hedonist is blessed, the lonely man a sinner.

KISS LA BOCCA, a kiss in the time of loneliness, the hedonists' commune. The laws there permitted no pressure of reproduction, no kinship, and therefore no human relationships. Single cells of sexual desire separated themselves from the yang world, congregated here, showed off their nakedness, and received a sexual feast that was still never enough to satisfy us.

So I returned to the yang world, to my work, my family, my place, my activities, and my social life. But I'd already been infected with the incurable disease of wanderlust and deracination. The older I got, the harder it was for me to adjust. Even if physically I rarely set foot in the nationless world of the homosexual, in spirit the yin world's beacon molded my tendency to reject all public systems. Being a member of society but asocial psychologically sentenced me to a life of exile, a lonely sinner.

One time, after Ah Yao had disappeared, there were shoe prints on his face and on his clothes when he reappeared.

He had come over to take me on his motorbike to the Taipei American School, where they were showing a 16mm black-and-white film by Luis Buñuel in a reading room. Ah Yao disappeared before the film was over and the lights came on. I waited for him until even the movie buffs who were reluctant to leave were gone. After they turned out the lights and locked the door, he finally ran out from the darkness, breathing heavily. He went straight to the motorbike, with me right behind, engulfed in the stink of urine that followed him. He handed me the key. He had dirt and shoe prints all over him. I asked what happened. Carefully dusting himself off, he asked me if he was clean. I pointed to the shoe prints on his face, but he kept missing them, so I cleaned them for him. He knew he was dirty and smelly, so he let me ride up front. From the seat behind me, he tried to avoid touching me. We went first to my place, then he rode his motorbike home. We didn't talk the whole way, didn't discuss Buñuel. With damp evening winds blowing over my face, I thought to myself that Ah Yao had probably left me to do "it."

But I was disturbed by his ghastly appearance for a long time. Had someone beat him up? Or was it S & M? Did he enjoy being abused? Details, details, I wanted details. Thousands of sexual fantasies entangled me like nightmarish demons, to the point where I was willing to try them out just to satisfy my curiosity.

It didn't happen until several years later, when I met and fell in love with Jay. Ah Yao was ready to go abroad, and I had just passed my dissertation oral defense and ended my job as a teaching assistant.

I still couldn't believe that Jay didn't love me anymore. I traveled back and forth, from south to north, to seek proof. I began to hope that the conscience of the betrayer would bring him back, but conscience was more ephemeral than the moon's reflection in water.

I still had Jay's housekey, and entered several times when he was out. But each time I felt more and more humiliated. I had become a virtual masochist, who would be content if only he were willing to talk to me, even a single word, a malicious curse. In the end, I begged him to kiss me, one last kiss, and I'd leave. I'd never, ever come back. But the word *never* so devastated me with its inherent truth that I was sobbing and trembling.

Jay turned his face to the wall, eyes to the ground; he wouldn't even bestow upon me his disdain or contempt.

I went up to hug him; it was like holding a frozen corpse and trying to bring it back to life with my body heat. But it was all in vain. David carved in marble. Holding his legs, I slid to the floor to kiss his feet with their light blue veins. Farewell, my lover.

I kept my promise and never went back to see him.

But I still traveled back and forth. Sometimes the weekend was so short I barely had time to make the round trip. Each stop took me closer to Taipei, or farther from Taipei. I still walked aimlessly for a long time, and invariably wound up in the alley where Jay lived. No longer agitated, I looked up at his window, which was sometimes dark, sometimes lit up. Whether he was home or not, there would be no miracle. Driven by the abyss inside me to return to this spot, I was swimming upstream, but all I spawned were absurdity and sadness. If I stood there too long, I worried that the neighbors, thinking I was a madman, might call the police on me; only then would I leave.

"My bitter infatuation was so deep and so stubborn that, even without soil or nutrients, it hung on stubbornly, struggling to survive." I read this much later in one of the letters from Jay's idol.

All night long I would sit by the pond in New Park, wearing a light jacket through nights of frost without feeling chilled; pain had dulled my senses. It wasn't a periodic sharp pain, but a constant torment that wouldn't go away. After a while it turned into a dull ache. I wasn't hungry, sleepy, thirsty, or tired. I couldn't see, I couldn't speak. In the dark, my eyes were good only for distinguishing the water from the roads: in the pitch blackness, the darker objects were trees and stones, while the even darker ones were hunters on the prowl. I followed people soft as mud, people whose skin sagged like shar-peis. I also followed some old guys whose arms were tattooed with the Nationalist icon of a bright sun and blue sky. They were like Old Li, who was in charge of answering the phone and making announcements in the housing project when I was a kid. I was shocked to discover they were still alive!

I grew obtuse and retreated into myself. I recall it was only in the strong, muscled arms of the young man I met on Hanover Street that I thought about Jay. Then, someplace inside me a crack opened up and the pain returned, as endless as a plateau, crushing down on me.

The pain also resurfaced when I oversaw soldiers under my command weeding or breaking up mud clods on the military runway, which reflected the sunlight like shiny metal under the vast, dark blue sky of southern Taiwan. I thought about northern Taiwan, and pain, awakened in my heart, spread out in the vastness. . . .

But most of the time I was numb.

Except for travel and sexual intercourse, I was completely cut off from the world during those years I served as an officer candidate. I closed myself up in the frozen grave I'd dug, then continued to dig it even deeper.

Only pain could provoke any activity in me. That's right, like the desire to live, only that kind of pain.

chapter eleven

Ah, the dusk of dog and wolf, MAGIC HOUR.

Ancient Hebrew texts call this the time when people cannot differentiate between a dog and a wolf; it is the hour when daytime is about to be replaced by darkness, the eight or nine minutes of magic.

Taking advantage of the constant changes of every second, the camera chases the sun and competes with it for light to catch shots of the glowing blue sky, the clouds still visible, and the outlines of objects and the red of human habitation below the horizon. Then the sky darkens in an instant. In the dusk of a city captured in the camera lens at this magic hour, neon lights flooding the landscape and buildings towering like trees create a decadent atmosphere of the city, a banana republic.

In that winter, an inner desire for self-destruction finally got so strong it erupted at this time of day. My blood sugar dropped dangerously, my breathing grew shallow, and all it would take was a single Let go! for my soul to die out. So I had to hold on to the last thread of will, already as tiny as a mustard seed, and force myself to eat a cracker or a piece of toast and drink a glass of hot water, then quietly wait for it to turn into energy. It was now dark outside; I had made it through another day.

In this way, I got through my entombed days. I shed several layers of skin and willingly bowed my head, resigned to my subjugation. I acknowledged my new identity.

I found a job, so I stopped going to New Park. I became very picky, seeking only pleasure and refusing to accept any accompanying burden or entanglement. Naturally, I kept my true feelings to myself. I paid close attention to my appearance, down to the last detail, which brought me immense pleasure. And I started working out, hypocritically joining yuppies who followed all sorts of health fads, and buying into the attitude, pushed by promotional ads, that your body is a temple and if you worship it, the whole world will follow suit.

I frequently strolled around the city and came to know its many secret entrances, which led to the temples of cults that performed all sorts of bizarre, grotesque rites.

For many days and nights, I walked along a tree-lined red brick road outside a wall that led to or away from one of those secret entrances. It wasn't until I stopped walking that I realized that the other side of the wall was occupied by a morgue and a crematorium for postoperation organs; it was directly across the street from the Legislative Yuan. At the time, newspapers were filled with stories about the Legislative Yuan's bad *fengshui*: there had once been a pond with landscaped hills and goldfish to frighten off the demons and evil spirits, and if any unclean objects headed in the direction of the Legislative Yuan, they would fall into the water and sink to the bottom. But then, during one of the legislative recesses, the compound was renovated and the dried-up pond filled in to build a central courtyard. The fengshui was ruined, bringing the peaceful days to an end in the Legislative Yuan.

I walked down Chinan Road toward the end where the

crematorium chimney sent wisps of smoke into the sky. In my befuddled state, my only thought was that at least I was back in Taipei, in the same city as Jay, hooking up with strangers, also in the same city.

I selected only those I desired, discarding and forgetting the rest.

Many people floated in and out of my life, faceless, nameless. He could be lascivious, wearing a pair of tight jeans low on his hips, the top button undone, and a black leather vest over his bare chest, an enticing, steamy invitation to poke at his belly button. I did it with him on an abandoned beachfront pillbox, where we could hear people playing in the water in the distance. The ocean and land framed the pillbox in light like a calendar page. Afterward, I rejoined the crowd; walking on rubbery legs, I stumbled across the blistering sand as if stepping on the soft, springy parts of a woman's body. I turned around, shielded my eyes from the sun, and watched him leap into a wave, soaking him and his clothes. Then he also rejoined the crowd, walking in the shallow surf. He turned to look my way, and in no time we became specks in each other's parting eyes.

Or he could be someone with a nice mouth and red, moist lips. The red of his lips was so unusual, it could only be likened to Dracula's lips after sucking on a human neck. So we kissed and sucked on each other. I was like the one whose blood flowed unchecked into the other's mouth, enduring every minute of it, squandering my life in extravagance.

Or he could be someone like faint perfume. In a bar, he smelled like a mixture of lemons, oranges, and tangerines. He seemed terrified of being ignored or forgotten, since he was constantly going into the restroom to replenish his scent. I'd rarely seen anyone so lacking in confidence. Then he gave off the fragrance of mild jasmine, rosemary, and plum. Toward the end, he emitted a strong meadowy mixture of oak moss, rock orchid, and sandalwood. He pushed me gently down onto the bed, closed my eyes with his fingers, and played me like an instrument. Emitting the perfume of all three stages, he started with a flute allegro, followed that with a piano festoso, then finished with chorus basso con gravita.

He was the clicking sound of tap shoes, reminding me of Bette Davis, who hated shoes that were catlike silent, who wanted people to hear her footsteps. After stripping off his clothes, with all their studs and chains, I saw that his neck and his arms were adorned with brass and silver rings and chains, like a slave. They clinked against one another while we were doing it and sparked a no-name lust that was associated with instruments of torture and bondage and whips, forcing out of me a dark shadow of consciousness that even I was ashamed to acknowledge, like the invisible reptilian tail we drag behind us.

He could be the flesh after a deep massage, more tender than Kobe beef. He oiled his body with Love Ointment from the Kama Sutra cosmetic line, made up of treasures from the sea floor. The bath salt turned a tub of clear water into turquoise and thickened the water. I intertwined with this flesh like rolling in gooey mud that didn't stick to the body, tasting Kama Sutra, the sexual flavor of ancient India.

He could be the cool, alluring boy on a BANANA REPUBLIC poster, or the fetching half-naked boy with neatly combed hair, wearing only a pair of jeans, in the Levi Strauss SILVER TAB commercial. He was a match for absurd daydreams, with whom I could reach the limits of imagination.

He could be the James Dean of our era.

Only *The Nazi Madman* [*The Damned*] of the Dusk Trilogy by Luchino Visconti was available to Ah Yao and me. We saw it in a small theater in Pan-ch'iao. The title had been changed to *The Nazi Madwoman,* and so much had been edited out that it made absolutely no sense to us. They even inserted a section on Swedish sex acts. He—Ah Yao sent letters and cards to me after he got to New York. My God, there he saw an uncut version of the movie, not a single shot missing. In the movie, a group of homosexual brown shirts are shot to death. He said, We've all been deceived, a phrase he loved to use while he was experiencing culture shock in the United States. In his letters, a crazy mixture of Chinese and English, he inserted the English comment, We've been deceived for thirty years, did you know that?

He could be Leonard Whiting playing the role of the lovesick Romeo, in a pirated copy of the film shown in a theater. His bare arms, disappearing from the screen in an instant, and his innocent, passionate, beautiful face emerged over and over during the theme song, which we quickly learned by heart. He was our undercover man, our spokesman in disguise.

He could be someone who took a potion that let him go at it all night without coming. Even when his cock was worn out, he was still hot to trot. The first light of day streaming into the room shone on his pale face, which was veiled by a blue haze. His lips, like a persimmon after a frost, opened to reveal bright red flesh, and the blood-red inner lining of his lower eyelid showed. He was a dead ringer for a geisha.

He could be a pair of eyes with lashes so long they hid everything but the sparkle. I could feel the prick of light on my back, but it vanished as soon as I turned to meet it. I decided to search for it, but provoked no response when I walked by and brushed past him. It wasn't a very big place, but it felt like a celestial maze when I moved about, for that light was there one moment and gone the next. Someone using his drunkenness as an excuse nibbled at my shoulder, but I was intent upon capturing that sparkle. Suddenly it meandered past; caught off guard, I followed it out anxiously. I was engulfed by a dense fog, finding no signs to point the way. Frantically walking and walking, I stumbled into a construction site encircled by warning signs and blinking red lights. Seemingly trapped and lost, suddenly I spotted the sparkle on the overpass. I clambered over steel reinforcing bars and iron beams like schooling sharks, eeled my way across the pitted ground, climbed onto the overpass, and spanned the city beneath me, following the sparkle that was moving down a dark street. Suddenly he turned around, passing me like a blind man and crossing to the other side of the street. With trepidation, I turned to follow him, my heart pounding. The street was like the Milky Way, divided into two sides, with me walking on this side, following him on the other side like a shadow seeking its mate. When he turned into a narrow street, I quickened my steps to catch up until I reached the end of the street, a dead end. It was just me and the overpowering stench of garlic and other garbage. Turning around, I saw a light materialize on the tip of a cigarette beneath an advertising kiosk. I walked toward it, smoke about to emerge from my burning eyes. Finally I'd grabbed hold of the sparkle that had been waiting so quietly and assuredly in the dark. He handed me his cigarette, which I dragged on. After catching my breath, I stared fiercely at the sparkle to keep it from getting away. He was mine now, and went with me where we should go.

I was a gold-digger, abandoning myself to sensual pleasure. I sought my fortune every night in the city, hoping to lay my hands on some dazzling nuggets.

At about the same time, I became hysterically obsessed with marriage.

I was tired of the endless, limitless feast of carnal delights. I had gotten so used to total abandonment, my combustion point had risen so high, that only the hottest fire could ignite me, and I was getting anxious about the possibility of impotence. I was afraid that one day, T. S. Eliot's prophetic comment would be realized in me: "I made love, but felt nothing."

I was like the girl's feet in demonic red shoes that couldn't stop dancing until they were lopped off. I longed for stability. My only salvation was marriage.

I decided to date Beibei in earnest. She had been my sister's best friend in high school, but they had drifted apart. Then Beibei and I, both single, became best friends.

But between us there was no—how should I put it?— no tension.

We were as close as family members, as comfortable as old slippers. Like brother and sister. She told me everything, even about the little spats she had with her boyfriends. Every time we went to a PUB to celebrate after she had gotten the OK on an assignment, she'd get drunk and hang all over me; that and her stomach problems amazed me—the way her work environment warped her personality wasn't much better than what we went through.

She told me how, as a girl, she had dreamed of a room of her own, one she could paint in her favorite color and furnish with a big desk and a tasseled desk lamp. She had shared a room with her two brothers, one barely big enough for two sets of bunk beds side by side and a desk with four shallow drawers. Given the upper bunk, she had to climb onto the desk to get into bed. At the age of fourteen, she began to detect a salty odor in the room, feeling that her body had a sweet and sour smell. She desperately tried to cover it up, like a cat burying its excrement so as not to leave any trace. She imitated her father by eating garlic and even hid a sachet of the stuff to create a false smell. She had learned to climb like a monkey, timing her getting into and out of bed when no one was around, so as not to expose her body to her brothers. She slept in one of the upper bunks; the other was piled high with a camphor trunk and winter bedding. At night she was afraid that monsters hiding inside the trunk would come after her, so she slept with her arms over her chest in the form of a cross to keep her safe. Whenever a cold front moved across Taiwan, requiring the use of heavy blankets and winter clothes from the trunk, her mother was always puzzled to find so much dried garlic and grass tied into crosses. Those were Beibei's amulets to ward off evil; she stuffed them into every crack, believing they had the power to protect her. There were two lights in the room: one a clip-on lamp shaped like an upside-down aluminum ladle, the other an overhead fluorescent lamp that would flicker for the longest time before finally stabilizing to give off a pale blue light. So she spent most of her very first paycheck on a lamp with a marble stand and a cream-colored, gauzy lampshade, no matter how out of place it seemed in her cramped, dingy room. Beibei had a lamp fetish that had turned into an obsession with antique lamps.

Beibei related her past and her present in great detail, and as her audience, I felt lonelier than ever.

She gave me so much, unilaterally, naïvely, unrestrained. And what about me? What could I give her? I kept my mouth shut; I was so stingy I didn't reveal one iota of the dark side of my life. She could have half of my world, but could never reach the other half.

In line with common practice, I initiated my courtship. I asked her out to a faddish restaurant for a somewhat overpriced steak dinner, which greatly surprised her. She tried to relieve the tension by teasing me about taking her to such a yuppie hangout.

I was so embarrassed. I never thought she'd guess my intentions so quickly. Pale, inarticulate, obtuse, humorless. Having made a mess of things, a hopeless case, I couldn't even look her in the eye. The meal became a dreadfully long dining ritual. Toward the end, I worried I might give myself away; like sticky dried seaweed, I had to keep the salty smell to myself. After paying the bill, I scurried off like a scared rat. I got the hell out of there.

I removed myself from Beibei's social circle, sure that I'd destroyed our innocent friendship in a single night. Full of remorse, I started to miss her. I couldn't get the image of her, dressed like Annie Hall in her three-piece pant suit, out of my mind. Had I fallen in love with her? The thought of romantic love between a man and a woman made me extremely happy. Maybe I ought to try again.

In the end, it was Beibei who came to see me. She'd already left two messages, but I was too ashamed to return her calls. She said, Did you fall off the end of the earth?

Tears of gratitude. I laughed out loud in embarrassment.

She asked *me* out to dinner. She was her usual vibrant self, talkative and energetic, while I did what I was good at—listening and responding. We returned to our comfortable, old way of interaction. What she said that night still rings in my ears: Women are like full sails waiting for the winds of history, while men are a bunch of idiots standing against the wind. That was a wake-up call for the world from a guy named Kuroi something or other.

Beibei was talking about the world of advertising. She said that male-centered industry had collapsed. In Japan, the company a man worked for was once his home away from home. With lifetime employment, the company, the *kaisha* in Japanese, was where a man spent his entire working life. The kaisha represented the concentric consciousness of the business world, the spirit of *bushido*. The last of the samurai—the postwar white-collar worker. Following the last oil crisis, men began going home. Gripped by insecurity, they went into the kitchen. Back in their studies, the joys of hidden corners.

She said, Japanese men have always been sheltered by their companies and their mothers. Their dependence upon their mothers has a particularly long history. In a group, they are cute little boys, but when they're away from the crowd as individuals, for some strange reason they become crashing boors.

She said, Women and children adapt easily to new environments, while men are slow to learn and slow to feel.

I astonished myself by agreeing with everything she said, assuming she had included me in the feminine nation and could openly air her views of men. But I made only a feeble attempt at responding by borrowing some phrases from Herbert Marcuse. Yes, once we have abolished all the social institutions, we can return to the utopian ideal of mother and son coexisting as one. That, however, only upset me, since I was uttering empty phrases that had nothing to do with what Beibei was talking about.

A long time afterward, I learned of a word in Japanese— AMAE—which means something like pampering, the feeling a baby gets when it curls up in its mother's arms. The Japanese have extended this notion into their everyday life, and it has become so much a part of that life that it is now a salient trait of the Japanese national character.

The systematization of amae is the Emperor system.

The philogical origin of the word *amae*—AMA—can be traced back to Japanese mythology recorded in the *Kojiki*. Descent from heaven, AMAKADARU, ascent to heaven, AMAGAKERU. In contrast to the notion among some nomadic tribes that heaven is fragmented, the Japanese believe that heaven is continuous.

The Sun Goddess, Amaterasu, lived in Takamagahara, the abode of the gods. Her younger brother, Susano'o no mikoto, rebelled and established his own male kingdom of the clouds, Zumo no kuni. Was this a sexual revolution instigated by a male god ten thousand years ago? But Amaterasu didn't recognize his kingdom, and sent her grandson to replace him by giving the youngster a stalk of grain to set up the kingdom of Yamato.

Amaterasu had a son, but didn't entrust him with the task because as an adult, he belonged to the male world. In contrast, her grandson could rule on behalf of the female world because he was still young and had lived and slept with Amaterasu in her palace. Ever since, the Japanese imperial line, unbroken for ten thousand generations, has included males, yet continues to represent the order of Amaterasu.

Amaterasu is worshipped at the Grand Shrines of Ise, where only an unmarried woman, a member of the imperial household, can be the *saishu,* the mistress of religious ceremonies. The saishu worships the Shinto gods as the Pope worships the God Jehovah. This can be likened to the ancient Chinese sacrificial rites to heaven and earth, for which the Son of Heaven was the high priest. Do you remember how, when Prince Shotoku wrote to Emperor Wen of the Sui Dynasty, he referred to his letter as a missive from the Son of Heaven in the place where the sun rises, to the Son of Heaven in the place where the sun sets?

The place where the sun rises, Naniwazu, was the Country of Women. The head of the household was a woman who

employed a man as overseer. But she remained inside, represented to the outside world by her son or grandson. The son was not
merely the overseer's overseer but the young ruler, who transmitted his mother's orders from the inner chambers in the same
fashion as Amaterasu entrusting her power to her grandson.

The young emperor, brought up by women, was very effemi-
nate; the dreamworld of Yamato was an artistic realm. No wonder the author of *The Tale of Genji* used the moon as a metaphor
for men. Most women had their places, which men frequented
for romantic purposes. The true foundation of Japanese literature
is women's court literature and women's ballads.

Feeling lonely, I said to my students, It makes more sense to
try to understand Japanese women before trying to fathom the
mystery of Japan's surge in productivity, which took the world
by storm.

The reality is, marriage is not, has never been, nor could ever
be, a private matter. Lévi-Strauss's maxim.

Lévi-Strauss pointed out that, whether the system dictates
marrying the brother of one's deceased husband or the sister of
one's deceased wife, there are only two kinship principles: intimate or distant, or intratribal marriage or intertribal marriage.

Intertribal marriage represents a group's allying strategy to
open itself up to all kinds of historical possibilities, but there are
dangers involved. Intratribal marriage, on the other hand, is a
strategy of consolidation, holding on to benefits passed down
through the years: the inheritance system, caste, titles, and con-
ventions. These two strategies are constantly interacting as a
matrix algebra model to unfold an intricate relational network.

One day, when my obsession with marriage had all but melted
away, Beibei and I went out to eat and talk—she talked and I listened, as usual. After dinner, we went to a small but charming
boutique across the street. Her eyes lit up like gemstones as she
fondled exotic foreign trinkets, inviting me to join her jubilant
tour with the oppressive zeal of an evangelist. I encouraged her
to buy something, but she said it was a waste of money. I knew
she was saving every cent to buy her own flat, where she could
live and work, since she wanted to move out of her parents'
house and live the life she wanted. Short in stature, she was
standing so close to me that I was seduced into revealing my

secret. I said we could buy all these things to decorate our house, if we got married.

Was she pretending she didn't hear me? Or was it because we were like brother and sister, and what I said simply didn't mean anything, vanishing as soon as it left my mouth? I sniffed the air, but couldn't smell anything. I wondered if it was something I'd said in a dream, and I was the only one who had heard it.

Beibei turned around to show me a white pewter pagoda-shaped clock studded with seashells, conch shells, starfish, and raised patterns of Pisces. The protruding portion was gilded in gold leaf, inlaid with a round face made of gypsum with wooden hands to tell the time. It was a handmade clock, inside and out. What it meant to me was, after digital clocks became so popular in the past decade or so, time began passing in seconds. But I used only clocks with mechanical movements, firmly believing that time should dissipate spatially, with the hands moving from one space to the next. Stubbornly, I wanted to take my long homeward journey into the night at just such a speed. Every time Beibei walked by, she'd go in to ask if the clock had been sold. Again I said, Let me buy it for you. We really should get married.

She said, No, it's too expensive. You're not making much more money than me.

I said, Yeah, it is pretty expensive.

She let it pass, misread my text. It seemed to me that I could see my rhetoric fall to the ground, a broken string of pearls that skittered and bounced off in all directions, like pachinko balls, among the goods for sale. Pewter sugar bowls; pepper mills; an antique silver spoon shaped like a rabbit, with rubies for eyes; mustard spoons; crystal glasses with enamel beetles; hand-painted pottery; a resin candelabra; a brass candlesnuffer; a copper mirror; a soldered mailbox with a rooster weather vane . . . my poor marriage proposal dispersed and was absorbed by all that imported bric-a-brac.

Over the coming years, I would see silver-haired grandmas invade fast-food restaurants in the morning, housewives become the primary customers for afternoon tea, and female empty-nesters turn into frequent flyers, traveling for pleasure and visiting relatives abroad. Beibei told me that since 1987, Japanese white-collar women have taken pride in buying themselves full-karat diamond rings. The very next year there were two-karat-diamond women. No longer were they waiting to get diamonds as a sign of love. The diamond trend was getting more and more popular, particularly in Taiwan, where female consumers were buying them for themselves, then for their parents, their husbands, and their friends, an obvious characteristic of a matrilineal society, and an unprecedented phenomenon in the international diamond market.

Heavy Metal, this year's hot fashion, Urban Knight Style, Postmodern Robin Hood, Farewell to Tokyo *Zoku*, Zip Chic. I witnessed strange, exotic boutiques sprouting up all over the city like grass in the spring.

China with blue floral arabesques, teardrop honey wax, transparent blood amber, blue-and-white dragonfly stone, fish bone beads, solid pearls, patterned amber from Russia, pine-green agate, old brass fingernail shields inlaid with cloisonné . . .

For modern people whose lives were sliced into broken fragments, fragrance was the ideal remedy to reunify their lives. Mix lime juice with salvia japonica to clear the mind; peppermint and orange to enliven the atmosphere at social functions; sandalwood, bishop-wort, and sesame to increase sexual stimulation. In 1792, a friar gave a formula for miracle water to his best friend, the banker Mülhens, who was getting married. This water, which differed from ordinary perfume and was the Mülhens's family secret, needed to be stored in barrels made of Black Forest oak for four months. When it reached maturity, the water was transported to places around the world in blue-green bottles with gold trim. It was called Worth 4711 perfume, and didn't reach this Asian island country for another two hundred years. It then became some gay friend's liquid memory, for using it would recapture the messy fragments of life attached to the scent.

Then I started reading the map of the city, made up of numerous shop names, interpreting them with no clear understanding, mixing and matching them at will. I tried to imagine their secret entrances, which led to places where many tribes and rituals were scattered like the constellations. A country of many scents, like the multiple rulers of India, three thousand kaleidoscopic worlds.

KISS LA BOCCA offered the trendiest red wine, Test Tube Baby, originally called KAMIKAZE, now bottled in red, white, and yellow test tubes. The bar made it in batches of fifty bottles, which sold for three thousand Taiwan dollars. Old customers and white-collar workers came to drink together. Sitting in a row, they lit up the bar with their happy moods, as if setting fire to barrels of gasoline. It was absolutely wild.

FRIDAY, CIRCUS, TOP, The Vendor, VINO VINO, Southern Comfort, Butterfly Feeds the Cat, Summer Blossom, Tricks, SOMETIMES, The Rest Stop, Rooster, Sunflowers, Hide and Seek, 4T5D, Postmodern Graveyard.

A salon bar à la Tokyo's Shinjuku district, Alien Dust, with a cathedral ceiling, lights and shards of glass livening up the atmosphere.

IR, U2, Mom's Cooking, Sun-Air-Water, A Streetcar Named Desire, Too Lazy to Give Change, You're Welcome, Stuffed Kitty, Light Fragrance Study, Teddy Bear Forest, HOMELIKE.

My Place, Cafeteria, Food and Drink, Alley 86, Grandma's House, Chat, Flowers and Food. Ah Cai's shop, with anticommunist slogans, steel tags for liquor and tobacco from the government tobacco and wine monopoly, and pictures of shaking hands representing the cooperation between Taiwan and the United States. Dad's Lover, which had a pedicab, used radios, old newspapers, and a vanity. Postmodern Chinese style PUB, Changan Boulevard. ABSOLUTE.

Alien KTV Palace, with alien monsters crawling up the sides of the six-story building. Waiters in fatigues like the American GIs wore during the Gulf War, threading their way along, as they lead you to elevators that take you up to the Kara-OK area, the KTV area, the Taiwanese cuisine area, the beer hall, the BB billiard parlor, the DISCO area, all under one roof.

Taipei's Dignity, Relevant Offices, Half of Paradise, The Sicilian. Every Once in a While, 4 minutes 33 seconds, Cultural Goods, Chasing Games, French Factory, Unarmed, Thirty-three Rooms . . .

Sitting at my desk, I saw the features and construction of the city composed by the arrangement of words materializing in front of me like icebergs rising out of the water, where the clouds and ocean met. The city appearing under my pen existed only in words, and when the words disappeared, so would the city.

Before the city dies, I make written note of our love. The contract and alliance between Yongjie and me.

Southern winds rise, blowing white sand,
Gazing at the state of Lu, its craggy mountains,
A thousand-year-old skeleton has grown teeth.

chapter twelve

I witnessed the flow of traffic, which Yongjie had gazed at, all dug up several years later to build an underground railroad and a rapid transit system. The sky was blanketed by dust from the construction, through which the city's residents struggled, covering their eyes and noses, enduring this daily inconvenience for a better future.

Automobiles crisscrossed a maze of streets partitioned by roadblocks or sheet-metal walls. At night, swarms of warning lights flickered all along the way. Carless and unable to hail a taxi, I took the bus. Sitting next to the bus driver, I looked down as we drove into the maze, with its flashing red lights, a sort of magic trigram. I felt as if I were walking past a Taoist prayer ritual requiring seven times seven lamps.

The residents of Taipei and I, naïvely believing that most of the surface traffic would eventually go underground, willingly cooperated and lived with the mess. Until one day we woke up to the realization that the ugly cement python running over our heads and blocking out the sun was the rapid transit system. Deceived again. Angry and aggrieved, I muttered the mantra of a madman and a philosopher: Why?! Why?! Why?!

Under the sandblown sky, people abandoned by their leaders opened their psalm books and recited, "By the rivers of Babylon, there we sat down, yea, we wept, when we remembered Zion."

I gave up the debate; instead, I concerned myself only with closing the windows tight behind thick drapes. Yet every day there was a thick layer of dust, no matter how industriously I cleaned the house. My greatest consolation was to be alone with words in a clean house.

Saeba Ryo, a strange combination of words, was the Japanese name of the *manga* urban hunter Meng Bo. Words secretly informed me that, in contrast to the common practice of using one or two pieces for the backs of clothes, Coco Chanel insisted on using six or eight, a trait that experts used to judge the authenticity of Chanel couture. Chanel believed that people's body movements started from the back, so only a finely crafted back cut could show off the wearer's demeanor. As for the attraction of psychedelic stripes, the words told us that the inspiration came from rainbows, which straightened out at the equator. And there's more, there's more. In the summer of 1918, Chanel returned from a holiday with a trend-setting souvenir that shook the world of fashion: an antique bronze skin tone.

Ah, the only thing I could do was arrange my place the way I liked it, my little mosque. Lévi-Strauss said that in India it took very little to create a human community. Life there was on the scale of a handkerchief: a square drawn on the ground as the site of worship; thus a prayer mat represented an entire civilization. To survive, everyone must maintain strong, personal ties with the supernatural.

Yes, supernatural. The residents in the sandstorm had their own personal supernatural.

My supernatural was words, writing. Medicinal hollyhock, coltsfoot, bitter tea, chrysanthemum, sagebrush, horsetail, rockrose, western milfoil, beer hops, myrrh, valerian root, privet, and benzoin. There was also storax gall: gall insects lay their eggs on the leaves of the storax tree. After the larvae hatch, they live on the leaves, which become what is called storax gall, an ingredient of tannic acid. There were also the buds of the prickly mountain orange and the sprouts of the mole plant, which are used as a spice after soaking in vinegar, perfect for smoked salmon.

Engrossed in all this, I frequently cut myself off from the outside world. Then someone erected the Lingyun Trade Building, with its white enamel sheet metal imported from Japan's Kawasaki Steel Mills and silver-blue reflector glass, which was double the cost of granite or mirror plate glass. The line above the skyscraper, south of Hsin-yi Road and Tun-hua South Road, was the migrating path of arctic birds that now had to climb higher when they flew over Taipei. People looking down from the building could see nothing but a murky yellow sandstorm even the sun could not penetrate.

Pulling back the heavy drapes, I gazed out at the overpass spanning the flow of traffic, the one Yongjie and I had walked across.

I went to see a free show with some friends who had VIP passes. After the movie we went out for a snack; then my friends went their separate ways, leaving only me, and Yongjie, behind.

We'd seen each other a number of times, and were drawn to each other, but neither of us was willing to make the first move—until that night, when I couldn't take my eyes off him. And he responded likewise. I asked him back to the place I was renting, and he said, Sure. But then he stopped, leaning against the overpass railing to look down at the flow of traffic below.

I leaned against him, savoring the smell of pine, tobacco, and sandalwood on his body. I'd seen what he looked like in the daytime and I'd talked to him before. But now his whole being had approached and knocked at the door to my heart. I could feel the pulsing of a small, defenseless, naked piece of flesh locked behind that door, wanting to answer the knock outside. The flesh was so soft, so fragile that the slightest tug would tear it with stabbing pains. It was he who helped me discover the existence of this piece of flesh. All the slivers of gold I had received night after night didn't add up to my feelings that one night.

I treasured the flesh, maybe a little too much, afraid it might turn to bloody water and disappear once I opened the door. For a long time I had carried it around, hidden deep inside me. It transformed me into a sensitive being with eyes, ears, nose, tongue, and a body, which tensed up to absorb everything in my environment. There were no boundaries between me and all worldly matters and objects, which came gently to me. My ears were exceptionally keen, my eyes sharp. In the world I saw, autumn dew was like beads, the autumn moon round like a jade tablet; the moon was bright, the frost was white. Time passed.

Whenever I reined in the wild horse of consciousness and stared at the person in my memory, I felt a warm current pass down below, turning it limp one moment, tingly the next. Just the thought of him was enough to bring me to an orgiastic state.

As he grew larger day by day and filled up my heart, my intentions changed. I no longer wanted a one-night stand, I sought something longer, something more permanent. What I wanted was that we remain friends even if things didn't work out somehow. I wanted to complicate our relationship, to entangle him in my social circle. Yes, with us, two people in love, I wanted to add more weight to my side of the scale, so we could maintain a relationship, even if there was no sex.

I approached him as if skirting the edge of an abyss, as if walking on thin ice. Now I understood what Yongjie meant when he described my coolness: like the sound of Miles Davis's trumpet, walking on eggshells. I didn't move ahead rashly; as the Bible says, Stir not up, nor awake my love, till he please.

He never wore a watch. He had childish single-fold eyelids. The camera hanging around his neck had become part of his body, his viewing instrument. He watched the flow of traffic for a long time, as if pondering how to retract his promise and decline my invitation, despite his unwillingness to do so.

In patient silence I waited for his answer, surprised by my own high-mindedness.

He said it. He said, I don't want to have to endure the loneliness after we're separated tomorrow.

My heart nearly stopped. I clasped his hands, which were as cold and as hard as ginger. The tremors in my body passed to him. I found his eyes and we gazed at each other. Uncontrollably, I kissed the sparkle in his eyes with the burning lights of my own, and he received them. He too began to tremble, groaning painfully, as if running out of breath. I asked, Are you afraid?

He struggled to say, as if swallowing, or choked with water, No, I'm not.

That's how it was, we were in sync.

We had run into each other at a crossroads before we knew anything about each other's past vicissitudes. It seemed too much like a dream. Holding hands, our fingers clasped tightly, we walked on, as if to keep the dream alive. Not wanting to say a word, we stumbled along, feeling ourselves burning. Our eyes were trained on each other; it was always he who, unable to stand it any longer, would turn his face to the sky, close his eyes, and exhale, then cross his hands over his chest as if mortally wounded, like a dying actor. He had no training in dance, but his body was music personified. Afterward, every time I saw him coming toward me, he'd do the same thing, as if displaying his sincerity, as if holding his heart so it wouldn't break. Yes, when you're in love, you know exactly where your heart is, so heavy, always about to split apart. You have to hold on to it to keep it from falling out. Later on, I saw the same gesture by another person. It was Ah Yao. When the lymph nodes under his arms were all swollen and discolored, he'd unconsciously cover them with his hands as if steadying a heart, the strands of his soul.

We continued along, oblivious to how long we had been walking and how tired we were. We walked all the way home.

Our sensitivity was so high, our boiling point so low, that we came just by kissing and fondling each other. I was secretly surprised. For the longest time, I took my cue from prostitutes, for whom kissing is taboo; anything but kiss, which is an invasion, since it means selling your body *and* your soul. For me, kissing was like chewing wax, insipid and nauseating, epitomizing the barrenness of sex.

But now the wheel had turned, and the pleasure was beyond description. We had returned to the innocent state of a boy's first love, soft, tender, brimming over, and juicy. The slightest touch made us ejaculate, we couldn't help ourselves. We were embarrassed and ecstatic. We needed no gimmicks or special techniques, and had no use for those elaborate touching rituals that exhaust you without leading to orgasm. We just held each other like a pair of hard nuts, sniffing and touching each other, fermenting and giving off ethereal odors that enshrouded us in their steamy heat until we were giddy. Or we'd lie facing each other, not saying a word, just smiling like lovestruck kids.

Ah, Looking at the Western Moon, a void appears/Listening to the South Sea Tide, silence exists. As I slept, Yongjie got up to look at me and draw my portrait in slumber, inscribing on it the past, the ephemeral, or that which was yet to come. . . .

Sail for Byzantium, sail to the erotic utopia.

Sail for the waterway, into an abyss with the sediment of time. Worms, insects, fish, and birds. In 48,000 years, a nation was created out of nothing.

Confucius, standing by a river, lamented, All things pass away, just like this.

I recall one time, when Yongjie had to be away for a while. He needed to check on a cover design at a print shop, but kept putting it off until it was nearly dusk. On the pretext of taking out the trash, I accompanied him downstairs. Residents on both sides of the street had set up braziers in front of their doors; the fires released sparks and charred, curling paper into the air. He walked into the smoke. Suddenly grief-stricken, I called out his name.

He turned around and began prancing backward, like one of those little cartoon space-age kids.

I shouted, Let me go with you.

Touching his finger to his lips, a kiss, he kept walking backward, a dancer taking a curtain call, until he disappeared around the corner.

The scent of transmigration—SAMSARA—begins with lemon and continues with jasmine, violet, iris, daffodil, ylang-ylang, and roses, then ends with vanilla, tonka beans, and sandalwood incense. I rushed upstairs, grabbed my wallet, some coins, and a bus pass, and ran after him. When I reached the corner I saw him at the bus stop, but instead of calling out, I just watched him board the bus. He would change buses at the next stop, a major intersection. I knew the print shop he was going to.

I waited till a bus came, got on, and rode it to the next stop, to transfer. As I was walking to the next stop, the bus he had transferred to came toward me. I hid behind a kapok tree and stood motionless, spotting him by a window, looking like a lily floating past a riverbank. Then I continued on my way to the bus stop, telling myself that if a bus didn't come by the time I counted to fifty, I wouldn't go to the print shop.

The bus didn't come, so I turned and walked slowly home on the brick-paved street. The evening sky darkened in the wind and the night brightened up with lights.

At the time, I was used to taking taxis, but Yongjie, who couldn't afford the fares, only took a taxi when he was in a hurry. And he was too proud to use my money. I was already plenty antisocial, but he was worse. He wouldn't even wear a watch.

When I went out with Beibei I took him along, and after a while, any time she asked me out, he was included in the invitation. Sometimes she and I would tell him about our childhood. She'd talk about my sister, I'd talk about my sister and me. But eventually the subject would come around to Ah Yao. Yongjie and Beibei loved to gossip, and sometimes even had minor disputes. I, on the other hand, Beibei's biggest fan, always sided with her. If she went to the bathroom or took a phone call, Yongjie and I would let our emotions run wild, flirting with our eyes until we were so turned on we could barely hide what we were up to when Beibei came back.

I asked Beibei to bring her boyfriend along, but she said, Old Zhang's a practical guy, not like us.

Yongjie said, Don't worry; we'll bring him around.

Beibei said, Don't, please don't. After all, he's my boyfriend.

They giggled, but I was embarrassed. I didn't think it was funny, and that only made them laugh harder, to my chagrin. I wondered if we were fated to provide entertainment for Beibei, to be her Dongting Lake or Boyang Lake, raising and lowering the level of the Yangtze River.

Our antisocial behavior was an elastic band, a security valve for a socially adept person like her. She came to us so she could let her hair down, then return to her world when she was reenergized. Playing the role of shaman or sorcerer, we paid a hefty price for revealing heavenly secrets: being mute, deaf, dumb, insane, widowed, alone. I'd already accepted my fate without complaint, and was willing to make people happy. But when Beibei wouldn't introduce her boyfriend to us, I felt used: when the hares have all been bagged, the hounds are killed and cooked. That made me very sad and very lonely.

She could be such a boor sometimes! We all opposed a certain Mr. Li's plan to build a Taipei landmark in competition with the Empire State Building, but she insisted on raising the stakes by calling it phallocentric, annoying me considerably. Of course I forgave her for being a lay person, but she didn't have to follow those stuffy academics who are always talking about this or that phallic symbol.

She said men have an uncontrollable urge to inscribe, on stone or on bronze; that a tiger leaves behind its skin, but a man leaves behind only his name. Men may be ambitious and eloquent, but they have a weak spot, and this is it.

She accompanied her aging father to visit relatives on the Chinese mainland. For twenty miles they traveled along the Hongze Lake while he taught her how to distinguish a poplar from a willow, two quite different species, both of which were sprouting and showing some green at the time. They rode in a tiny imported Toyota van with right-hand steering, and every time a car passed coming the other way, she was terrified that they would die in a hideous crash. Gazing out the window, she spotted some fishing boats anchored in a cove and a stone tablet with an inscription that read, We are determined to repair the River Huai, Mao Zedong. Both her father and the driver said it was erected in the fifties, when Mao was still clear-headed; the calligraphy wasn't bad either. But she said it was a far cry from the legacy of Empress Wu of the Tang Dynasty, who left no stone tablet, letting later generations judge her solely by her accomplishments and her failures.

I recall that the three of us once took Beibei's Honda Civic to Aoti for some of its famous sea bream. When the meal was over, we walked around the harbor and gazed out at Turtle Island. It seemed like ages, a whole lifetime, since Ah Yao and I had gazed at the island, and now it was gazing at us; but everything had changed. Yongjie was leaning against an abandoned skiff, and when I turned around, I noticed his dark, pensive eyes, looking at me as if he had been with me at some particular moment in time and was reading my past. And I felt Beibei, for the very first time, sizing up Yongjie and me from a distance. It was only a split second, but I saw the look of aloofness in her eyes. Three of us at the seashore, all facing a mid-life crisis. I recalled a poem by Goethe: We young people, sitting in the cool afternoon breeze ...

I also took Yongjie over to my sister's place.

She could never forget how warmly Ah Yao had treated her, and that led to a strange animosity toward Yongjie and his place in my life.

Most of the time she was, if anything, overly friendly with guests, preparing things for them to eat and drink to cover up her shyness and nervousness. She'd always been like that. Once people stopped taking notice of her existence, she'd calm down and carefully observe movements in the house with her bright, squirrel-like eyes. When something was needed she quickly supplied it, so there'd never be a shortage of anything. If she had nothing else to busy herself with, she'd hide in a corner, smiling enigmatically like the Mona Lisa. Even then she'd only show her guests her profile, as if trying to make herself completely invisible.

Yongjie tried hard to win her over, praising her patchwork cushions and asking if she'd made them herself.

That caught her off guard, like a hermit on a deserted mountain hearing someone calling her name. Blushing immediately, she decided not to respond, looking my way and tossing the job of socializing to me. I'd already told Yongjie that my sister did fine needlework, but I repeated it now. She was angry that Yongjie had brought her out of her comfortable, inconspicuous corner and thrust her into the center of attention. She departed the site of conversation and remained in the back of the house for a long time. When she came out to warm our tea, her face was still red; even the whites of her eyes were red, unforgiving of Yongjie's rude trespass.

The instant you stepped out of her little mosque, it was difficult to tell where the residential district ended and the red light district began. She had worked hard to grow vines on the patio so as to block out the dirty, evil world beyond. The outer layer of her handmade cotton drapes was printed with daisies; the inner layer was made of an opaque lacy fabric that let in muted sunlight. The house was full of DIY [do-it-yourself] stuff, all skillfully arranged to capture the aura of a British countryside mediated through Japan. She kept everything she'd ever collected as a girl. The annual Christmas cards from Ah Yao alone formed a good-sized bundle; then there were the souvenirs he had bought on his trips around the world, which he'd bagged up and asked me to give to her. She'd framed all the pressed-flower bookmarks Ah Yao had given her and hung them on the wall above the shoe rack. Three here, five there, all arranged nicely. On one of the cards Ah Yao had quoted Pushkin: Don't say the roses have wilted. Show us instead the blooming lilies.

Once I lifted four pieces of taffy from Ah Yao's place for her. It was the wrapping that appealed to me: plastic paper, each a different color—golden yellow, burgundy, opal blue, and peacock green. Inside the plastic wrappers was tinfoil that you opened to reveal a piece of pink or creamy white candy. Of course, she didn't eat them immediately; she just looked at them until they turned sticky. Then, after finishing them off, she washed and dried the plastic wrappers and wedged them inside her textbooks. For a while they were the most magnificent colors in our house, the colors of the dazzling treasure we imagined Ali Baba would see after calling out, Open Sesame.

She accompanied me to Ah Yao's place, where she stayed in my shadow, hoping no one would discover her. She went to look at Mama's room. The vanity on the tatami floor, a white camellia in a china vase, and a swivel ottoman were all things she'd never seen before. Mama, who was putting on make-up in front of the mirror, called her over. Surprisingly, instead of shying away, she walked over. Mama put some lipstick on her and let her look in the mirror, smiling and saying how darling she looked, how very cute. That day, my sister refused to eat a thing, so she could return home with the lipstick intact. There she watched ruefully as the color slowly disappeared.

Mama used make-up all her life. Her cosmetics, from the time I was a boy all the way up to the day Ah Yao died, never varied. It was as if she could transfer all human emotions into her make-up and turn them into a symbolic Noh mask. I had no way of knowing if any real emotions lay beneath it.

When Ah Yao left the country and stayed away, Mama's only connection with our house was broken. We'd never seen Ah Yao's father except in photographs. The only traces of him were a violin, a box of Columbia classical records, half a plaster cast of Venus, and a book of charcoal sketches of Mama in a school uniform with a middy collar. The sketches were full profile, face front, three-quarter profile, and head lowered, which showed the part in her hair. Before World War II he'd been a literature student in Kyoto, and when the War in the Pacific broke out he was detained in Japan. After the war, he returned with a Japanese wife and a disease that had been romanticized by writers ever since the eighteenth century—tuberculosis.

Mama later returned to her homeland.

Ah Yao wrote to tell me that Mama was returning to Tokyo for her inheritance. He said if I was free, I might want to give Infinite Mother a call to SAY GOOD-BYE.

During those days of self-entombment, the letter disappeared from my memory. I had no recollection of when my sister graduated, found a job, had a boyfriend, or grew up. I didn't even recall my father, who had been stationed on the offshore islands nearly all his life, then was hospitalized soon after he retired. When I went to see him in the hospital, he was in the final stages of stomach cancer, with tubes sticking out of nearly every orifice of his body. When he occasionally came home, his shadow was enlarged by light bulbs at night, but he had shrunk to the size of a bundle of firewood. I was given five days' leave to attend the funeral, but I spent most of my time in Taipei taking long walks. I went to Jay's place, where I stood silently for a long long time. My father's death had not affected me as deeply as my lost love. Vaguely recalling that Mama was leaving the country, I tried to put the thought out of my mind, like a debtor fleeing his creditor. But my own Jiminy Cricket, down deep in my gut, said, Pick up the phone and call Mama. Maybe she hasn't left yet.

That annoying little bug gave me no peace until one day, during those dreary afternoons when I called every number in my address book, I dialed Ah Yao's number. His family had two numbers, one for the clinic, which I'd never used before. I asked to talk to Auntie Huang, saying I was a classmate of Huang Shuyao [Ah Yao]. Not getting through, I repeated myself in broken Taiwanese. It turned out that Mama had already returned to Japan.

Ah, Mama's tatami room, with its subtle fragrance and white camellias. Many years later, when I was at her place in Tokyo, I heard a folk ballad about a crane-wife. A crane that transforms itself into a woman marries a man out of gratitude and presents him with a suit of clothes woven from feathers as a token of love. His neighbors are astonished by the splendid fabric and urge him to demand more clothes from her. She agrees, reluctantly, but forbids anyone to look while she weaves. She produces several suits, but grows thinner and thinner in the process. One day, the man peeks at her and sees that she is a white crane, plucking her feathers to weave into the fabric. The crane discovers the man before he has time to hide; her feathers nearly gone and her feelings for him dead, she soars into the sky with a shrill call and disappears without a trace.

My sister yelled out that Ah Yao's mother had left at the beginning of last month. She'd read Ah Yao's letter, and had called Mama to say good-bye.

Sitting in the dark, I looked at her in total shock.

Having overheard my phone call to Ah Yao's place, she'd come out to clue me in, then turned and headed right back to her room. She'd seen through me, knew everything about me, my true identity, the things I did. Everything. She knew everything.

I was ashamed to suddenly discover that she now had waist-length hair. For such a long time, I'd forgotten I even had a kid sister. Did she resent me for that? We had once relied on each other for support, so why had I abandoned her when I was going through such a tough time?

As kids, we'd often had to eat at Auntie Chen's house across the way, since no one was home to cook for us. Our mother was forever being called to school or the police station because of our older brother, and our older sister was assigned to an entertainment troupe after graduating from the Military and Political Academy. Their adult world was so complicated, so chaotic, that my kid sister and I, the two kids born after our parents came to Taiwan, lived an independent life.

In the corner of Auntie Chen's living room, with its cold, slippery terrazzo floor, we watched movies from south China with superstars of the Run Run Shaw Studio. Auntie Chen's daughters, Baohua, Baoli, and Baoqian, and my sister and I each had our own favorite star, and we argued about them all the time. We even marked up the pictures of their favorite stars by crossing their eyes and adding moustaches, until the Chen sisters refused to let us back into their house. But we knew that the next time their older brother brought new pictures home, they'd drag us in excitedly to see them. When one of them wrapped herself up in a bedsheet and towel, pretending to be superstar Lin Dai playing a femme fatale in ancient China, like Da Ji or Diao Chan, they needed me to plant myself in a chair and play the king, so they could dance and sing. Opening her sheet, which took the place of a bathrobe, like a bird spreading its wings, Baoli said, Master, look at me. She actually pronounced it Mister. I had to say, Good, very good. Then she fell down and passed out at my feet, and I had to look up and laugh. My sister and Baoqian ran out, helped her up, and took her into the bedroom.

Baoli also pretended she was another superstar, Li Jing, playing a mermaid. She rolled on the tiled floor until the carp turned into a human. My sister played the Goddess of Mercy, who sprinkled water from a cup over the carp with an oleander leaf. But after a while my sister tired of playing the role, so I took over. Holding a duster made of stripped silvergrass tassel, I recited incantations at Baoli, who flapped her legs like the tail of a fish, rolling back and forth from one side of the room to the other. She cried out in pain, asking me to help with my magic powers. I brushed her with my duster as she drew me into the part with an earnest look on her face. She kept rolling around, sweat beading her twisted face, which made me nervous yet cruelly violent at the same time. I beat her savagely with the duster until I felt something getting hard between my legs. Panicky, I dropped the duster, stood there stunned for a moment, then ran off.

I left Auntie Chen's house with a burning face, wondering where my sister and the others, who had been inside just a moment earlier, had gone all of a sudden.

It was bright daylight outside, but there was no trace of them, nothing but chalk drawings on the cement ground for hop-scotch and treasure-hunt, and drawings with red bricks for games of attack-and-defend on the shiny, crisscrossed ground.

My sister was already home when I got there.

She was making paper-doll clothes. After tracing the outlines, she pressed the paper against the screen door and lightly ran a crayon over the paper to trace the patterns of the screen, a new fabric design for her. She experimented with a variety of imprints: straw mats, nylon sofa covers, rattan chairs, bamboo steamers, uneven wall surfaces, baskets, plant leaves, even a fly swatter. Pretty soon she had collected a whole bookful of color-ful imprints. I'd even seen her squat outside the Chens' house by a new bicycle to rub the pattern of its tire.

Without actually intending to, we closed the book on that period of games we'd been playing. One day after school I took a shortcut home through a narrow alley, where I ran into Baoli, coming straight at me. Too late for me to get away. Wild lights leaped out at me from her eyes, which made me hot and nearly suffocated me. I shrank into a human shell and clung to the wall to let her pass. The strong odors of her body and her blood swept by like a flood, washing away the foundation under my feet. After she had passed by, I felt as if I'd fallen into deep water and was drowning, until I floated to the surface and caught my breath.

Just like that, with neither rhyme nor reason, a barrier was thrown up between the Chen sisters and me. When we met on the street, we pretended we didn't know each other and never exchanged a word. Boys on one side, girls on the other. I had no one to play with on holidays anymore.

But I never joined in with the big boys, not the group who

hung out at the entrance to the housing project to smoke, nor the group that played basketball. In eighth grade, Ah Yao and I were put in the same class. He asked me to go to movies with him, and because of him, I started watching Western films. We saw every one we could and collected pictures and posters; Ah Yao bought every issue of *Eigo no tomo* and SCREEN. When Alain Delon's first movie, *Purple Noon*, came out, we watched it five times just to see him. In the movie, there's a song by Paul Anka— DIANA—and years later, when I sang it to Ah Yao on his sickbed, he was moved to tears.

My kid sister watched *Waterloo Bridge* with us and fell in love with Vivian Leigh. She collected black-and-white glossies of Leigh, which were displayed at a newspaper stand under a West Gate overhang. Anytime I saw one she didn't have, I bought it for her. Ah Yao took her to Mei'erlian for her first Western meal. She had steaming rice like beads of jade on white china plates, over which she poured bright yellow curry chicken, like gold nuggets, from a silver gravy bowl in the shape of Aladdin's lamp. She was tentative and polite, enjoying this meal from the Arabian Nights in a very affected manner. After that night she often tried to eat off a plate at home, laying out army crackers, crystallized ginger, and powdered orange juice.

Her mannered attitude also showed up when she was at Ah Yao's house that time, as if she wanted everyone to know that she was not intimidated by the formal atmosphere of a big family. Bravely she let Mama put lipstick on her—you should know that our mother never used lipstick, as far as we knew, and there was certainly no vanity at our house. As for our big sister, I recall her dressing up, then standing on her tiptoes and moving around in the narrow space between the closet and the dresser, trying to see her full figure in the closet-door mirror. She rushed out the door with her head held high, leaving her clothes, her belt, and her slippers scattered all over the place, a pile here and a pile there. She'd forgotten to flush the toilet, in which the water was bright red; I fled in terror when I saw that.

My sister only went to Ah Yao's house that one time. We entered through the rear. Actually, I never used the front entrance, which was reserved for patients and special visitors. It was a three-story building whose entryway had a brick front, terrazzo floor, and cast-iron banisters; with its clean, horizontal lines, it echoed the minimalist style of modernist architecture. The back entrance was typical Western style: red bricks from Ch'ingshui, a balustrade lined with green glazed vases, and arched windows with floral lace curtains pulled to the sides. The building was close to the street, but long, and divided into three sections, with a front thoroughfare, a back alley, and two courtyards for sunlight.

We crossed the courtyard by the kitchen, which had a stove and a furnace, and entered the dining room in the middle section to wait for Ah Yao. There we stared at the deities and scarlet longevity lamps on the altar, something we'd never seen in the project. On the dining table were a new shipment of medicine and some calendars from pharmaceutical companies; the air was pungent with the smells. Ah Yao came rushing down and led us to the second floor. It was their living room, bright and spacious, with scrolls painted with pines and cranes hanging on the walls. Ah Yao, his mother, and his cousins all lived on the third floor. Looking down through the window of Mama's tatami room, we could see a small yard by the back door planted with Chinese magnolia, camellias, Japanese camellias, cherry trees, and perilla mints. Ah Yao had slept in his mother's room until the summer before high school. Then all the kids in the house changed rooms, and he began sharing a room with a younger boy, his cousin. But he was so used to his mother's room he'd spend whole afternoons there sitting on the tatami and playing his guitar. When I came to see him, Mama would say he was upstairs, and I'd just follow the sound of the guitar.

Once he insisted on dressing me up in his favorite clothes—a white turtleneck sweater and a leather jacket—then pushed me up to the mirror so we could both enjoy the sight.

Sprawled out on the tatami, he asked why our classmate Qin never wore a tank top in P.E. I didn't know, but I thought he cared a bit too much about Qin. He said it was because Qin was growing hair under his arms.

He lay his head on his folded arms on the low table. I thought he'd fallen asleep, but he was weeping.

Since I was riding over to Ah Yao's place, I asked my kid sister if she wanted to come along. She seemed taken by the arched windows and their lace curtains. The houses in the project all had open doors and windows, and we could determine what anyone was having for dinner just by sticking our heads in through the window. I invited her along.

I can't, she said. I have homework to do.

Yes, she'd never go back there again.

But years later, she called Mama to say good-bye. Knowing how lazy I was, she carried out Ah Yao's request for me. She didn't want Mama to think we were uncivilized. How thoughtful, proud, and proper she was!

And how hard to please. Yongjie said, Your sister doesn't like me.

I said, Not to worry, that's just how she is.

Yongjie and I carefully built our spiderweb nest, spinning threads into each other's past to wrap together all the memory fragments floating in the flood of time, tie them into knots, then braid them into threads and weave the threads into a net. For sure, ancestors and the living were equally important, and the souls of both the dead and the living had places of their own.

We didn't publicize it, we just secretly attached our nest to the periphery of the social forest, carefully walking the fine line between coming out and staying in the closet. We willingly humbled ourselves, modestly saying our prayers, like the line in the popular song, "I don't want much. I really don't." We hoped that with our submissiveness, our insignificance, our harmlessness, even our clowning around to please others, we would be able to toady up to fate, which would reward us with a long life together. We didn't care whether people knew or not, or whether we could tell them; we just wanted to live in this world of norms and mores.

And so Ah Yao's radicalism, his anger, and his grudges scared the living hell out of us. In my view, he was Xing Tian of Chinese mythology, who fought the Yellow Emperor. After his head was lopped off, Xing Tian continued to fight with his battle-ax, using his nipples as his eyes and his navel as his mouth. We covered our eyes, not daring to look at him, then turned and walked away coldheartedly, not caring to know what came of the battle.

Falling in love turned us timid, and we would become progressively more so. A worthless life had become two, and now that we were responsible for the birth, old age, sickness, and death of another person, we tasted the loss of freedom. That loss was so severe that I'd even give a wide berth to the pythonlike elevated rapid transit line to avoid the possibility of cement blocks falling down and crushing me. In order to enjoy a long life with the one we loved, we became indescribably neurotic, doing everything possible to stay alive, to avoid danger and flee from disaster.

And so I felt that life and death shared the same face, right in front, looking down at me.

It was often there, when I crossed a street, or when I was in an elevator, or right now, while writing. The face wasn't all that scary; it even had the hint of a smile, like a Noh mask hanging on a wall looking down on me—or that's how it felt. If it had grown more vivid, it would have been the picture of an Indian goddess, a sword and a human head in two of her outspread arms, while the other two promised blessings and protection. I was right in front of her, coexisting with her. Therefore, death is not the Angel of Death, who wore a black cape and a black robe and played chess with a knight in Bergman's *The Seventh Seal*. It was, instead, life, who looked down on me.

The ancient Greeks said, You can never place your feet in the same river twice.

Yes, the kalpa gone, the kalpa now, the kalpa to come.

The past, the present, the future.

chapter thirteen

Mountains and rivers like paintings. In ancient times, they say, the sea was green.

Seaweed floated up from the visible bottom of the sea, one patch after another, swaying savagely beneath my chest, like countless souls of the dead or the living reaching out welcoming hands to pull me down. Yongjie was swimming beside me, dragging me along by my life vest. Through my diving mask, I saw his legs, sometimes flapping like a fish, sometimes hanging straight as he treaded water. As long as he was there, I wasn't afraid. He led me out to deeper water, very close to the warning rope, so I could

see all kinds of different fish. I bit down tightly on the mouthpiece, the snorkeling tube rising above the surface. The bottom of
the ocean was getting farther and farther away, almost impossible
to see now, and the seaweed was swaying even more violently. My
life was in Yongjie's hands. I could hear his voice above me, saying,
Don't be scared. The shore isn't far. I saw a school of flat yellow
fish that looked like the pickled radishes in lunch boxes sold on
the train when we were kids. Then a school of shiny blue fish
flashed by like lightning. I saw Yongjie's strong, vigorous torso and
legs in the water, and couldn't believe they belonged to me. He
led me along like we were a pair of mating fish. Suddenly we
entered a bright area where a school of small fish scattered like
pieces of silver, then fused back together. Yongjie let go and dove
under the water to smile up at me through his goggles. That made
me nervous until my head suddenly broke the surface and I realized we'd made it back to shore.

I thought back to Susano'o no mikoto, who rebelled against
his sister to build his own country, Zumo no kuni. He was Japan's
first balladeer, with a song that went, "There are multicolored
clouds in the sky/The clouds shine down on my city/They
shine down on my wife/We live here together."

The most glorious days of my life: on the shore, my sister and
her family resting and eating snacks, Yongjie and I frolicking in
the water. We were doing everything possible to enjoy our ideal
kingdom, a painting of eternity.

Ocean Park, where we'd already taken her kids twice, but it was
so inviting, the whole family decided to come along. My sister
didn't want to go into the water, probably having her period. Out
of consideration for her, Yongjie replaced his tight, sexy bikini with
a pair of conservative boxers. He'd thought of everything: snorkels,
diving masks, goggles, life vests, and life preservers, for both the
adults and the kids, plus sunblock. With incredible patience, he
showed the kids some fish in the shallow surf and taught them
how to hold their breath under water. My brother-in-law swam
back and forth between shallow and deep water, while I kept my
sister company. She brought me up to date regarding our older
brother and sister—our mother was living with our brother at the
time. Looking out at the slanting shadows under the setting sun, I
sighed. It was the same sun that always set in the west....

It was always during my happiest moments that I felt the inconstancy of life.

We traveled through the city where skyscrapers created hurri- canes in the interstices, like deep gorges, while the sky was sliced into angular strips like circus tents, cleaving the air as hurricane winds blurred our vision. Thank God, we were both alive, not sick, not disabled, not HIV-positive. We had to make good use of the rest of our lives, not making love so often and spreading our love around to others—was this yearning the aspiration of the last saints?

We needed order, because we were violators of rules.

Fellini said, I need strict discipline in order to transgress norms. I have encountered taboos—rules of morality, religious rituals—every step of the way, but am protected on both sides by the hymns.

We arrived in Rimini, a place that disappeared in winter. In the movie *Amarcord*, when the fog shrouds everything in the Rimini winter, the piazza disappears, the city hall disappears, so does the Malatesta Temple. In the summer the shadow of the Emmanuele Theatre cuts the piazza in half, but in the winter the theatre is completely swallowed up by the fog. On his way to school, Fellini suddenly saw the head of a cow materialize in front of him. The surprised cow stared at him with its big eyes. They confronted each other, then circled around to move off; in the fog the cow lowed deeply, loudly.

We traveled among the super-skyscrapers in the West Station District of Shinjuku, which formed a mass, a unit, a city, like the latticework in the Dunhuang Caves, giving us the vague feeling that we were passing through the Valley of the Kings on the west bank of the Nile, looking out at cave tombs that covered the mid-slope of distant mountains. At lunchtime, crowds of people poured out of every opening, walking in groups on ground formed from connecting overpasses. Every man wore a suit and tie, every woman a two-piece dress. We felt as if we'd stumbled into a futuristic space station; or could it be Orwell's *1984*?

Our train carried us along a narrow strip of land surrounded by a vast body of water dotted far and near with buoys and pilings. We couldn't see the shore in front or behind. If the tide rose just a bit, the tracks would probably be submerged. That was how we entered Venice. When we turned to look, we saw the campanile that rises 99 meters into the sky, its tip seemingly carried along by swift-moving clouds, until it appears about to tip over. We thought we were in Delft, a 700-year-old town where the clouds also skitter past, threatening the tip of a new church in the center of the marketplace. It was getting dark, and the evening sky was turning blue. Delft was the setting for Werner Herzog's *Nosferatu*. Dracula squeezed out through a door, his bald head glowing in the bright daylight, a dead ringer for that last photograph of Foucault I saw in the newspaper.

Delft's nights are the blue found in fairy tales. The only comparable sky is the one soared through by the incredibly popular *Starlight Twins* feature from the SANRIO studio in 1976.

I brought gifts back from Japan for the kids: HELLO KITTY items, big-eyed frogs, Mommy Rabbits, WINKI PINKI. My kid sister bought SANRIO toys for the kids, because they were *her* favorite. I got lost in all these cute toys, searching for the vanishing Starlight Twins and the blue night sky behind them. I once wondered if they were the Martians of ancient records, born into the human world in the guise of little boys in scarlet to spread a prophetic song. "The moon is rising/The sun is setting/The arrow and the quiver nearly destroyed the Zhou." All the little kids on the street began singing the song.

We left Saint Mark's Square and took the ferry to the Lido to visit DES BAIN, the main setting for *Death in Venice*. On a hotel stairway, Visconti met the lovely young boy, Tadzio, for the first time. During the fifteen-minute ferry ride, Venice began to fade into the light sunset, floating above smooth, peaceful blue waters. This city without a foundation is full of artifacts. A white-haired old man was absorbed at his worktable, blowing glass beetles, spiders, ants, and miniature deer. The place was filled with perfume bottles and vases like soap bubbles. Standing amid an array of eerily beautiful masks hanging from the ceiling, a young girl was painting a mask with silvery powder under a halogen lamp. We walked down a vine-covered cobblestone lane, hugging the wall and stepping softly so we could hear the people talking on the other side. We emerged from the walled lane into a street steaming with all kinds of food: pizza, sausage, fresh seafood. The shop signs hung like fruit on a tree. An arched bridge rose steeply, until the crescent moon was so close you could almost touch it. The city floated on water. On the sunny side the water rippled like gold coins; on the side away from the sun it was smooth as glass. Terraced buildings on the city's shady side were emerald green, crystal purple, deep-forest green, swan-velvet black, and scarlet red, but on the sunny side they were all maple gold. The city was sinking millimeter by millimeter every year, eroded by mosses and by water.

The sinking metropolis, the Seven Treasures sparkle.

The indulgence in beauty of the *Rubaiyat*.

The pessimistic epicureanism of an oasis civilization.

Yongjie's team was setting off on the Silk Road, starting at Ürümchi and proceeding to Turpan, into the Yanqi Huizu Autonomous Region, then to Korla, Kuqa, Aksu, Kashi, Varkant, and Sanchakou. He'd taken the Silk Road twice before. The last trip took him through Xi'an, Lanzhou, and Dunhuang. He returned after a busy schedule that had kept him away for several days. As we lay in bed, I pretended I didn't know he wanted to make love, and turned over to go to sleep. The next day he packed his sleeping bag, canteen, down clothing, sand goggles, a turban, a powerful flashlight and long-life batteries, moisturizer, and an array of medicines. Every time he went on one of his trips, I considered him to be dead and waited quietly to be so informed. That's why I didn't want to make love—I needed to owe him something, and if our contract had not yet expired, fate would send him back to fulfill his obligation. If the contract *had* expired, we'd just have to owe each other—there'd be no next life, only another death to carry with me until I died.

He came back. He was darker; he'd lost weight; he looked tired, and five years older; but his eyes brightened, because we were together again. He told me about the sandy purple of Fire Mountain, and the cliff nearby where the Tang monk Tripitaka had tied his horse to a stone pillar. The waves of sand on Sounding Sand Mountain rose dozens of feet in the air, and the wind blowing over the desert produced a drumbeat.

Starting with the first oasis in the east, Hami, you travel westward; every time you see sand dunes, every time you see a patch of green at the edge of the sky, once you cross the Gobi desert, you enter a land of fragrant flowers and singing birds. Leaving

Xinjiang like this, you pass through Central Asia, Asia Minor, Egypt, and North Africa until you reach Casablanca, having walked through hundreds of sections of desert without seeing another soul, and hundreds of oasis cities. Desolation mixed with bustle, silence mixed with noises; the last saint has completed his pilgrimage of Islam. He contemplated the traces of his ancestors. The desert was vast and constantly changing; only the starry sky and his well-paced journey produced a monotheism in the desert. The oasis created 1,001 Arabian nights with the mysterious fragrance of roses.

Monotheism destroyed all the idols, and vigorously introduced the practice of asceticism. Hence, human senses had to be content with transforming themselves into fragrance, gardening, embroidery, mosaics, and laces. It was a mirage in the hot air, a city in a sinking land.

We came to the ancient city of Kamakura when the cherry blossoms were in bloom. People everywhere were offering sacrifices to the flowers; all over the city lanterns swayed and people sang. Where there are people, there are flies, and Buddha. Beneath the blossoming cherry trees, no one was a stranger.

This was where the Ofuna Film Studio was located and where Ozu Yasujiro shot many of his films. We recognized the shots that appeared so often in his movies: the five-level tower and its wind chimes, the hills, the streetcar stops, also the God of War Shrine and the Great Buddha, which were filmed during the wheat harvest. And Ryu Chishu and Hara Setsuko, whose relationships were constantly rearranged in different films: father and daughter, brother and sister, uncle and cousin, father-in-law and daughter-in-law—Ozu's ideal people. The ideal man and the ideal woman.

According to the theory of authorship, every director makes only one film in his life. In that case, Ozu's films are all about marrying off a daughter. An entity is separated from one group and joins another, to establish and continue the world. As the Bible says, A man shall leave his father and his mother. Ozu never filmed the marriage of a son, which proves that the marriage of a daughter was a reduction, a severance, and a loss, which caused so much turmoil and bitter disappointment that Ozu spent his whole life in exploration; even when he died at the age of sixty, there was still more he wanted to say. His first sound picture, *Only Son,* opens with an epigram stating that the first act in the tragedy of human life originates in the relationship between parents and children.

Ozu never married. I wondered if he was a closet case or a transcendent comrade. He lived with his mother near the Jochi Temple in northern Kamakura, where we went to pay homage with deep emotion. We passed through the tunnel that normally took Ozu forty steps to negotiate. The small path beside a rocky wall was planted with persimmon trees. The bamboo grove underneath housed the residence of the painter, Ogura Yuki, into which he often collapsed when he came home drunk. So we also bought a volume of Ogura's paintings. At the foot of the stairs leading to the second floor of Ogura's house she had hung a line of poetry in Sanskrit, personally calligraphed with a writing brush by Tagore when he came to Japan. Ozu's mother wore the same kind of eyeglasses as the painter, Ogura, looking like all the mothers in the world. Ozu often joked that he would not get married as long as the old woman was alive. When reporters asked him why he remained single, he replied that he had missed the time for marriage, because he was drafted into the military just as he was considering starting a family. That was true. He was sent to China right after the Marco Polo Bridge Incident. Two years later he returned to Japan, but was immediately sent to the South Pacific, where he remained until the end of World War II. He said that the issue of marriage became too complicated after his discharge, and he was happy to be with his mother.

When he was directing his maiden film, *Sword of Penance*, he met the scriptwriter Noda Kōgo, with whom he worked for thirty-six years, through his last, posthumously released film, *An Autumn Afternoon*. Both famous drinkers, they toasted each other the first thing every morning. Many of their scripts were finalized during long hours of drinking, as they spoke the dialogue out loud, until they were both drunk. The most common phrase in his films was, Sō desu ka? Is that so? The old couple in *Tokyo Story* invariably used this phrase in their conversation, not as a question but to show agreement; that created the pace, atmosphere, and state of indecisiveness akin to that of the Noh.

Ozu employed Shigehara Hideo as his cinematographer for the first decade of his career, and Atsuta Yushun for the last decade. People teased him, saying that the cinematographer was his wife. When talkies became popular, he persisted in making five more silent films, like Charlie Chaplin on the other side of the Pacific. He did it because Shigehara was doing his own research on sound projectors, and Ozu promised to wait until Shigehara produced a machine, no matter how long it took. So he quietly stuck to his silent films while being bombarded by questions about why he didn't make talkies.

His locations were always extraordinarily quiet, for he was a peaceful man. Only once did he scold an actor who was hamming it up: A popular song goes, You smile with your face, but crying comes from your heart. You run and jump when you're happy, and weep and wail when you're sad. That's what the monkeys in Ueno Zoo do. Saying the opposite of what you're thinking and expressing emotions the opposite of what you're feeling is what makes us human!

He had broad shoulders, a straight nose, and a handsome moustache. He had the eyes of an elephant when he wasn't smiling, and even more so when he was. Throughout his life, he looked at the family from a distance; since family was precisely what he lacked, he invested it with limitless fondness and rationality. When the body of a family was on the verge of separation and disintegration because one of its cells was confused and unable to see its own role clearly, he was able, given the advantage of his position, to see the whole picture. He became a man of vision, a thinker who created his own allegories.

He preferred to use medium-range or close-up shots of the upper body of a character facing the camera and smiling or talking, distinguishing qualities of polite femininity, just as the language of Japanese women is markedly different from that of the men. Hara Setsuko's innocent expressions, which showed her fearlessness of men, and her smiling face always reminded me of Jay, who described his lover's manner this way: "I belong to no man, and am comfortable and happy in that." I admired the femininity of the girl in Miyazaki Hayao's animation, and the language, the accents, and the laughter of the Japanese children in his *Kurenai no buta*, who were kidnapped and subsequently rescued; they embodied the characteristics of a country of women.

We happened upon the cherry-blossom festival. A country in love with festivals.

A people in love with flowers, beauty, and the arts.

In the garden of the Shrine of the God of War alone, there are festivals for peonies and sweet flags. Festivals for all flowers, in all seasons; there are festivals for all things, for all things are gods and all gods are symbols. Whatever we can see exists, and nothing else. And women in particular love festivals.

Listen, the high-pitched sounds of a flute came and went as if creating musical signs in the air. Enchanted, we looked up to decode the signs; we chased after drum troupes amid the sea of cherry blossoms day after day. Listen, heavenly drums and earthly flutes. The musical signs in the air confiding their secrets: three thousand kaleidoscopic worlds, a thousand rulers, a country of many fragrances, the femininity of India.

See, there's Lévi-Strauss. He said, Islam, on the contrary, has developed according to a masculine orientation.

Yes, the abstract, the unified, the monotheistic.

The destruction of idols started with Abraham, and when the Ten Commandments appeared, all other gods disappeared.

We left the drum troupes and stood before a high platform, enchanted by dancing shamans in vermilion robes and short white coats. It was an unknown shrine, with the musicians sitting on both wings of the platform, dressed in ancient clothes, playing flutes and beating drums.

The vermilion of the shamans' robes was that of the caste mark between an Indian woman's brows. The white of their short coats was that of a Yin dynasty carriage, the white of the Shang Dynasty. The white of the white robe and headdress worn by Hatshepsut, Queen of Egypt, who ruled upper and lower Egypt in the fifteenth century B.C. The vermilion and white were a white ox pulling a vermilion wagon in *The Tale of Genji*.

The two shamans were seventeen and nineteen years old, wearing the court dress of the Nara Period, short white coats with baggy sleeves, vermilion robes with flared skirts, gold head-dresses, and white hemp decorating their flowing hair. They had bells with handles tied with long, wide ribbons. Each holding a bell in her right hand and grasping the ribbons with her left, they opened their arms and raised them to shoulder level, like cranes spreading their wings, ready to fly away. Standing straight, they shook the bells, flapping their wings, and began dancing to the gods as the drums and flutes played.

Their flared skirts and baggy sleeves billowed with the movements of their bodies, so simple it was almost like the earth breathing. Suddenly they turned to dance toward the worshippers

beneath the platform. Three steps, five steps, like tides rising higher and higher, overflowing, menacing. The Nara Period in Japan;
in China the South and North Dynasties, the Northern Wei,
and the early Tang. Erect a stele, and in a thousand years the crane
will return.

A pillar was a stele, used to measure the shadow of the sun.

We visited the Hypostyle Hall in the Temple of Amon in
Thebes. A hundred thirty-four giant stone pillars were lined
up like men on a chessboard. During the New Year in July, the
floods came with tons of rose granite and snow-white gypsum.
The God-Welcoming Festival was held during the second
month of the flood season. The inspiration for the pillars came
from the papyrus grass in the Nile River, so the tops flowered,
some like water lilies, some like closed buds.

Of the many obelisks, one was taken away by Napoleon and
now stands in the Place de la Concorde. Another stands in front
of St. Peter's Basilica, where Yongjie and I held our wedding ceremony. We looked at St. Mark's Cathedral, Venice's landmark,
from a distance. We could see the face of the royal blue clock,
with its roman numerals and the gilded figures of the twelve
constellations; the hands and the hour marks were gold. Bronze
statues of two Moors stand on the tower beneath the clock,
which has kept true time for five hundred years.

We were ignorant when we watched a Noh play; we knew
only that the impressive costumes belonged to the Heian period,
which flourished at the same time as the elegant and subdued
Song Dynasty in China. Later we saw two Kabuki plays: *The
Maple-Leaf Gatherer* and *The Dissolute Monk on the Sixteenth Night*.
The hem of the female lead's dress was tapered like the three-inch
golden lotus, the bound foot, for the tastes of Osaka merchants
during the Edo Period tended toward understated beauty.

Wabi, sabi, iki, lonely, quiet, refined. A clandestine tryst in order
to increase the charm, an aesthetic extramarital affair.

We went to the Valley of the Kings to visit the tomb of Queen
Hatshepsut.

The queen's father had no sons by his queen, so she inherited
the throne. But women couldn't be kings, evidence for which is
found in the absence of a cuneiform term for female king, so she
married her half-brother, who became the legitimate pharaoh.

The pharaoh died young, without a son by the queen, who then picked the young son of one of the concubines, Thutmose III, to succeed her, while actual power rested with her for twenty-two years. She wore the pharaoh's robe, decorated with bees and lilies, his wig, and a faux beard, under a towering white crown with snakes or eagles. In all the documents she was referred to as King. Dovish when it came to war, she was fond of exotic objects and treasures. Grand expeditions returned from all over the world with monkeys, leopards, ivory, ebony, and ostrich feathers, all of which the Egyptians had never seen before. She was also fond of building temples, and erected two obelisks at the Temple of Amon. After Thutmose III ascended to the throne, he led sixteen conquests, expanding his territory all the way to Palestine and Syria. When he returned to Thebes, he erased the queen's name in the temples and replaced it with his grandfather's name, while starting construction on his own temple. The walls of secret rooms were inscribed with the history of his conquests, a chronicle in stone.

On that summer night, we returned to the city of Karnak, which we had visited earlier that day. It was located on the eastern bank of the Nile, where sound and light shows enticed the tourists. A voice seemed to come from the riverside, beckoning us to enter Karnak, which was guarded by 124 sphinxes. The voice said, You needn't go any farther, for you have arrived here, where time begins.

Then the sound of flutes, as the voice said, It's here, Karnak, where a god named Amon sat on the hill. This is the first place touched by the rising waters in July, where wild ducks roost during the flood season.

Voices gushed from all corners: from a giant boulder, ruined walls, crumbling city walls, damaged columns, secret passages, the opposite bank of the river. The lights shifted to the statue of a pharaoh with his arms crossed, a staff in one hand and chains in the other. The voice said, I am a pharaoh whose name has been lost. People argued at the foot of my throne. I left behind this giant statue.

The clarion call of a horn sounded, then an old man's voice: I, Ramses II, the flame of the nineteenth dynasty. Three thousand years ago, I built the second temple door through which you will pass. I wore the crown of unification of upper and lower Egypt. Three queens slept in my bed, the third of whom was the daughter of the Hittite king, hegemon of Asia Minor. Later I married four of my own daughters. I have 93 sons and 106 daughters.

Another voice said, I am the king of declining ancient Egypt, Ptolemy Euergetes III. I built this door with genuine Lebanese fir, inlaid with Asian brass. Tonight the door will allow you entrance into the most wonderful and moving areas of the Karnak maze.

A young voice said, I am Tutankhamen. In the courtyard, I left only a calcite sphinx.

Tutankhamen, who died at the age of eighteen, is more famous than all the other pharaohs because his tomb was raided and great treasures and frescoes were excavated. We went deep inside, to his burial chamber, where we looked at him for a long, long time.

I went to Kusinagara in northern India, where Sakyamuni died. I also crossed the Ganges Plain to Bodhgaya, where he attained enlightenment. I made the trip during the longest separation between Yongjie and me, when he was in Sichuan, Yunnan, and Burma to film the southern portion of the Silk Road. It was winter break at school, so I joined a pilgrimage to Nepal and India.

On our visits to the sites of ancient civilizations, we sat in front of the Parthenon to watch a sound-and-light show. We saw purple dandelions blooming amid Olympian ruins, and the windswept sandstone relics of Troy. Groves of squat olive trees bent in the wind, waves of dark-green leaves, or a sea of silver gray when the wind blew the other way.

As for the other side of the Taiwan Straits, where Yongjie, passionate about his work, had trod nearly every inch of land, I have never been there, not once.

The dark mountain roads are heavily traveled. But I have never been there.

Yes, on my map of the world, I skipped only that vast piece of land.

Now it was there, like the sloughed-off skin of my youth, like the remains of a love, cast into a heap. I walked by it indifferently, sensing it to be more alien than all the distant countries of the world. I had no intention of ever going there.

I use its language. I am using it right now. It, it is here.

It is here, containing everything about it that language represents, still flowing at this very moment, after tens of thousands
of years.

No chance, no chance at all. I can only be here.

I finally realized that the place I'd longed to visit, the place I'd
dreamed about, does not, cannot actually exist. It is an unattainable place that has always existed only in the written word.

chapter fourteen

Perhaps it was as Fellini said: Music is cruel, it fills me with
homesickness and remorse. When the tune is over, I never
know where the music has gone, only that it is in an unattainable
place, which saddens me immensely.

When Yongjie returned from that unattainable place, he told
me he'd seen peach blossoms in Shandong. Groves of peach trees
covered the countryside, a bewitching sight. In the Yimeng
mountain area, nearly every family had a martyr, not soldiers
who had died in battle but laborers sent up to the front line,
where they were formed into columns to set off mines and
exhaust the firepower of the Nationalist army. He trembled as he
walked through the groves, fearing he'd never see me again.

Yes, those peach groves. Three thousand years ago, King
Xuan of the Zhou was defeated by the Quanrong barbarians.
On the way back to his capital, he heard children singing, The
moon is rising/The sun is setting/The arrow and the quiver
nearly destroyed the Zhou. Three years later, during a royal sacrifice, he saw a beautiful woman walk slowly from the west and
enter the ancestral temple. She laughed three times, wailed
three times, then bundled up the ancestral tablets from all seven
temples and slowly walked east. King Xuan ran after her, then
woke up and realized it was a dream. Its meanings were revealed only later. Laughing three times referred to the tricks
played on the feudal princes by the concubine, Daji, with

warning fires. Wailing three times was for the son of King You, who was killed by the Quanrong; the ancestral tablets going east; and King Ping moving the capital to Luoyang.

The groves of peach trees. According to legend, when Daji was to be beheaded, the executioner raised his arm three times but wasn't able to complete his mission. In the end the son of Zhou, Yinjiao, covering his face with his sleeve, carried out the execution.

Peach trees chase away ghosts, peach amulets ward off demons, and the Peach Lady tried her magic powers on the Duke of Zhou.

The demon Ba wore black clothes, and droughts occurred wherever she stayed. Chiyou, who fought the Yellow Emperor for domination of China, was aided by the gods of wind and rain, who sent storms down on the land. The Yellow Emperor sent Ba to perform her magic; the rains stopped, and he slew Chiyou.

There was also the thunderous sound of yellow ants at war, and the weeping of the stone man at Zhongnan Mountain. Bloody rain poured down, and the stone man predicted the appearance of the rebel Huang Chao.

Within the span of a thousand years, there were three southern dynasties: the Southern Song, the Southern Ming, and the Southern Nationalists. The Qin Dynasty kept no retainers, so thousands of tigers and wolves were scattered in the streets. The world was plunged into chaos: radicals and ultraconservatives engaged in debates and disseminated heresies; the common people undermined governments and launched revolutions. The Goddess of Mercy wept copiously. From red to green, the homosexual has no motherland.

Is that why I didn't become a patriot during my innocent and pure youth, when I believed in only one truth?

I had always brushed up against all sorts of organizations and beliefs, whether it was the ultranationalism of Yukio Mishima and his Tatenokai comrades or of the passionate students at Tokyo University who flirted with communism and stuck up posters that said, Don't try to stop us, Mother. The ginkgo tree behind you is crying.

Or was it because I was born with the face of a sycophant, a good listener, so people mistakenly assumed that I was a believer and entrusted me with their deepest secrets? But before long the differences would emerge, and I could sense the other person's disappointment, as well as my own regret that I wasn't worth teaching. So I usually distanced myself before the other person cooled off.

Yongjie was the same at the time.

Particularly during those years when everyone was taking video cameras up to the mountains and down to the seas to shoot documentaries, and Yongjie was sent to film the Taiya tribe in Hualien. After he finished filming, he fell in love with a young man called Abei, and stayed behind to live on the mountain for more than half a year. Abei and his fellow tribesmen, not permitted to keep their original names, had to choose Chinese names to satisfy census requirements. Yongjie herded sheep, climbed betel-nut trees, and shelled the nuts alongside members of the tribe. From Abei's grandmother he learned how to cut ramie, remove the fibers, thread them into strips, and boil them in water mixed with grass ash to bleach the yellow threads snowy white. He also learned how to identify dyeing materials, such as the plump roots of yams, crepe myrtle, corn, aubergine, Java cedar, dye-hue flower, UNTSUM grass, and WAYAI TASH grass. He even learned how to use a weaving machine to mix colored threads with hemp to make red, blue, and black fabric. His love for Abei was innocent; the most they did was fall asleep holding each other after getting drunk.

We often strayed from the main course of life. When we looked back, we realized that we had followed a diversion to reach the point where we were at the moment. Early on, our sexual orientation had always taken us on different paths.

What we lacked was not just a motherland. We, the rule breakers, with our transient lifestyle and socially unacceptable behavior, were pagans, who likely had no fathers or ancestors either.

So, was ours a society with no father? Paul Federn said that revolution was a kind of patricide. But what about Fan Lihua, the woman warrior of Tang China, who killed her brother and her father? What about Natha, the impulsive son of a god, who cut off his flesh to return to his mother and carved out his bone to give back to his father, in order to sever ties with his family? None of the above count.

Ancestors who had long since passed away!

Eighteen years ago, on a humid evening in mid-spring, after Ah Yao and I had finished watching the movie *The Bicycle Thief* in a screening room, I accompanied him back to his house instead of returning to my dorm room. As we lay on our cots, he listened to music from the U.S. Armed Forces Radio station. The night was so hot and humid you couldn't help having bad thoughts, so we decided to go downstairs for some fresh air. Leaving though the back door, we walked toward Chung-shan North Road. There was no wind. The darkness hid everything; it was a night for cats on the prowl. A sudden downpour caught us by surprise, and we quickly ducked under the eaves of some stores, where we saw army trucks rolling toward the Grand Hotel area. The downpour was so spooky, it gave us goose bumps. We didn't know until the next day that the Great Man had died. The butchers' union announced a three-day moratorium on slaughtering.

My kid sister wore a black armband. For a whole month, the three TV stations showed programs only in black and white. When I went home, a group of people had gathered at the entrance to the project. An old friend, Liao, came up to hug me as soon as he saw me; he nearly squeezed tears out of my eyes. I stayed with these friends, although some of them went home but came back out, hanging out, not knowing what to do. Several years before, I'd seen the Great Man with my own eyes for the first time, though it was only an image as small as a grain of salt, with waving white gloves and a mumbling voice. A great man is, in the end, a man. But all those gorgeous doves and balloons, and tens of thousands of boys and girls crowded into the plaza . . . and when they dispersed it was like a tide receding, one group after another leaving the plaza and flooding the neighboring alleys. Paper garlands everywhere, belonging to girls who, reluctant to leave, cluttered the streets. Ah Yao left his group to look for me, then dragged me over to see a boy who looked like Jimmy Dean. Ah Yao said the boy went to the high school attached to Taiwan Normal University. I followed him the best I could, but my mind wandered and I lost him. Then I ran into a bunch of girls from some school or other creeping toward the plaza, taking up half of the street. They all wore flowing dresses in peach red, carrying flower baskets like the fairy Ma Gu presenting peaches to the Queen of the West. Captivated by their appearance, I fell in behind them. But with crowds of people coming toward me like schooling fish, I was going against the human tide. Everyone on the street, it seemed, was staring at me with murderous intent, so I turned and fled, walking aimlessly, unwilling to accept that this was all there was. Fewer and fewer flags hung by the street, and the crowds were thinning out. I'd walked a long way but could still hear the music from the plaza. It was like a circus after the performance, a deserted playground in the winter, which always, always depressed me; I couldn't have felt worse. So whenever two or three of the girls with garlands appeared in front of me, I was so moved I felt like going up to greet them, as if they, like me, had been left high and dry on the beach after the tide went out.

I felt very sad about the people who congregated at the entrance to the project. We no longer hung out together, for lack of common interests, and had gone our separate ways. Some of the families, whose homes were to give way to low-income housing, had already moved away, but were driven back by sentiments caused by the death of the Great Man. We huddled together for mutual support. Maybe this was the last night we could be so open about who we were, for tomorrow, truly everything would be different.

For a whole month, the project went into a collective hypnotic trance, temporarily forgetting what day it was. Through repeated shows on TV about the life of the Great Man and bombardment by a host of memorial activities, programs, and interviews, we entered a state of recollection. Overlapping memories of the Great Man and ourselves, coupled with patriotic songs and poems repeated over and over, became a farewell rite for people in the project.

Myth and forgetfulness.

Continuity and the destruction of this continuity.

The future, the present, and the past share the same errors of memory.

And I had already witnessed how the living interpret the dead based upon their own needs, so that the dead continue to change in the living. The dead are dead, but come back to life with every change in definition.

I tried to solve my own mystery of life and death with this type of meditation. The only problem was, a dead man like this had to have been a great person to begin with. For people like me, what extraordinary definition did we have to force the living to keep revising? A definition for people like us could be summed up in a word. If there were to be an epitaph, it would be: A slave to carnal pleasure who died before his time.

Yes, indeed, a slave to carnal pleasure. Yukio Mishima wrote his last novel, *The Decay of the Angel*, to chronicle his own predicted death—the five decays: appearance, speech, eyesight, hearing, and thoughts. He went with his comrades to Ichigaya, headquarters of the Self-Defense Forces, where he harangued the Jieitai soldiers, calling upon them to transform society by acting in the spirit of *bushido*. He then committed *seppuku*. He was our greatest martyr, one who died for carnality.

Then there was the one who typified those who died young, Nijinsky, who was famous for his amazing jetés and the way he could hover in the air. Jay once said, Nijinsky descended more slowly than he ascended.

Dancing rhythmically to Debussy's *Prélude à l'après-midi d'un faune*, he would stop abruptly and hold the pose like a Greek statue. To achieve this effect, he violated the classical rule requiring a dancer to bend his knees and step down on his heels. Nijinsky asked the dancers to turn their heads to the side while their bodies faced the audience and to bend their arms in a variety of angles. The dance came under savage attack as soon as it was performed, disappearing after its first performance, along with *The Rite of Spring*, which caused a riot on the day of its premiere. Only the music was left for later generations of dancers to perform and interpret.

After less than a decade on the stage, at the age of twenty-seven, he was diagnosed as a schizophrenic, and remained hospitalized for the rest of his life, dying at the age of sixty-one! At the time, his wife of only five years described with extreme sorrow how he was gradually taken away by an invisible, incomprehensible force, away from his art, his life, and her. Confused and flustered, she fought against this terrifying force, which she could neither understand nor explain. Her husband was still good to her, still magnanimous, endearing as ever, but he was a totally different person.

And so, later on, I desired to know nothing about Jay, like with that sole lost continent that showed up grayish yellow on my map of the world.

Many years later, Yongjie invited me to a performance. Calmly I watched Jay dance, understanding him completely; no mystery or incomprehensibility. With the karma removed, I could see that, as a dancer, he was dead once his trustworthy, powerful body could no longer perform the movements he expected of it.

A dancer practices in front of his mirror, where his movements are displayed for all to see; he can hide nothing. After a long time, he comes to believe in his body and uses its writing to communicate with the world. When his physical abilities leave him, he must remain silent as a salmon. Unlike most other people, he knows what it's like to die twice.

Everything grieves for its own kind. Tears ran down my face.

Yongjie comforted me by saying that Jay could still choreograph.

But I was still sad, knowing that one day he would no longer be able to express himself directly with his body. He was his own creation, which he exhibited again and again. Exhibition was a kind of existence, exhibition was self-sufficient. He was a dancer and a choreographer. But before long, his body would be the first to die, leaving his ideas and skills to be expressed and transmitted by others. He could only be a choreographer. He could only accept and adjust to this role and this fate. To borrow what he said to me: You have to get used to all this.

Yes, he'd experienced everything I'd experienced.

His teacher's teacher danced till the age of seventy-six, when she performed the Queen of Troy. With the image of all her lovers dying before her eyes, one after another, the aging Hecuba bade farewell to the stage. She was lucky; she was also unlucky.

If I managed to live to that age, everyone I loved would likely no longer be around. Fellini, for example, slipped into a coma in October. Two months earlier, he'd suffered a heart attack in Rimini and was paralyzed on one side when he left the hospital. This time he was hospitalized again. Giulietta Masina went to see him daily, but he was no longer conscious. In today's newspaper, Giulietta was reported to have collapsed from exhaustion.

Satyajit Ray died last year, and this year Ozu will have been dead thirty years. Recently I began to comprehend that the members of what is called "your generation" includes childhood playmates, the bridesmaids and best men who give you a hard

time on your wedding night, and the people who organize your funeral. If I lived long enough, till I was the last funeral organizer, then I'd be the blind Tiresias of Greek mythology.

Tiresias was the only person in mythology who had been both a man and a woman.

Zeus and his wife Hera were debating whether men or women enjoyed orgasm more. They both believed that the other gained more pleasure, and the one who gained more pleasure had to compensate the one who gained less. In a word, the one who gained more pleasure became the debtor, and neither wanted to owe the other anything. They asked Tiresias to be the judge. He answered candidly that women's pleasure was nine or ten times more intense than men's. Outraged, Hera blinded him. But Zeus gave Tiresias two things, longevity and the ability to predict. Tiresias then became Thebes's prophet.

Ah, a prophet who suffered insomnia! Like an old man, he got up in the middle of the night; the Son of Man had no place to stay. He had lived long enough and saw that what had occurred before was about to occur again, so he had to tell people what he knew; but of course, no one would listen. A voice in the wilderness. Yet words cannot hurt, so he kept talking and talking, and eventually was silenced for his talkativeness. Otherwise he would have to keep his mouth shut, dying alone and lonely in an age when all witnesses were dead.

If longevity for us was to be with the one we loved, then when one died—Yongjie said his chin was more pointed, so he would die before me—what happened to the other one?

I thought about that for a long time. One day while we were eating, I said to Yongjie, My heart is definitely stronger than yours, so I'll outlive you. Which is why I'm going to stare at you for a long, long time, to memorize the entire process of your death, not missing a single moment. Afterward, it will resemble what I read in the Eastern Wilderness chapter of the *Classic of Mountain and Sea*: There was a deep gully beyond the Eastern Sea, which was in reality an abyss, and was called Return to Ruin. I would live on the cliff above the deep gully, watching countless people and numerous generations pass me on their way into the gully, never to return. I would shrivel up day by day until

I became a mummy squatting there, pen in hand. And I would continue to write, ceaselessly.

Yongjie, you see it, the scene of my last moment in this world, when, weathered by the wind, I turn to stone.

Before he slipped into a coma, Ah Yao was converted to Christianity and given the last rites. When I rushed over to the Fussa Clinic, Mama gave me the news with great joy and excitement. It's wonderful, just wonderful! I said. But both Ah Yao and I knew that conversion means nothing to the dead, that its only function is to comfort the living. Why not convert? In the end, he relented in his treatment of his mother.

chapter fifteen

Yes, myth and forgetfulness.

I joined a pilgrimage to Bodhgaya, the place where Sakyamuni achieved enlightenment. The old bodhi tree spread its umbrella of branches over the Diamond Throne, and no matter how I sized it up, it looked just like the surroundings in any rural Taiwan spot, with a big banyan tree and a local-god temple. The ground was covered with bodhi seeds, or they could have been banyan seeds, which were stomped into pulp. A Sambodhi Tower had been buried there by Buddhists during an eleventh-century Muslim invasion. Traced through descriptions in Xuanzang's *Travels to the West*, it was later unearthed. Pedicabs and poor people packed a vacant lot near the site of enlightenment.

I came to India only because, after enduring half the time Yongjie was to be away from me, I still had to get through the second half, which included the winter break and Chinese New Year. Afraid I might die of loneliness, I left a message on the answering machine informing callers of my trip to India and my return date, an insipid message for Yongjie in case he called. I recorded it many times, but no matter what words came out, they all sounded like a final farewell. I felt as if I were leaving my body in the house and sending my soul out to look for Yongjie, who might not even be alive.

That's how I came to be in India; it was like arriving at the wasteland inside my heart. The farther I went, the farther behind I left the society I lived in, and the closer I got to Yongjie, it seemed.

So I witnessed, on that late night, Sakyamuni waking up next to his wife and son and staring at their faces under the moonlight. Those faces were exactly what he had long been contemplating, ever since returning from his latest trip outside the city, the faces of all living creatures. He had fallen more and more in love with this collective, complete, semiotic being, all living creatures. But these living creatures—birth, adulthood, family, decline, emptiness—living creatures, a history of destruction. Fatigue, ENTROPY, thermodynamics. Several thousand years later, Lévi-Strauss said that anthropology could be changed to entropology, a study of the decomposition process at the highest level. Sakyamuni, unable to extricate himself from his obsession with this semiotic being, was about to bid farewell to his wife and son under the moonlight and go off to a distant place.

I saw him walk out of his palace and wake up the royal attendant, Chandaka, get out the white horse, Kanthka, and leave the city. He removed his fancy clothes and ornaments for Chandaka to return to his father, then walked toward the snow-capped mountains.

The mountains were just over there, on the horizon. A ridge with no angles, just two rounded peaks.

The water from the snow-capped mountains became the Nairanjana River. Nothing remained before me but a desert many miles wide. On the other side was a village, wheat fields with billowy green leaves, trees, and betels. I crossed the dry sand, walking with local residents carrying baskets on their heads. Under the sweltering sun, the sand seemed to be mixed with gold dust. In the middle of the desert was a small puddle of water where someone was rinsing clothes, which were then spread on the ground, decorating the white-hot desert with a few dots of red. The clothes were wet when I came and dry on my return trip. The leader of the pilgrimage led them in performing the rite of *Vairochana* on a sandbar, facing the sun in an act of visualization, drawing solar energy to turn into their own. When they were done, the leader consecrated everyone by sprinkling water on their heads. This group performed *Abhisecana* throughout the trip.

I saw Sakyamuni, after living on a snow-capped mountain for six years, turn into a bag of bones, like an AIDS victim. Having gained nothing, he abandoned his formal asceticism and came down from the mountain. He walked alone and passed out when he reached the river.

According to the records, the man led an ascetic life for ten days after performing a fasting rite.

The writings describe how, on the fourth day of fasting, he lost consciousness. On the fifth day, he awoke to a windowful of bright sunlight. His vomiting stopped and he gradually regained his hearing and eyesight. On the sixth day, he heard morning prayers on the field, and while trying to follow the prayers he heard his own voice. His body regained its senses, and his thoughts began to unravel gradually, like finding the first thread in a ball of tangled thread. The past slowly came back to him like a ship emerging from a vast ocean, first a small dot, then the white mast, the cables, then holes in the sail, and finally the eyebrows of the sailors. The boat sailed toward him, then sailed off to the distant sea, leaving swells in its wake. Little by little, stage by stage, it disappeared without a trace. Sadness or joy, it was hard to tell.

On the morning of the seventh day, he got down off his hammock, walked over to a little table, sat down, picked up a book, and read over a dozen pages. That night he slept soundly. On the eighth day, he tried opening the door to his room, and walked a bit. At that moment he felt strengthened and fulfilled. On the early morning of the eleventh day, Gandhi prepared breakfast for him, giving him a glass of grape juice and some orange juice, telling him he had completed his ascetic rites and it was now time for him to eat.

I witnessed it, it was right here, where I was standing, that the village shepherd girl helped Sakyamuni up and fed him some milk gruel. His mind cleared and he regained his strength. He thanked the girl, saying, All human beings must eat.

Yes, yes, all so-called living creatures need food to survive.

Sakyamuni crossed the Nairanjana, entered the city, and sat down by a bodhi tree, where he comprehended the ultimate formula of the universe.

I climbed to the top of a small hill in the village. White oxen, their bells ringing, walked past me. The day before, I had traveled through the Ganges Plain; the road was so straight it seemed to merge with the horizon. After five hours on the road, the car made its first turn; half an hour later, it made its second, and we were there. The trees were cassia fistulas; the fields were planted with wheat, yellow-flowered rape, and sorghum with tassels that looked like purple smoke. Rows of white oxen dotted the black, fertile soil, and there were people on every inch of empty space.

This was a country without cities. In India, I didn't sense the existence of cities, only congregations of houses on the ground, or houses that were actually just expanses of dusty ground. A blanket was placed on the dusty ground, and in the middle sat people with smudges of incense ashes on their foreheads and vermilion caste marks between their brows. Everything in the civilized world was here.

And so India had virtually no antiquities, no relics, neither buildings constructed by human beings nor the universe of material objects. Everywhere you went and everything you saw was people, nothing but people.

Did you know that thousands of years ago, India endeavored to solve the population problem by means of the caste system, to change quantity into quality, that is, to differentiate between human groups so as to enable them to live side by side?

Lévi-Strauss said sadly that vegetarianism was the failure of India's great experiment. In order to prevent social groups and animal species from encroaching on each other and to guarantee each group its own particular freedom, the means chosen was to force the others to relinquish the enjoyment of some conflicting freedom.

Then Sakyamuni began from the negation of the negative and the negation of existence, right?

India was the boiling hot dust on the plains and the cool starry sky over the plateaus, the humblest resignation to fate and the unrestrained freedom of imagination, a gaudy, decadent world of desire and its complete opposite—a land of loneliness. The

Visva-Bharati University founded by Tagore would be India's last land of loneliness.

And the India I visited was where Buddhism had vanished. Over a thousand years after Sakyamuni died, the Arabs invaded India and the monks were incorporated into Brahmanism; five hundred years later, Buddhism disappeared from India.

At Varanasi [Benares] I crossed the Ganges in an early morning fog. I bought two rolls of pot marigold wrapped in bodhi leaves, lit the little drops of wax on them, and set them on the water. In the mist, the little flames left the boat, floated away, and flickered out, leaving bright yellow flowers on the water.

Some of the early risers from the pilgrimage were also on the boat. The leader, seasick after Abhisecana—the daily ritual of sprinkling water over the pilgrims—had weakened his body, was flanked by two pretty female disciples, who wore down jackets, oiled tights, and high-top sneakers, sort of like space-age warriors. The members of the group sought divine revelation for everything and prayed whenever they came to a temple. They even fought over the leader's leftover water, adding it to their canteens. I envied them their staunch belief in a mundane world. They traveled to exotic places and spiritual realms, but were more middle-class, more firmly rooted in reality, than anyone else in their own society.

Ah, Varanasi, Hinduism's holiest of cities, with statues of gods everywhere, which I'd already seen in Satyajit Ray's movies: the yellow terraced landings, the *ghats* that extend into the sacred river, the people standing in the water bathing themselves, the crows perched on the canopies, and the people on blankets by the river, reciting prayers after bathing. The ghats represent a vast crematorium; on the opposite sandy shore there are no houses, nothing but a sunrise.

Bodies of the dead, wrapped in coarse shrouds and anointed with fragrant oil—orange red or peach red for the women, white for the men, and yellow for the children—are carried to the sacred river to be washed, then burned on wooden pyres that line the river every few feet, guarded by relatives until the pyres turn to ashes. Day and night, lighting up the sky, forming a fiery city. People who set up their pyres here must pay a certain family whose right to charge has been passed down by inheritance, beyond the jurisdiction of the government. In the city and along the riverbank are multistoried red-brick buildings, the so-called dying inns, which are divided into networks of caves for use by those who have come from far away to live out their final days and for their relatives.

I saw the living come to the sacred river, the Ganges, to bathe and cleanse themselves, while the dead were washed in preparation for their ascent to heaven. Was the god here the real god and not a mere symbol? Did the god really live here? Small flames and flowers drifted on the misty river, like so many spirits of the dead and so many living souls, giving them real outward appearances and real substance to make it a true field of life and death.

I watched Mama's shoulders heave when the thick, heavy cast-iron door closed after the box containing Ah Yao's body was sent in. A current of warm blood surged up from my startled heart.

We went up to a tatami room on the second floor to drink tea while waiting quietly for Ah Yao to be burned to ashes.

The first-floor prayer hall had a shiny marble floor and crystal chandeliers, much like a hotel lobby. There were two incinerators marked by pitch-black doors with polished brass handles.

The other women, all parishioners from Mama's church, sat around chatting casually. Of the four or five men in attendance, one, the maternal nephew of Mama's natural mother, was the only relative. Mama had been raised by an aunt and her husband, who had married into the family and taken her name. After returning to Japan, Mama looked after her aunt, since all the men in the family had died. Not long afterward, her natural mother moved back to live with them. Two sisters, who both had Alzheimer's, sometimes smeared their feces on the wall, and sometimes walked to a neighboring village, where they fell into a ditch. Mama sold the house she inherited after both her mothers passed away, and moved into her present Western-style house, of the type so popular among nuclear families. I became the representative of Mama's side of the family in witnessing the cremation.

Every time Mama cried, she first dabbed her right eye, then her left with a neatly folded handkerchief. By the third dab her eyes would be dry. She wore an ink-black kimono; her tears were like a Noh gesture, a dance, or a symbol.

I was puzzled by the peaceful look on Mama's face, like the three-quarter profile of Garbo, and anyone of the Fellini generation seeing her face could not help but be reminded of the Last Judgment.

After about twenty minutes, we went downstairs.

The public crematorium in Varanasi that day was located on a large platform, on which a wooden pyre had been erected. After five or six hours, when the cremation was finished, the ashes were swept into a dustpan with a bamboo broom and dumped into the river, along with other remains. For the sake of sanitation and appearance, the government provided a free power-operated crematory, but no Indian was interested.

We went downstairs to wait by the furnace. The door was open but the furnace was still red-hot. When the box was pulled out, Ah Yao's ashes looked more or less like a burned-out stick of incense that had been laid flat on the floor. Just a line of ashes, much less than I expected, much much less.

I'll never forget, when the nurses pulled back the bedsheet, how Ah Yao looked when dead—there was nothing left of him. All that remained on that naked bag of bones, eaten away by AIDS, were two bony knees and a superfluous, rumpled penis. As the only fleshy part of his body that remained, it looked abnormally, even shockingly big.

A clean-shaven, neatly dressed undertaker swept the ashes into a shiny, square steel pan and picked up a ring-shaped bone with a pair of pincers, showing us that it was from the throat. The skeleton looked like a person sitting cross-legged, meditating.

In groups of two, we picked up bones with long chopsticks and put them into a round container.

The container was sealed and placed in a square wooden box, which was then covered with thick, snow-white paper and tied with knotted tassels. When the process was over, the undertaker tipped his hat slightly toward the box as a show of respect.

The box was given to me to take back to the house in Fussa.

Ninety-one kalpas, and only three of them had a Buddha. The rest had nothing, which was rather sad and pitiful. Hence, being born in the same age as the Buddha is as unlikely as chancing upon a blossom on the udumbara tree, which blooms once in

3,000 years. His appearance is rare, yet often goes unnoticed.

I had seen Ah Yao off to be cremated. It was just the beginning; he was the first one.

As time passed, I would see one after another off to be cremated. Like today, the newspaper reported, Fellini Dies. The last day of October, Taipei, a clear autumn sky.

I put down my pen to rest for a while, for the death of a Buddha, and went out for a walk.

Look, under a sky covered by sandstorms, a frenzy to build a city of skyscrapers; we hadn't seen the sun for a long time. Four el cars painted blue and white glided past in the dusty gray sky. Yongjie and I pointed at them and vowed that, once the rapid transit started running, we had to remember, we had to remind each other not to take it, so as to keep from being burned to ashes.

Time cannot be turned back, nor can life. However, in the process of writing, I am able to turn back everything that otherwise couldn't be.

So my writing, it continues.

notes to *Notes of a Desolate Man*

1   Thou shalt not tempt: Matthew 4:7.

1   Master Hongyi: The religious name of Li Shutong (1880-1942), who gained fame as a poet and calligrapher. He became a Buddhist monk at the age of 39. Upon his death he left as his own epitaph the words *Beihuan jiaoji* (grief and joy mix together).

3   norms of the human world: *Gangchang*, an abbreviated form of the traditional, patriarchal concept of *sangang wuchang*, the three cardinal guides—ruler guides subject, father guides son, husband guides wife—and the five constant virtues—benevolence, righteousness, propriety, wisdom, and fidelity.

14 "The cat has fainted": A nonsensical evolution of a phrase when passed along from listener to listener, as in the children's game Telephone.

19 It is not good: Genesis 2:18.

25 The revolution: The quote is from Sun Yat-sen's last will and testament. Here the revolution refers to the gay movement; the comrades are gay members of society.

28 *Tristes Tropiques:* Here and throughout the novel, the Chinese translation of Lévi-Strauss does not always square with the French original or English translation, either in the order of the text or in certain terms or phrases. Our rendering generally follows the latter (John and Doreen Weightman, trans.; New York: Atheneum, 1973).

29 red shoes: Hans Christian Andersen, "The Red Shoes."

34 "neither consciousness nor unconsciousness": Obscure as this extended passage from the *Ksitigarbha Sutra* may seem in English translation, it is no less bewildering to the narrator, whose real concern is articulated in his question at the end of the paragraph. The sutra must be read in its entirety to make any sense to the uninitiated.

38 The flag of the Republic of China is red, with a white spiked circle on a blue field in the upper left corner. It is described poetically as "Blue sky, white sun, the ground is red." "Double-Ten" (October 10) celebrates the founding of the Republic of China in 1911.

47 A man shall leave: Genesis 2:24.

47 Stir not up, nor awaken my love: Solomon 2:7.

48 I've always relied: Tennessee Williams, *A Streetcar Named Desire*.

52 one good poet: The "good" poet is, of course, Mao Zedong, the "red sun" in the following paragraph; the lousy one is Chiang Kai-shek.

53 Great Northern Wasteland: That area of Heilongjiang near the Russian border where intellectuals and others were sent to work, and sometimes die, in opening up new lands during the Cultural Revolution.

53 mainland music: Prior to the lifting of martial law in 1987, listening to music (as well as all other public "contact") from mainland China was illegal.

56 Montaigne: "Of Cannibals."

61 KTV: Similar to a Karaoke bar, but with individual rooms for "sing-along" guests.

64 reds and greens: Here and below, the color terms have been taken from a book by Xu Tianzhi entitled *Zhongguo gudian shi zhong "diaohong kelü" de shangzhe yanjiu* (On the appreciation and analysis of "reds and greens" in classical Chinese poetry). In the context of the individual poems, the meanings and interpretations could vary.

71 Adam's rib: The narrator's "logic" in establishing a sexual identity for gay men has led to this distortion of the biblical myth.

110 banana republic: A pun on Taiwan's famous banana-export industry, combined with the island's status as a "republic," and on the "banana republic" nature under the Chiang Kai-shek rule.

123 By the rivers: Psalm 137:1.

124 Saeba Ryo: A character in a popular Japanese comic book (*manga*). In Taiwan, the character's name was changed in Chinese comics to Meng Bo.

127 Confucius: *Analects* 9:16.

142 Starlight Twins: Characters in a popular Japanese animation film.

152 Huang Chao: An untranslatable calligraphic pun that describes the construction of the written characters for *Huang Chao* has been omitted.

152 red to green: Socialism to environmental concerns.

153 Paul Federn: (1871-1950), author of *The Psychology of Revolution: Society Without Fathers* (1919, in German; English translation from the Chinese).